For permission requests, contact:
Field Note Fiction Publishing
inquiries@fieldnotefiction.com

ISBN: 979-8-9991058-1-3

Cover design by GetCovers

A Warm Welcome To Our Town

There's Just Something about North Riverbend ©
From the moment you arrive you'll feel it. A mix of hometown charm, small-town chaos, and the kind of connection you don't always see coming.
The North Riverbend City Tourism Committee -no dizzy chicken members in sight- is thrilled to welcome you.
Whether you're here for small town gossip, string ensembles, varsity basketball games, or friendships that hit you like -70 below windchill—you're one of us now. And we'll all be there to help you get your car out of the snowdrift that wasn't there twenty minutes ago.
Start your visit with exclusive insider's loot: stories, lists, and a peek behind the scenes.
(The creatives of North Riverbend have plans-all good.)
Your Honorary Citizen starter pack awaits →
https://mcdanielsenyaauthor.com/ → Newsletter Signup

All the Roads Leading to
North River Bend

Want more heartfelt YA rom-com inspiration, book updates, or behind-the-scenes extras?

Visit www.mcdanielsenyaauthor.com

or

instagram.com/mcdanielsenyaauthor
pinterest.com/mcdanielsen
facebook.com/author.mcdanielsen

DEDICATION

To my family,

What Evan said is still true,

"You have to be weird to belong."

Thankful to be weird with you. All my love.

Almost

Missed Our Shot

RIVERBEND HIGH
HAPPY ENDINGS
BOOK 1

M.C DANIELSEN

TABLE OF CONTENTS

Late May to Early June

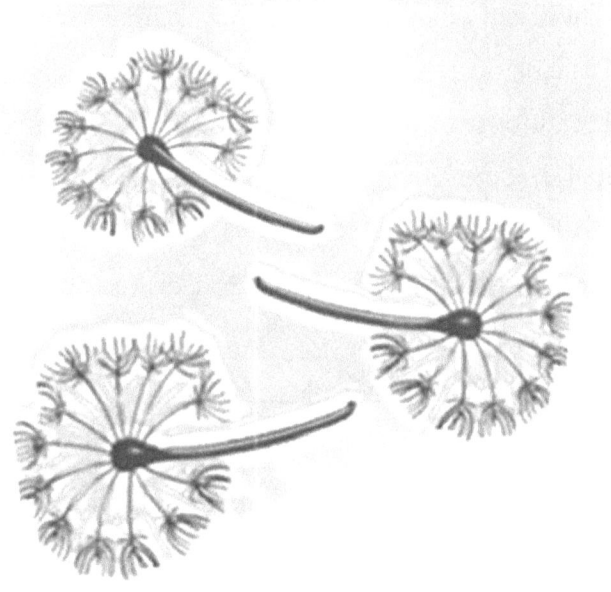

1

AT THE COPA

Ivy

Is it possible to have a good day when it's Barry Manilow waking you up? My *it's-been-busted-for-two-years-clock-radio* came back to life. The alarm I had been using to wake me? Well, it made no sound. Music blaring from the radio woke me up.

I slapped the snooze button, the power button. The music wouldn't stop. I shot upright as the time registered, twenty minutes behind. Late for the first time all school year. I scrambled from bed, knocked over music theory books, and jammed a toe on my cello case.

My day started with Barry Manilow and a full band. A disco-Latin music mashup syncopated to the max. Peppy, filled with strings, horns, congas, and backup singers - *Copacabana*. I knew that Lola the show girl would be dancing in my mind all day. I checked my phone.

Aiden: You up?

Sent 24 minutes ago.

I yanked a brush through my hair while grabbing my backpack. I stuffed a granola bar into my mouth while "*Her name was Lola; she was a showgirl...*" looped in my head like a curse. A high-kicking, boa-draped curse.

I bolted out the door chewing and yanking my right shoe on mid-run. I spotted Tyler and Aiden several blocks ahead. They laughed and ambled along in stupid long-legged sync. I pushed away the urge to catch up.

There'd be no matching their strides, Aiden's especially. He grew taller overnight and woke up with his legs already taking him somewhere. I had no chance to catch up; I was too far away to call. I missed a chance to tell Aiden what I needed him to know.

***

Things that Messed Up My Morning Plan
-Barry Manilow and everyone responsible for *Copacabana*.
-My alarm clock.
-My own feet.
-Aiden and Tyler's ridiculous growth spurts.

Lunch

Lunch would've been the prime opportunity to grab a chat with Aiden-five months ago anyway. When we still ate lunch together, before basketball took over. I spotted Aiden surrounded by teammates at a far table. Basketball boys being basketball boys, tossed grapes into each others' mouths. I hovered, direction undecided, then heard, "Ivy! You have to see this!"

Jenna waved me over to see a viral cheer routine. Aria had a group chat screenshot I had to read. Someone asked about music camp. Chris Olsen tried to flirt with me, which I completely missed. I looked up. Aiden was gone.

***

<u>*Things That Got in the Way During Lunch*</u>
-Jenna's emergency TikTok analysis.
-Aria's group chat drama.
-Chris Olsen and his inability to flirt transparently.
-Me—I got in my own way.

What I needed to tell Aiden? It wasn't a confession, an uncomfortable truth. Just a fact. I'd be gone all summer. Why couldn't I say it?

Two Days Before the Last Day of School

We had a plan to walk home after eighth period, like old times. Aiden texted at 2:47.

> Coach added a meeting. Rain check?

I said sure to a rain check that never came. He said he'd meet me the next day.

> I'll meet you by the front door.

He didn't show. I waited long enough to memorize the slant of sunlight through the trophy case.

***

Back in second grade, we started walking to school. We had our own rhythm. Aiden would hop sidewalk cracks and walk backwards while cracking jokes. I didn't need that much movement—I liked a steady pace. We were different, but our steps matched. Now? I wasn't sure how many of my steps equaled one of his. Wasn't sure I'd get a chance to figure it out.

***

My four-year-old cousin, Miggy, managed to text me goodbye. My preschool cousin who didn't even have a cell phone.

> **Miggy:** Bye Ivy!! Why do you need a camp for music? Do you sound way, way better far away? Don't forget socks and string.

***

People Who Actually Said Goodbye

-Miggy – aged 4
-Aria
-Emilia (twice)
-Tyler
-Maddie
-Jenna
-My dentist
-My cello teacher
-Mom, repeatedly
-Dad – he'd say it at the airport. I felt it now in his hugs.

People Who Didn't

-Aiden

***

Way back on the first day of kindergarten I was scared. Aiden showed up, helped me find my cubby. He was excited that we were cubby next-door-neighbors. He sat beside me at snack time. When my hands shook that first day, he handed me a string cheese and said, "You got this, Princess." He wrapped his pinkie around mine on the way home. Now, I couldn't even get a reply.

***

Last Day of School

I saw him in the hallway, digging through his backpack. I opened my mouth to call his name just as someone bumped into me. The bell rang. He looked up and saw me, I think. Tyler pulled him into a side conversation, and he disappeared into the classroom. I could've chased him. I didn't.

***

After Supper, My Last Night Home

I started typing:

> I was hoping to get a chance to—

I meant to delete it. Reword it, make it sound casual. Instead, I hit send and panicked. Immediately followed up with

> Never mind, Aiden. Hope you have a great summer.

Read. No reply.

If he thought about what it meant, he didn't say.

***

I kept thinking we'd get back to normal. One more week; one more walk; one more laugh. But we hadn't been normal in a while. Not since spring break—maybe before. Walks shortened. Texts went unanswered. Plans fell through. I kept waiting.

***

Reasons I Signed Up for Summer Music Camp
-To develop my cello abilities further.
-To meet people who understand key signatures.
-To NOT spend the summer waiting to be remembered.

***

He used to call me Princess. Not in a sparkly, tiara way. It started when we were little—something he picked up from my dad, but made his own. Building mud castles. "You rule this kingdom, Princess." I gave him a snack I'd brought for a walk. "Royal delivery!" He noticed I was nervous on the first day of school. "You got this, Princess."

It wasn't a throwaway nickname. It meant something. Said I was more than the quiet girl next door. I don't remember the exact moment when he stopped saying it. But I noticed.

***

That last night, I wandered into the backyard. Felt the still sun-warmed grass. Heard birdsong in the air like background music. I found the tallest dandelion and held it between my fingers. I was too old for wishes. Too old to think a single breath could change anything. I didn't care. 8I closed my eyes and blew. Each seed lifted into the air like it had somewhere better to be. Somewhere else to go. Each one carried a piece of me I was forcing myself to let go, a memory, a wish, a maybe.

I didn't want to leave without saying goodbye.

But I guess he didn't need one.

2

TIDAL WAVE OF GOODBYES

Ivy

I was mid-spin, belting out the wrong words to a song no one under seventy had listened to in years.

"I'm gonna pack my bag and pack up my jeans, and send myself out to caaamp." I sang to the tune of *Wash That Man Right Out of My Hair* from *South Pacific*. I'd watched the movie recently, now it was stuck in my head. I added dramatic dance moves. My bedroom door flew open.

"Surprise!"

A girl tidal wave crashed in—Jenna, Maddie, Aria, and Emilia. No knock. No warning. I yelped and dove for my phone. I attempted to kill the music before they could get bad-music-judgey on me (btw, musicals are not bad music). Too late.

Maddie laughed from the floor. "Were you singing a showtune?"

"Musical neophyte," I muttered.

Jenna shoved a polka-dot container in my face. "Emergency cookies for camp survival."

I shook my head, grinning. "Didn't I already say goodbye?"

"A week ago, you really thought was enough? No way, mamá!" Emilia said, kicking off her shoes. "My mom drove us here."

I pulled Emilia into a hug. *Te amo, prima.*

"Hey, we got in the car too," Aria said, mock offended.

"I love the rest of you for getting in the car," I said.

A living group hug swallowed me in limbs, hair, laughter. At one point I had Emilia's braid in my mouth. The hug untangled and collapsed onto my bed. Aria leaned over my perfectly packed suitcase poking my folded shirts.

"So, this is it, huh? Fancy cello camp for our little prodigy?"

"It's not fancy," I said, swatting her hand. "And I'm not a prodigy."

"Please," Maddie said, spinning in my desk chair. "You're basically the cellist in this town. Don't turn all snobby and start wearing berets."

"Berets?" Emilia laughed. "You think she's joining a secret society of French musicians?"

"No berets," I promised. "And North Riverbend isn't big. Hard not to be the person here."

Jenna scooted closer. "For real, though—we're gonna miss you. Eight weeks is a long time."

Her words welled up in me. I'd miss them too. The teasing and comfort, having them only a text away.

"Don't worry," Maddie said, nudging my shoulder. "We won't tell your mom about your camp romances or when you text us about your skinny dipping."

I hurled a stuffed animal at her. "I'm not skinny dipping, you dork."

Emilia wagged a finger. "We'll keep it secret when you sneak out for midnight forest walks and stolen kisses."

"Or when you flirt with the drummers—"

"Percussionists," I interrupted Jenna, tossing a second stuffed animal.

"Or break the hearts of the trumpets and tubas."

"The brass section," I corrected Aria, flinging another stuffie.

"The braaasss," Aria repeated in a fake posh accent. "Their poor brassy hearts crushed by the hot cello diva who couldn't choose but collected kisses from them all."

"We'll keep it a secret when you find the best make out spot," Jenna added, hugging the stuffed animal I'd thrown.

"Good grief! I'm not going wild at music camp!" I laughed. "I'll be practicing, not making out. I'll be fine if I can make a couple of friends so I'm not alone all summer."

They mobbed me again.

"You'll make friends!" "We love you!" "They'll be drooling over curly blonde cello girl!" "Be yourself!"

"Off, off, off," I gasped, pushing them away. "I need to breathe."

Emilia scooted closer, softer now. "Oh, chica, you never give yourself enough credit. Those music mutants? They'll see what we see."

"Mutants? That's a little offensive," I said, nudging her shoulder.

"Or Note Nerds, your choice." I huffed and gave her a shove. She leaned back in draping herself on my shoulder.

Jenna popped up and peeked out the window. "I think your mom's here, Emilia."

Aria handed me a little bag. "Emergency gum. Emergency chocolate. Emergency pen. Emergency notebook. Emergency lip gloss. Emergency paperclips."

"Paperclips?"

"Don't ask questions," she said.

I pressed the bag to my chest, smiling. "You guys are the best. Hopefully not too many emergencies, but thanks."

"That's what friends are for. We'll keep you from perishing in the wilderness fromn lack of chocolate," Maddie said, hugging me.

"You take such good care of me," I said as I returned her hug. One hug turned into four.

"You're gonna kill it at camp," Aria said with confidence. "We'll count the days till you're back."

"Miss you, Ivy," Jenna said.

"There'd better be some summer left for me when you get back," Emilia added. Her hug was the tightest.

"Miss you too. Love you," I whispered.

The door closed and I sat on the edge of my bed, smiling but aching. Their chaos echoed in the air. Quiet followed shortly, with it the awareness of one person's silence. Aiden hadn't said goodbye. Would he even bother now?

How long was I supposed to listen for something he wasn't saying?

3

EMOJIS WITH AGENDAS

Aiden

Mom and Dad came and sat at the kitchen table. I was immersed in a book about shot mechanics. I greeted them vaguely, but didn't top reading. Dad cleared his throat. I lifted my head to find them looking at me. *Okay, family meeting time.* Not sure what it was about what? Not grades. My room was clean, chores done. Maybe basketball camp?

Dad rested his hand on Mom's. "Hey, Aiden. Before we head to camp, we need to talk." My eyes snapped to Dad. He was beaming, Mom was too. *Okay, so not bad news.* I still didn't relax.

Dad leaned in. "You're going to be a brother." He paused. "Your mom's pregnant—with twins."

My brain shorted. Twins? I was going to be a big brother...to *two* babies? The words hung in the air like a buzzer beating shot I couldn't block.

"You're...what? Twins? I'm a brother? Whoa. How—uh—how did this happen?" I stammered out then felt instant regret.

Mom laughed, a mom-look on her face. The same look she wore when I was four and asked about belly buttons. Dad grinned and started to open his mouth.

"Stop! Don't answer that!" I cut in fast. "No need for details." I held up a hand. "It's just a...surprise. When are they due?"

"October 26," Mom said. "Mid-June we'll find out if we're having boys or girls. I'm hoping for girls. But it doesn't matter really."

October. Tiny babies, little ankle-biters. In a couple years at Halloween, I'd dress them like famous basketball players for trick-or-treating. They'd be here a month before basketball season. I'd teach them to dribble, read them my favorite bedtime stories.

If they were girls I could see pink basketballs, glittery basketball kicks, tiny hands with polished nails shooting free throws. Mom had dealt with stinky gym socks and sweaty jerseys for almost sixteen years. If she got girls, she'd go full glitter mode—the sparkle equivalent of DEFCON 10.

My thoughts bounced everywhere—like someone knocked over the basketball cart in gym. I couldn't hold a thought for more than a second. I managed to say, "October."

Mom looked at me gently. "How are you feeling, hon?"

I felt the real question she was asking. Was I excited to be a big brother? She wanted me to be and I was. I was surprised. Underneath the surprise? Yeah, I wanted this.

"It's good. A big surprise, but...I'm good," I said finally, with a smile. Behind my smile, worries crept in. Would I be patient with messes? Grabby fingers? Crying for no reason?

Would I be any good at being a big brother? Fear edged in. I shoved it back. No fear. I could do this. I *wanted* to. Especially seeing my parents beaming. I took a breath, steadied myself. Then grinned.

"You're gonna need a couple of NRHS Mustang jerseys in size XXXXS. I expect to see them repping at my games."

Mom's grin widened. "Oh! That reminds me, I had something made for you."

She reached into a bag and pulled out a navy T-shirt, unfolding it with flair. BIG BROTHER TO TWINS—bold white letters across the chest. Beneath it, two identical yellow faces stared at me. Blowing kisses.

I squinted. At first glance, the smileys looked normal. At second glance? Nope, not normal. They were smug, smirking. As if they knew something. I tilted my head, didn't help. Their puckered mouths smirked at me, like I was a joke.

Mom beamed. "You love it?"

I swallowed and forced a nod. "Yep. Love it."

The T-shirt itself was fine. The faces? The faces had an agenda. I glanced at Dad. He was grinning, unaware I was having a full blown emoji-triggered psychological crisis.

"You'll wear it, right?" Mom asked.

"Yeah! Of course. Just...not right now." I folded it carefully and set it out of sight but not out of mind. I still felt their emoji eyes sizing me up and making plans.

Ivy
Summer Harmonies
Music Camp

Early June to Early August

4

ORIGIN OF THE KAZOO KULT

Ivy

Prepared for boarding I had my pass easy to access on my phone. This was solo traveling, no parents, friends, familiar faces. Just me, my suitcase, and my cello. The Dickinson gate agent assured me my cello would be safe as oversized baggage. I couldn't find the chill, or trust, to stop worst-case scenarios from looping on repeat.

A long legged boy with wavy black hair slouched in a chair by the gate. A bass case stood beside him. His T-shirt read *Low End, High Impact*. I glanced again. Yep, cute in a bad boy meets concertmaster way. I whipped my gaze back to studying my boarding pass, not before his eyes slid to my cello case. Heat crept up my neck. I focused hard on picking out a playlist.

I forgot to follow the Playlist Golden Rule; *first, the earbuds, then the playlist-always preview the blast*. I tapped before checking the connection. *Clair de Lune — Kazoo Orchestra Edition* buzzed through the air like a swarm of killer wasps racing to a connecting flight.

Startled, I dropped my earbuds. On hands and knees, I scrambled grab the earbuds while fumbling with the volume. It took too long. The entire gate area now knew I was a kazoo cuckoo.

I snuck a glance at bass boy. He was laughing. I slunk to a seat, giving my best impression of someone who would never share questionable classical music in public.

Kazoos hummed in my ears. Cello worries poked at my brain. What if the baggage handlers dropped it? Pulled it out for an impromptu hoedown, just to lose it during a suitcase emergency? My flight hadn't even started, and I had an instrument obituary half-composed. *Dearly loved stringed companion, survived by Ivy Preston, who vows never to forgive the airline for its crimes.*

Boarded and seated and buckle in, I faked being a stellar passenger. I worked on powering down my phone. The device betrayed me and blared *Eine Kleine Nachtmusik*, the meowing cats version. I poked at all the buttons and mashed the volume. The old man across the aisle glared.

The flights from Dickinson to Denver and Denver to Seattle were uneventful. Turbulence occurred only in my mind—bad flying weather as a cello worry front collided with a cell phone malfunction temperature spike. In Seattle, I followed the crowd to baggage claim. My suitcase was flung out onto the carousel. Good. But my cello? That's what I needed.

A sign pointed to oversized baggage where a crowd had gathered. The instrument cases everywhere made it obvious—we were music campers. I spotted every size and shape of case, bassoons, trumpets, even a harp surrounded by campers as varied as their instruments. My cello had survived.

I kept myself from hugging but crooned, "Not a single scratch. I almost wrote your obituary, you know." I heard a laugh and looked up. Dickinson Airport Boy, from now on D.A.B., stood nearby.

"Hey, I talk to this big guy too. Helps him stay calm," he said.

"Cellos and basses, big babies of the strings. They need emotional support. Unlike narcissistic violins who think they own the world."

He laughed, looked about to reply. *The Elephant* from *Carnival of the Animals* started playing. I turned toward the music. A man in a Summer Harmonies T-shirt waved a *Campers This Way* sign while holding up his phone, music source.

"Get the musical zoo moving!" he shouted. "Summer Harmonies' campers, follow the zookeeper!"

A few campers chuckled. The group shuffled toward him as he barked out more directions. It felt like we were being rounded up, herded—which fit, I guess. I joined the instrument herd, toting my belongings. I imagined a couple of border collies nipping at our ankles.

The camp bus pulled up to a large building with Camper Orientation signs posted everywhere. The herd, I mean, campers were offloaded. First thought? *Trees.* Trees, so many trees in shades of green I didn't know existed.

I should've journaled something deep. Instead, I posted a shot of the Summer Harmonies camp sign—weathered wood, bright musical notes, and a suspiciously chipper treble clef.

***

@ivy.celloforce

Caption: Traveling —

Don't get lost at the airport. [check]

Don't break cello. [check]

#MusicCamp#HopeICanKeepUp#CelloTravels

@ivy.celloforce

Image: A trail disappearing into trees, sunlight filtering down.

Caption: Best kind of sensory overload. Music everywhere—better energy wings than Red Bull. Forest aesthetic: 10 out of 10, would get lost in again.

#WelcomeToCamp #StringNerdsUnite #MusicEnergy

@ivy.celloforce

Image: Ivy's cello lying on lush green grass.

Caption: Survived Day One. Not expelled yet. What I know so far: The talent = intimidating but inspiring. Camp = a foreign country where the language is music.

I get to play - Tchaikovsky's Serenade for Strings.

Tours, rehearsals, new bunkmates: check, check, check.

#MusicCampDiaries #StringLife

5

D. A. B.

Ivy

The Senior String Symphony rehearsed in the outdoor pavilion. I spotted D.A.B.—Dickinson Airport Boy—setting up behind me. He looked completely relaxed—like his bass weighed nothing and nervousness wasn't a thing. I tried to look chill too, like I hadn't been sneaking obvious peeks at him.

Rehearsal started with a slow dissection of the first movement. I focused on bowing, shook off my nerves, and let the music pull me in. Playing here felt bigger. Like the music mattered more. Shortly after our break started I heard a voice.

"Hey, you handle your cello well."

I turned—and boom, D.A.B. was right there. Leaning on his double bass like he did it for a living. Tall. Relaxed smile. Definitely cute.

"Oh," I said, too breathy with surprise. Was I wearing a too-tight corset? "Thanks," I added. *Impressive conversationalist, Ivy.*

"I think we both got came via the Dickinson airport."

"Yeah, I was there. I noticed the double bass."

"The double bass not the boy?" he teased.

My brilliant reply? "Uh..."

"Sorry," he said. "I'm a bass player. Always need extra attention."

"Big double bass baby," I blurted—then slapped a hand over my mouth. "I meant...uh...well, I meant what I said."

He barked out a laugh. "Figured you might be heading here. You looked stressed—didn't want to bother you. Thought we'd cross paths eventually."

"I was stressed. My only thought was, 'My cello's going to die.'"

"Near cello death. The reason for the emotional greeting in oversized baggage claim?"

"Embarrassing. Forget the crazy cello chick, please."

"Forgotten. But what about kazoos and cats? Forget that too?"

I groaned dramatically.

"Ah, don't bother—it's bound to happen again. Flew out of the Dickinson airport because you live in...?"

"The one and only Dickinson."

"North Riverbend for me."

He held out a hand. "Jordan Scott."

"Ivy Preston."

His smile deepened. "Nice to meet you officially, Ivy."

The conductor clapped for attention, ending our conversation. Rehearsal continued. I stole a few glances at Jordan. He didn't seem bothered by my weirdness—he rolled with it. That kind of ease pulled me in.

A couple weeks into camp tucked into my bunk I smiled as I thought. Camp—nothing like I expected. I was different too. Surprising myself. I couldn't wait to share more. The girls would eat up my posts. A feeling stopped me before I hit post. A pinch of guilt twisted in my chest—like I was abandoning Aiden. I'd always felt best-friend emotions about him. But at some point, that changed. Shifted into something more—something I couldn't take back, even if I wanted to. I'd started feeling more for him while we started feeling like less.

Now I had no clue what we were. Best friends who hardly spoke? No, "Hey, how's camp? Not even a stupid "R U OK?" Aiden and I were only friends—if that. He used to bring adventure and feel like freedom. I missed the way he called me "Princess" like it was my real name, the way we built imaginary kingdoms and ruled them.

I wondered what people at camp saw in me. I was making friends, drawing people in. I'd always thought I borrowed magnetism from Aiden and our friendship.

Getting to know Jordan was it him that drew me in, or just how he made me feel seen? I enjoyed the ease he had, the way he didn't take himself too seriously but still had presence. The friendship we'd started...it was growing from joyful ground. A place I'd forgotten. Aiden used to make everything feel easier than breathing. Now, breaths felt heavier. He was layers of silence glued together by everything unsaid.

It would be easier with someone who felt open. Someone who made life feel simple. Liking someone just for feeling like Aiden's opposite? Not how I wanted to be. Especially when I knew one thing without a doubt. If Aiden reached out, tried to pull back the complicated layers—I'd be there. I'd help him peel it all out of our way.

---

ivy@cello.force

Image: Ivy holding her bow in front of her face, crossing her eyes dramatically.

Caption: Facepalmed myself. While holding my bow. Yes, it hurt.

Trigger: remembered that I once shared a recording of classical music interpreted by—wait for it—kazoos and cats. And by shared, I mean played it on a plane, onboard, with other passengers. But might have gained a new member of my kazoo kult that day. Shoutout to Jordan, bassist, fellow ND traveler, still speaking to me after hearing my Yoda impression.

#kazooforthepeople#facepalmingwithABowHurts

---

ivy@cello.force

Image: Ivy pretending to hold a soccer ball, looking skeptical.

Caption: Fun facts -I'm not an athlete, I ended up at a soccer game, I was rescued from having to run. New

---

friends=my summer heroes. So much gratefulness. True heroes.

#MusicOrSportsforme?#MusicHandsDown

---

ivy@cello.force

Image: New camp friends, Jordan in the middle

Caption: Current status—still not playing soccer, am gossiping in the great outdoors,

telling nerdy music jokes-getting pity laughs. Confirmed I will not be in the talent show.

Are all bassists chill or just Jordan Scott?

#SurvivedAnotherDayMusicCampVibes#ChillwiththeBassist#NDClass

---

ivy@cello.force

Image: Ivy performing a bicep curl showing zero muscle definition.

Caption: Chill-but-mean bassist shared my bow facepalm story with new friends.

I threatened him. My incredible strength shut him up. Okay, he stopped talking so he could laugh.

#MusicianStruggles#EmbarrassingStory
#StrengthIsAnIllusion

6

MUSIC NERDS AT NIGHT

Ivy

I'm a girl from small, rural town. I've been to a hundred campfires – backyard birthday parties, late summer s'mores, or, "It's Tuesday night light 'er up." This was a first; twenty music nerds shouting, "Jug band!" into the darkness.

"Time for a game," Jordan said, standing up and waving his arms for attention. I knew him better and I realized this was on brand—Jordan liked people. He liked watching people enjoy each other. Starting a group game was something he'd do without thinking twice.

"Here's how it works," he said. "I'll call out a category—like musical instruments. Someone else yells a letter—say, S. The first person to shout a word that fits starts a countdown from ten. Everyone else has to name something before time runs out. If you don't get one in time, you're out. We keep going until there's one person left."

Someone yelled, "Let's go!"

Jordan shouted, "Genres of music!"

Someone called, "J!"

"Jazz!" I shouted, kicking off the countdown. "Ten, nine, eight—"

"Jug band!" someone across the fire called just before I hit three. Laughter broke out around the circle.

The musical J words kept flying until two campers didn't answer in time.

We moved on. "Classical composers." "Songs with colors in the title." "Instruments smaller than a shoebox." Countdown after countdown, the group shrank. I barely survived a round that hinged on *Quena—thank you cello teacher for your insistence on well rounded knowledge base.* Eventually, it came down to me, Ella, and Ryan from brass. Jordan grinned. "Final round: musical terms. Letter: T!"

"Tremolo!" I shouted before anyone else could blink.

"Ten, nine—"

"Trill!" Ella got hers in.

"Tacet?" Ryan guessed—right after my countdown hit one.

Jordan threw his hands up. "We've got a winner—Team Strings!"

Cheers erupted from our side. Someone tossed a marshmallow in the air like a victory confetti pop.

"We demand a rematch tomorrow night!" Alex shouted.

"Anytime, anywhere!" I called back, laughing.

It wasn't basketball, but maybe now I understood a little of how Aiden and Tyler felt after a win—that shared spark-in-your-chest feeling.

***

Later Jordan nudged a log with a stick. "No talent show solo, no midnight pranks—what's your version of the camp experience?"

I hesitated. "I think... just doing it. Getting through Tchaikovsky's *Serenade for Strings* without messing up. Figuring out who I am, musically. Belonging here."

Ella rolled her eyes. "Okay, but you *do* belong. You play like someone who actually feels it."

"Thanks," I said, a little embarrassed. "Sometimes I forget that matters."

Ryan shrugged. "It's the only thing that does."

Jordan nodded. "And hey, you've got me in the back holding the bass line together. Emotional support bassist. Very niche."

I laughed. "What about you guys? Why are you here?"

Ella leaned back on her hands. "Honestly? I needed to remember I still *liked* playing, not just performing. "

Ryan smirked. "I came to be around people who don't flinch when I say 'double tonguing.'"

Jordan grinned. "I came for the late-night ensemble magic. And the snacks. No one talks enough about the snacks."

We all laughed. For a second, the fire crackled louder than we did. The quiet between us wasn't empty. It felt like something settling.

"I think I needed to hear that. That I'm not the only one figuring it out."

One by one, campers stood and stretched, the night winding down. We scattered to our cabins, still laughing, still teasing each other about dramatic guesses and missed notes. As I walked back in the dark, my hoodie zipped tight and my fingers brushing my jeans in time to some leftover melody. I thought, *"This is what I'll remember."* Not clean bowing or perfect pitch, but the games, the bonfire. Sharing a love of something bigger than any of us. We'd come here as strangers. Around the fire we'd started to become a brand new composition.

***

JOURNAL ENTRY

Today wasn't about rehearsal or technique or getting every note right. It was about the fire. The game. The way people laughed without holding back. I didn't expect to feel like I belonged this soon. But tonight, something shifted. We didn't play a single measure of music. And still, it felt like we were in tune.

7

WELL ROUNDED MUSICIANS

Ivy

At Summer Harmonies, being a well-rounded musician meant more than just scales and sight-reading. Rhythm was something you were supposed to feel in every part of life. Which explained why camp offered enrichment activities like:

- Swing Dance — a.k.a. trusting someone not to spin you into the dessert table

- Disco Night — because nothing builds confidence like platform shoes and questionable dance moves

- Introduction to Pointillism — for when all you want to do is *dot, dot, dot, dot, dot, dot.*

- Rhythm in Fiber Arts — org the experience of tangle thread, rage-quit, repeat.

- Improv Comedy for Musicians — confirmed I am excellent at panicking in any scenario.

The camp director said it best at orientation, "You can't sit in a practice room all day. A well-rounded musician needs experiences. Needs movement. Needs to feel the rhythm in every part of themselves."

So I let Jordan talk me into swing dancing. Yep, swing dancing. *It'll be fun,* everyone said. Turned out swing dancing strangely resembles a dysfunctional relationship. One person leads. One follows. Simple, right? WRONG. If the leader isn't clear? You just stand there like, "Uh, what now?" If either of you hesitates? Twenty car pile up from black ice.

@ivy.celloforce

Caption: Swing Dancing = Relationship Metaphors?

The moves:

The Swing Out = "Go away! Wait, come back!"

The Tuck Turn = "Trust me. I won't let you fall (hopefully)."

The Sugar Push = "Give me space but also don't leave me."

Don't even get me started on dips. They're just trust falls in disguise.

Jordan: "Follow my lead."

Also Jordan: *Spins me into orbit.* So yeah. Relationships. Suspiciously similar. Discuss.

#DeepThoughts #RhythmAndRegret

@ivy.celloforce

Caption: Whoever let Jordan on the dance floor made a mistake.

Me: "Think we can actually do this?"

Jordan: "Not a clue."

Me: "Cool. Let's go."

We created a new genre of dance- Survivor Reality Swing Dance. Pretty sure I barely survived.

#realityswing#realwivescanttouchthis#voteJordanoff

@ivy.celloforce

Me: "I give up. You win Worst Dancer."

Jordan, bowing: "Thank you, thank you."

Me: "If dancing is inner expression, you're channeling Post Malone doing the Carlton." And then he did the Carlton. Someone come get him. I'm embarrassed for both of us.

#DancingDisasters #SwingAndMiss

@ivy.celloforce

Caption: Jordan, "I'd dance better with my bass."

Me: *Please don't let that happen.*

Also me: *It happened.*

He swing danced with an imaginary double bass. I backed up five steps. He spun it like a yo-yo. Dipped dramatically (nearly took himself out). Whispered to it like they were sharing secrets. Patted the air and said, "Almost lost her."

#SwingingAndStringing #JordanAndBigBertha
#PublicHumiliationAsTherapy

Later on Jordan said the dumbest thing ever, "My bass, high
strung like every instrument I've ever dated."

I was stunned into silence by his stupid joke. Not true. I was
laughing so hard I couldn't form words. I'm waiting for someone
to pop out of the woods and tell me they want to cast me in a
musical comedy.

8

TRAIL RIDE OR TRUST EXERCISE?

@icy.celloforce

Image: Candid shot of Ivy on Beethoven the horse—nervous smile, sitting slightly too up right in the saddle. In the background, either a blurry squirrel or another camper's mock-dramatic finger pointing at the trail.

Caption: Hoping *Roll Over Beethoven* doesn't become the soundtrack of my life with me crushed by ahorse whose first name is Ludwig. Trust is a work in progress. Half-ton of muscle vs. one-pound squirrel. Guess which one freaked out.

#BeethovenBetrayal #BadMusicMoment #TrailRideDrama

@ivy.celloforce

Caption: Final Trail Ride Stats

Image: A squirrel, smug as can be.

Caption: Final Trail Ride Stats:

Beethoven—terrified of squirrels

Me—terrified of falling off

Unnamed Warm-weather State Boy—terrified of North Dakota women

Jordan—trail ride MVP and cracking stupid jokes

#TrailRideSurvivor #BeethovenHasTrustIssues #RegretsWereMade #JordanEqualsDumbJokes

---

@icy.celloforce

Image: Ivy staring straight into the camera with a formidable expression.

Caption: Public Service Announcement-Do not call me "North Dakota" unless:

-You can say something about ND that isn't "cold" or "corn"

-You've personally survived an Alberta Clipper

-You understand NDSU football superiority

Otherwise? Prepare to be frozen out.

#KnowYourStates #NorthDakotaDefense#AlbertaClipperIncoming #Midwest Survival Guide (For the Warm-Weather Delusional)

@ivy.celloforce

Image: A photo of the North Dakota Badlands, looking dramatic and very much not cornfields.

Caption: Unnamed Warm Weather State boy says, "North Dakota is just cornfields."

Ivy says, "Excuse me??"

North Dakota says, "Hold my coffee, I've got this. Teddy Roosevelt trained here -More national football titles than your state -Blizzards that could END YOU, Home of the Badlands, Rough Riders. Anyone?"

Warm Weather State: Alligators -Theme parks -Traffic

I'll take my chances with the blizzards.

#MidwestPride #FrozenButFierce#Cow-WomanEnergy

@ivy.celloforce

Image: Slightly more intense selfie (think-I ran through a blizzard in flip-flops).

Caption: Thoughts of those warmed year round.

Unnamed boy from a warm weather state: "I think I could handle a little snow."

Me: Impromptu TED Talk. And go...

Frozen car doors? Standard.

Eyelashes turning to ice? Obviously.

Nostrils frozen shut? Duh.

Entire personality shaped by horizontal snow? From birth.

Stay warm, buddy. The prairie doesn't care about your theme parks.

#ColdHardFacts#FloridiansArentReady #FrozenOut #JSis #NDTough

9

TEXTING NODAK

Me: Trail Ride Survived. Also, sorta spending time with someone.

Emilia: Ivy? What??!

Maddie: Explain. Immediately.

Aria: Drop a name or we riot.

Me: Jordan, from Dickinson. He was in the Dickinson Airport. Didn't talk to him until SEA-TAC. He's chill, nice. Experienced a specific type of chaos and didn't get scared away.

Jenna: Define *"specific type of chaos."*

Me: Accidentally blasted kazoo music in the Dickinson Airport. Followed by Cats Classical music on the plane. He didn't flinch.

Aria: He's either unshakeable. Or secretly weirder than you. Of course your weirdness is adorable.

Emilia: Either way, I like him.

Maddie: Need a vibe check and visuals. Now.

Me: Also, weird. I guess I was flirted with. ???

Me: Selfie with a very confused expression.

Me: Jordan told me, "I think Unnamed Boy from Warm Weather State was flirting with you.

Me: I said, "huh???"

Me: Then, "Oh well. He got hit by an Alberta Clipper. Wasn't dressed for the weather.

Me: I kinda gave him a TED talk about the superiority of ND.

Aria: Full blown sideways snow mic drop courtesy of Ivy Preston.

Maddie: I just snorted smoothie. You TED talked a flirty guy into submission. Bet he's still running.

Aria: He got Dakota'd. There's no comeback from that.

Emilia: Did he insult ND chica?

Me: TED talk trigger=ND's just corn. And there's no real college football played in ND.

Jenna: Nobody survives getting ND schooled by Ivy. Also, don't dis our football.

Jenna: Do we need to worry about Jordan? He experienced Ivy at Full Peak

Me: He egged me on, so more peak than me?

Jenna: So you're saying Dickinson Dude brought on Peak Ivy on Purpose?

Maddie: 1. Nose + smoothie, still Ouch!
2. GIRL, he chaos whispered Peak Ivy appearance? Thinking soulmate possibility.

Emilia: Possibility of an Ivy + Jordan ship now makes me worry about nuclear armament.

Aria: Noooo!! 2 much 2gether. Dickinson's not ready. North Riverbend's not ready. ND isn't ready. The world's not ready. We aren't ready. I'm not ready and heading to shelter in the basement.

Emilia: Already called the nuclear weirdness, but seriously—if you kiss him, we'll need to update the group chat name and maybe evacuate a five-mile radius.

Jenna: Is Jordan cute-cute or just cutest guy in the Dickinson airport cute? Important distinction.

Maddie: I'm just over here planning your future wedding playlist. Looking for cats singing The Wedding March. Kidding! (Unless.)

Me: We're literally just hanging out.

Aria: Hanging out. With vibes. In a post-kazoo dystopia. Sure, okay.

Jenna: It's like Katniss with Kazoo instead of arrows. Survival and Soulmate found.

Me: You all need to. Take. A. Breath.

Me: Just friends. Just hanging out.

Me: Probably will stay Just Friends.

Maddie: Wedding March played by bagpipes? Dystopian feel?

Emilia: Music camp=Strings and Soulmate.

Me: Do you want me to go reverse-flirt Warm Weather Boy? Fall in love? Move away to warm weather state?

Me: Cause this is how it happens.

10

War of the Weeds

Ivy

The path between activities curved along a grassy knoll dotted with tenacious,r little dandelions. Here, in all this lush greenness, they popped up—stubborn reminders of everything I couldn't let go.

I kicked one of the white seed heads, scattering fluff. Was I making wishes? Destroying them? I didn't know. All I knew was every time I saw one, I thought of Aiden. And every time, an ache followed.

I kicked another. Seeds scattered like memories. Aiden. My best friend. The boy next door. The one whose world revolved around basketball. And my world followed a sad little orbit around his—present in his galaxy, but invisible.

I remembered how I used to send a whole patch flying. He'd run laughing through the fluff, trying to make a wish on every seed before it disappeared. Always claimed he got them all. Always insisted it worked.

Aiden didn't make wishes anymore. He drilled and he practiced. Me? I wavered somewhere between hope and loss. I stomped another dandelion, watching the fluff scatter like smug little ghosts.

"You wish-flinging weed goblins! Why do you pop up everywhere? Mocking me with your fake-deep symbolism?"

Another kick. More fluff. I threw my hands in the air. "Massive piles of buffalo dung ! Could you at least try to be less poetic while ruining my day?"

I glared at the next one, bent down, and yanked it straight from the ground. "Stinky hairy buffalo butts!"

A beat of silence. I exhaled. "Okay, wow. That might've been a bit much." I brushed stray fluff off my leg.

"You didn't ask to be the weeds of false hope," I told the survivors. "Scattering your little maybe-wishes across the breeze like you've actually got a plan."

I picked another. Held it up. "No hard feelings?" I blew the seeds into the wind. "Now I feel like I owe an apology to the God of Noxious Weeds."

I cleared my throat. "Okay, God of Weeds, hear me out while I list the virtues of your fake flower."

I twirled a stem between my fingers. "First off, people make wine out of you. You're basically the champagne of weeds. Respect."

I sat up straighter. "Let's not forget your nutritional résumé. Salads. Teas. Stir-fries. People pay actual money for organic dandelion greens. Meanwhile, here I am—committing mass dandelion-icide."

I gestured to the battlefield. "I don't recognize myself."

Dramatic sigh. I flopped onto my back. "I'm the villain in a very niche plant documentary. I promise no more violence against your people, dandelion deities."

And then—rumble. Not wind. Not bees. Bass. Strings. Ominous orchestral buzzing. Cosmic intervention? Divine punishment? I sat halfway up, blinking at the meadow.

"Ivy Preston," a voice intoned above me—low and grave. Deadly calm.

DAAAAAAAH! DAAAHHHH! DA-DAAAAAAAAAAAAHHHHHH!

Brass. Tympani.

BOOM, BOOM, BOOM, BOOM, BOOM

I screamed.

Heart racing, I scrambled upright and braced to face a shimmering god of photosynthesis. I was ready for the Curse of Chlorophyll-*To the end of your days, your succulents will rot and your houseplants will die overwatered deaths.*

It was Jordan.

Phone in hand. Deadpan expression. Narrator voice fully activated. "You seemed like you were having a moment. I gave you the perfect soundtrack."

I yelled with what breath I had left. "You Straussed twenty years off my life!"

He shrugged. "It felt spiritually aligned. Anyway, I'm usually mistaken for a god of stringed instruments, not a dandelion deity—but I can flex if necessary."

He gestured toward me. "You've got dandelion guts all over you. Looks like you barely survived the great dandelion massacre."

I scowled. "Yeah, well, it was me or them."

Jordan tilted his head, watching a few seeds drift by. "And yet, they're the ones floating away. Living their best lives."

I glared at the fluff. "Keep floating, you useless white, whisps of false promises."

I gestured to the field. "I'm done being fooled by the sunshiney, fake-flower charm of this weed."

I turned to Jordan. "This is war. And there's no Switzerland in weed war."

He grinned. "Hey, not my fault I caught you mid–dandelion genocide."

We locked eyes. He grabbed a dandelion, twirled it dramatically, and blew the fluff straight at me.

"War it is."

For five minutes, we battled. An epic, slow-mo, fluff guts in the wind face-off that honestly needed *Yakety Sax* as its soundtrack, and I think it might have kazoos.

"Well, false weed god, are you going to judge my dandelion destruction?"

Jordan picked up another stem, twirling it. "Are you going to tell me what the weeds ever did to you?"

I picked at the ground. "I was on my way to rehearsal when these fluffy little weeds ambushed me. I hulked out. You showed up mid-destruction. I used to see wished, now? Just weeds. Stubborn ones. The kind that remind you what you should let go of, but can't"

Jordan nodded and blew the seeds from his dandelion. "Yeah, I get that. I've got some stubborn stuff too."

I looked at him. "We're both hanging out on the deal with stuff plane? Need to deal, but putting it off?"

"And I thought getting away for the summer would help. I feel more confused."

He nodded again. "Yeah. I get that."

"Do you?"

He laughed, rubbing the back of his neck. "Maybe not exactly the same, but I know what it's like to want something to make sense—and it doesn't."

"Is there a name attached to your stubborn?" I asked.

"Is there one attached to yours?"

"Let's say it on three. One, two, three—"

"Aiden." "Sarah."

We blinked at each other.

"Details?" I asked.

Jordan exhaled, staring at the sky. "Sarah's not a weed. She's funny. Snarky. Kind. But she's seen me as a good buddy for so long. I thought I'd finally left buddy status, but nope. I don't know if she got scared—or if I was never anything but the safe guy."

I nodded slowly. "Sounds familiar. Aiden lives right next door. We've been best friends since diapers. He's fun. Adventurous. Amazing. And completely clueless. He exists in a basketball-playing bubble. That's all he can see."

Jordan groaned. "Next door? It's hard even being on the same block. So we're both stuck on people who don't see us the way we see them? Who live irritatingly close?"

I nodded.

Jordan smiled and nudged my shoulder. "Crazy odds Preston. But we don't have to figure it all out today."

I leaned back. Let the tension ease. He was right.

"I'm glad I met you, Jordan Scott."

We settled into the grass, conversation drifting between jokes and something real. Camp had given me exactly what I needed—not only for music, but for me. I wouldn't leave with all the answers. Or a boyfriend from Dickinson. But I'd found some clarity. And a real friend.

11

IT'S YOUR THING

Ivy

The bonfire smelled like burnt sugar and smoke—one of those scents that clings to your clothes for days in a way you don't mind. Half the group tried to sing along to a song no one fully knew. I hugged my knees, picked at the frayed edge of my sleeve, and watched Jordan nudge a log with the toe of his sneaker.

"So, Preston," he said, voice light but pointed. "What's the move?"

I blinked. "The move?"

"Yeah. What's next?"

I hesitated. "You mean...like, going home?"

He rolled his eyes. "No, I mean are you actually gonna do anything about...ya know."

He gestured vaguely.

"Global warming, mosquitoes, black holes?"

"No Preston, your unresolved, super obvious thing."

I scowled. "That's a terrible name."

"Fine. Your *Denial Spiral™*."

I sighed and looked at the fire. "I don't know what you want me to say."

"The truth about where you're at?"

I tilted my head back. "Ugh. I feel like if I start something, it's gonna turn into a *thing*. And I don't want a thing."

Jordan gave me a flat look. "That's the dumbest thing you've said all summer."

I frowned. "Thanks?"

"Ivy, everything is a thing. Avoiding stuff? That's a thing. Pretending you don't care? Also a thing. Acting like you can just go home and keep everything the same? Yeah. That's a thing, too."

I chewed my bottom lip, stomach knotting. Jordan let the silence settle, then nudged me.

"Hey. You'll figure it out. And if you need a distraction, text me. I've got plenty of bad decisions to make about *my* Denial Spiral™."

I managed a small laugh. "You're an idiot."

He grinned. "A supportive idiot."

I raised an eyebrow. "Well, you supportive idiot, I'm happy to support you with your Denial Spiral™. Or is it a *thing* now? Because, remember—everything's a thing."

He shrugged, unbothered. "But that's a whole other thing."

I pointed at him, smirking. "That was my point."

After the bonfire, the things didn't disappear. But they felt lighter.

I feel kind of melancholy today.

Like a piece marked mesto—that soft, aching sadness woven into the notes.

Is it the end of music camp catching up to me?

Or the blank space next to Aiden's name on my phone?

It used to be full of him.

Silly, spontaneous messages.

Inside jokes.

Plans that turned into little adventures.

Now? Nothing. Just an empty chat bubble where his voice used to live.

Sometimes I think I should've texted him first.

Should I have?

No—his silence started long before camp.

For fourteen years, I've lived next door to the sounds of his life.

The echo of basketballs.

His laugh through the walls.

Doors opening, closing, slamming.

Music. Movement. Now? Silence.

He's still there.

But I can't hear him anymore.

If my life were music, I'd be caught in a rest—suspended, soundless.

But I won't stay there forever.

I'll find my way back to the melody.

Even if he never hears it again.

Because my music still matters.

And it deserves to be played.

With or without an audience.

***

Final Concert Tonight

(A surprising number of classical music fans live in the forests of Washington State)

It was so late by the time I made it back to my bunk after the final concert.

Tonight is hard to describe.

Like any other performance—but not.

The concert hall buzzed with nerves—last-minute tuning, deep breaths, fingers stretching.

Jordan looked at me.

I must've looked green.

JS: looks like you're about to spontaneously combust or barf.

Me: Arrrghh. Both.

Then we played.

That first note—God, so beautiful. Bittersweet.

Like a memory I almost recognized but couldn't hold.

I was playing. And not overthinking.

It had been a long time since that last happened.

Unbelievable.

Not overthinking. Just playing.

And then it was over.

The last note faded.

Applause came crashing in.

I didn't want it to end.

The reception was a blur—photos, lukewarm punch, all the usual.

Jordan dropped into the seat beside me.

JS: Well, Preston, you didn't combust.

Me: Nope. Internal organs remain intact.

JS: Low bar, but a win.

JS: You're not gonna disappear when you get home, right?

Me: ?????

JS: don't turn into Wild Horse Girl running with the herds in Teddy Roosevelt National Park. If you do, at least send a postcard.

Me: I'll teach the herds hoof tap. Morse code. You better start learning and listening.

***

And because I can't leave camp without a few last lists:

Best Things I Learned:

• Music is a language I can speak without overthinking

• It's okay to mess up—it's part of playing

• Some people are worth getting to know, even when it's hard to trust

• I can handle a lot more silence than I thought

Hardest Things:

• Letting go of how things used to be

• Facing the fact that nothing stays the same

• Feeling like I don't fit—not even with the people I've known forever

• Getting past my own fear to do something anyway

Best Music Moments:

• The feeling of bow on string—like everything I've been holding in gets released

• Losing myself in a song and forgetting to worry

• The way music can hurt and heal at the same time

• The final note of the concert—the quiet after the chaos

AIDEN

Dakota Hoops Basketball
Camp & Clinic

Early June to Late June

12

Basketball White Noise

Aiden

Basketball camp was practice on steroids—and I loved it. The gym echoed with sneakers slapping, and basketballs bouncing. Coaches shouted drills to position players. I ignored the sweat dripping down my face. The mix of sounds was familiar, comfortable. The white noise of where I wanted and needed to be.

"Heads up Pedersen!"

I turned to catch a fast pass from Jake, my drill partner.

"Thanks, Reiman." I handled the ball and finished the drill.

Coach blew the whistle. "Good work, boys. Take ten."

I pulled back, leaning against the wall, breathing hard. My mind buzzed with the last drill, already replaying it. Free throws need work. Footwork needs to be quicker, cleaner.

A list. The thought caught me mid-breath. An Ivy list. Like she was standing there beside me. She'd shake her head at me. *As if you'd write any kind of list, Aiden—unless it's about the wonders of Kevin McHale.*

I wondered—had she listed the joys of her music camp? Ranked her top ten cello pieces of summer? An annotated list, obviously, because she was Ivy. The thought stuck. I gave in. I imagined saying: *Ives, you and your lists.* She'd give me that half-smile, one eyebrow raised to dare me. I never could back down from her dares.

So I made one.

Basketball Moves to Improve:

• Free throws — stop overthinking and shoot
• Footwork — keep drilling speed
• Shooting range — find weak spots and work them

I grabbed my water bottle. Ivy would've added commentary.

"Don't forget passing to your teammates instead of being a three-point hero."

I froze. I heard her voice so clearly when I'd hardly talked to her this spring. Could I list the last conversation we'd had? Anything we'd said to each other since school ended? I knew I'd blown it at the end of school year. Screwed up badly. I didn't know what to say to her. So I let it go knowing I was making it worse everyday.

***

This morning, I woke up hyped. Drills. Skills. Sharpen. Polish. Ball was all that filled my head. Last night? I'd passed out. Too tired to overthink. Before I fell asleep, my brain shifted toward Ivy. My best friend and I'd barely spoken to her in weeks. I started to worry about us, our friendship then stuffed it down and let exhaustion claim me.

I could've texted: *Hey Ives. Sorry I'm a jerk and didn't say goodbye. But you know basketball takes up all my bandwidth, right?* I didn't reach out. Didn't text. Didn't check in. Didn't know what to say. Can't fix anything. Can't draw up a play for this. Messy scares me. Messy makes me feel.

Guess the easy path's my specialty.

***

Mornings for drills. Afternoons for scrimmage. A shrill whistle from Coach. We're back on the court. We ran, wove between cones, made impossible passes. That was the plan. But then I saw it. A flash of white and green at the edge of the court. A half-smashed dandelion. Its white seeds clinging on, ready to scatter at the slightest breeze. A strange feeling hit me. I wanted to jog over, pick it. Blow it apart and send a wish flying, like Ivy and I used to do. Back then, those wishes felt real.

Magic.

I didn't move. Wishing felt soft and out of place. I was on the court. A place for hard work and focus. For grinding. Not wishing on fluff. I shook off the memories. I wasn't here for dandelion wishing. I was here to prove myself. To push harder. Be better.

Something about the dandelion stayed with me—a loose thread I couldn't pull free from a frayed edge. I was locked in. I knew my goals. Yet, something felt off balance. Like the solidity I thought I had was false.

13

THE JOSH HARLOW

Aiden

A week into camp I saw him. The Josh Harlow was standing in the coaches' huddle, arms crossed, leaning against the wall. He looked relaxed but locked in. It didn't look quite right. The scene needed a neon arrow pointing at him while flashing, LEGEND IN THE MAKING.

I kept my mouth shut. Didn't want to let out the Jenna-level squeal I was fighting off in the presence of The Josh Harlow. *Dude*, my inner cool guy told me, *chill*. Josh grew up around Dickinson—farm kid. His high school play got him a full ride at the University of Minnesota. He was kind of my varsity ball equivalent of a K-pop band.

Coach waved us over. I ended up right next to Josh. He exuded cool but not untouchable. He was one of us, but next level. The kind of guy who said, *Yeah, I know I'm, well, me. But hey, I'll lean down and lend you a hand.* We exchanged a nod. I did not squeal. Internally? Maybe. But externally? Calm. Mostly. He gave me a quick once-over—like he was reading my stance, my energy, my

DNA. I suddenly wanted to fix my hair, flatten the cowlick that never stayed down.

"Pedersen, right?" he asked, voice casual but confident in a way that makes you want to stand straighter. I felt inner cool guy wheeze and whisper, *"He knows my name,"* before he fainted back on a chaise lounge that my psyche provided.

"Yeah," I said, clearing my throat. "That's me."

"Coach K. pointed you out. Said you're running shooting guard. Wants me to get in some time with you."

"Sounds great. Cool. Yeah. That'd be great. I—uh, yeah, look forward to it. That'll be good."

Inner cool guy revived to shout at me, *"Shut up, Pedersen. Shut up."*

I panic-thought back at him, *"I can't shut up. I can't shut up."*

Now inner cool guy used a psyche loudspeaker, *"SHUT. IT."*

Josh let out a small laugh and nodded again. "I'll catch you later." Then—shoulder clap. My idol thumped my shoulder. I would never wash that shirt. Or that shoulder. Probably.

We hit drills again. I dialed in. I poured everything into the reps. Every pass, every cut, every shot. I was going to train with The Josh Harlow. Was this... a Josh Harlow effect? I wanted to text Ivy. She'd laugh at me. Call it *The Josh Syndrome* like a science fiction title. She'd mock my reaction to a manly shoulder thump, but she'd understand. Even while teasing, she'd be supporting me. She always supported my game. The thought withered. I'd chosen the easy way. Avoided the messy. Let her head into summer with nothing from me.

The realization hit—heavier than the ache in my muscles.

14

Josh Has a Molly Dolly

Aiden

The whistle blew for the hundredth time—sharp and shrill. Coaches and refs. Holding the power of the whistle definitely went to their heads. This time, the sound brought relief. I bent over, hands on my knees, taking a moment to confirm I'd survive the walk to my water bottle. Sweat dripped down my face, but I wasn't ready to let up.

Okay, yeah. The Josh Harlow watched our drills today. No big deal. Just another day of practice. Not trying to impress anyone. A whistle pierced the air again.

"Yo, Pedersen! Over here." The Josh Harlow called me to work one-on-one. I nodded, totally unfazed—then tripped over air. Smooth, Pedersen. Now recover. Regroup. Play it cool.

"Right on," I said. *Right on?* My inner cool dude shuddered. I grabbed my bottle and took a swig.

Josh clapped his hands. "Anytime today, rookie."

I could've tossed out a clever remark. Should've. Didn't happen. I gave a nod and trotted over like a golden retriever. Be cool. Be cool. I was actually training with The Josh Harlow.

"So, here's what I'm seeing, Pedersen. Push harder on those cuts. Defense is watching your hips—if you're predictable, they'll shut you down."

I nodded, breathless—from the drills, obviously.

"You've got good, clean footwork." Inner cool guy gave a foot shout out. *Way to go toe-bros!*

You've gotta keep your eyes up. Attack the lane like you mean it."

Attack like I mean it. I felt like I should salute. Yell Sir, yes, sir. Inner cool guy screamed. He'd gotten access to a to a tornado warning siren. *DO NOT SALUTE!!!*

I listened. Took the ball. Stepped into position. ne-on-one with The Josh Harlow. I had the ball. The second I moved, Josh was my shadow. Had I been playing with a shadow ball? I swear the ball dissolved into nothing—or that's how The Josh Harlow made it seem.

"Eyes up, Pedersen!"

Right. I shifted left, faked, then cut right. He stayed with me, fast and fluid, barely sweating. I tried to drive past him, but his hand was already there, reading my move before I finished it.

"Too slow," he said easily, stealing the ball like it was never mine. He dribbled back out and tossed it to me again. "Try it again."

Deep breath. Reset. This time, I pushed harder. Drove my shoulder in. Forced my way to the hoop. I was fast—quicker than most guys my size—but Josh was next level. Still, I went for the layup. He smacked the ball clean out of my hands.

"Good drive," he said, tossing it back. "But you need to sell it more. Change speeds, change angles—make me believe you're going one way, then go the other."

"Got it."

He watched. "Okay. Go."

I attacked the basket. Slowed. Hesitated—just enough to sell the pullback—then exploded past him. He didn't recover. I made the layup.

"Better," Josh said, nodding. "Do it ten more times."

I swallowed my exhaustion and got to work. By the end, my lungs were burning, my legs lead. I was eighty percent sure I'd sweated out every ounce of hydration in my body. Josh jogged to the bench and grabbed a towel. I collapsed beside him, breathing so hard it sounded fake.

He chuckled. "You'll live, Pedersen."

"Bet," I muttered.

A phone chimed. Josh checked it. His whole face changed until he looked like a living heart-eyed melty face love emoji.

"Sorry, gotta take this," he said, standing.

I nodded, draining my water. His agent? A scout? No, not with the heart eyes.

"Hey, Molly-Dolly," Josh said, voice dipped into syrup. Wait. What? "Yeah, I can't wait. Soon, baby." Oh.

"Mmmhmm. Me too. Love you. Nope, I love you more. Okay. Love ya, babe. Bye."

I sat there, bottle mid-air. The Josh Freaking Harlow just cooed. The same guy who blocked me into another dimension now looked like he'd walked off a chick click movie set. He hung up, totally unfazed.

"All right, Pedersen, up on your feet. Let's hit the paint."

I shook off the secondhand romance haze.

"Not your agent, I guess."

Josh grinned, stretching. "Nope. Better. My girl."

I blinked. "I—uh—what—"

Josh clapped his hands. "Less talking, more drilling, rookie. Let's go." I pushed up, still mentally processing that The Josh Harlow had a Molly-Dolly. That was a plot twist.

Later, in my bunk, I spotted one of my teammates grinning at his phone. Not quite Hallmark-level dopiness but close. I glanced at my phone on the nightstand. No texts from Ivy. Because I hadn't sent one. I hovered over her contact. Opened the screen. Blank.

What would I even say? *Yo? Wanted to say all I can think about is basketball? Have a good life?* I clicked my phone off and dropped it. My head hit the pillow. I was asleep in five seconds.

***

I was at the U of M. Josh said I had potential. Gave me tickets. I was courtside, watching him float to the basket—slow-motion dunk magic.

The crowd exploded. Confetti? No. Emoji reactions. Kissy faces. Sparkles. Heart eyes everywhere.

Josh stuffed the ball. Landed. Started blowing kisses into the stands.

Wrong. The Josh Harlow did *not* blow kisses.

He pointed to the crowd, thumped his chest. *Mouth moved and said, "That was for you, babe."*

Then—It was me. I'd dunked the ball.

A heart-eyed emoji tried to smooch me. I swatted. Missed. Swatted again. Smacked myself.

I woke with a jolt, heart pounding. Full emergency mode.

Except—Not an emergency. Worse.

I'd just dunked for Ivy. Blown kisses. Said, *"That was for you, babe."*

Nope. Nope nope nope.

I sat up, dragging a hand down my face. I needed to shoot. Needed to reset my brain. Not because of the dream. Definitely not because of emoji nightmares. Outside, in the cool night air, I started to shoot. Dribble. Breathe. Focus. Shoot. Repeat. Footsteps echoed.

"Couldn't sleep?"

I shook my head. "Nah. Needed more reps."

Josh stepped onto the court, grabbed a ball. "All right. One-on-one. First to seven."

I nodded. "Let's do it."

We played hard. He was better. But I held my own.

After the final shot, he clapped me on the back. "You've got skill, Pedersen. But you need to trust yourself more."

I dribbled, frowning. "I feel like there's always more to prove."

Josh nodded. "There always is. But don't let it consume you."

I frowned. "Isn't that the point?"

He gestured to the bench. "C'mon. Sit a sec."

We dropped down, catching our breath. He pulled out his phone, flipped to a photo. Him and a girl with a violin, both laughing.

"That's Molly," he said, voice softer. "She's a musician. Kind of a nerd. Keeps me grounded."

The word *musician* sparked something. Ivy's face flashed in my mind—lost in her music. I shoved it down. Josh kept talking.

"She's tough. First time I tried to impress her, I dribbled around at lunch. She didn't blink. Just went, 'Nice ball. Do you take it everywhere or is it for dates with yourself?'"

I winced. "Damn."

Josh groaned. "I strutted to a bake sale in warm-ups. She said, 'Did the NBA call? Or are you flexing for the cookies?'"

I laughed. "Brutal."

"She kept me honest," he said. "That's why I love her."

He rolled the ball between his hands. "You thinking college ball?"

"Yeah. That's the goal."

Josh nodded. "Then grind. But it's not just skill. You need resilience. Humility. Balance."

I looked up.

"You remind me of me," he said. "I thought I had it figured out. But when I wasn't the best anymore, I shut everyone out."

I bounced the ball. "But you figured it out."

"Because of Molly," he said. "She reminded me I was more than a stat. That life's bigger than a box score."

He looked at me. "You think it's about proving yourself. But sometimes, the real fight is remembering who you are when no one's watching."

I stayed quiet. It stuck, too much. Josh clapped my shoulder. "You're good, Pedersen. But don't just be a player. Be a person. You're allowed to care about more than basketball.

Doesn't make you weaker. Makes you better."

15

DRIVE HOME DREAM

Aiden

The gym smelled like sweat, rubber, the lingering burn of competition, and the pursuit of dreams—Kidding. It was one hundo rank, sweaty dudes.

We were pushing hard on the last day of camp. Wringing out every last second of practice before heading home. Josh wasn't taking it easy on me. At all.

"Feet quicker, Pedersen! You're moving like you haven't woken up from a nap."

I pushed harder, shifting left, then driving right—Josh read me again and cut me off before I could plant my foot for the shot.

"Predictable," he said. "What have I been telling you?"

I exhaled through my nose, frustrated but focused. *Trust yourself.* That's what Josh had been telling me. This time, I didn't fake a move—I let instinct take over. I shifted my weight, dropped my shoulder like I was driving left, then suddenly pulled back.

Josh bit on the fake for a second—enough time for me. I pivoted on my back foot, created the space, and stepped back for the jumper. The ball arced, smooth, effortless. Swish. Josh nodded, a flicker of approval crossing his face.

"Much better. You didn't overthink it. You trusted yourself and playeeyd in the moment."

We cycled through more drills, a blur of sprints, layups, and shooting reps until my muscles burned and my shirt stuck to me. Josh jogged over and slapped me on the back.

"Good work, Pedersen. You'll be solid if you keep this up."

I rolled my shoulders, catching my breath. "If?"

Josh grinned. "If you don't let your own head get in the way."

I huffed out a breath, letting the words settle. Josh stretched his arms overhead, glancing at me.

"Hey, I never asked you, you from around here?"

"North Riverbend," I said.

Josh looked at me. "No kidding. You know Whitney Harlow?"

That name caught me off guard. "Yeah, I know her," I said carefully.

"She's my cousin," he said like it was no big deal. "Small world, huh? I'm visiting her family for a couple of weeks after camp."

Whitney? Josh Harlow's cousin? Whitney, who lived for drama like it was a competitive sport? I took a second, trying to reframe everything I knew about her.

"Didn't know you two were related," I said, keeping my tone neutral.

"Yep," Josh said, his smirk softening into something almost amused. "Whitney's complicated. I'm guessing you've never seen the side of her I know. Man, she's the mean girl in your class, isn't she? I'm not surprised... it's not my story to tell either. Like I said, complicated."

I didn't even know where to go with that, so I nodded. Josh checked the time, then pulled his phone from his pocket.

"Give me your phone. I'll add my digits. Text you when I pull a pickup game together."

My brain short-circuited. Josh Harlow wanted my number. Wanted to text me for a pickup game. I absolutely did not give an embarrassing squee, though it was a close call. I unlocked my phone so fast I nearly dropped it.

"Yeah, okay, cool."

Josh tapped his number into my contacts, then texted himself.

Trying not to sound too desperate, I casually asked, "Cool if I bring a friend?"

Josh smirked. "Yeah, Pedersen. Bring a friend."

I had to help spread the Josh Harlow effect around. Right? First to get the experience? My bro Tyler. He was going to lose his mind. I could already hear him now, "Did he make you his mini-me? You realize this makes me, like, Josh Harlow-adjacent, right? That's elite adjacency." Followed by, "If you pass him the ball before me, I'm taking your Christmas present back."

Josh was still watching me, waiting. I cleared my throat, shoving down the ridiculous mental image of Tyler grinning like an idiot and me pretending I didn't know him when he inevitably started talking trash. I played it cool and did nott grin like an idiot myself.

I looked at the text Josh sent. "Uh...any reason you texted me this, Harlow?" He looked at my phone where the blowing-kisses smiley face emoji stared back.

"It's doing that again? Damn it." He shook his head. "Don't worry about it, Pedersen. Stupid phone sometimes randomly inserts emojis."

Josh pocketed his phone, tossing me a ball. "All right, one last drill before you go." I gripped the ball, feeling the weight of it against my hand.

"Let's go."

***

I grabbed a shower and a change of clothes before Dad showed up. Camp was only a couple hours from North Riverbend. The road hummed beneath the tires—steady, rhythmic, the kind of sound that lulls you into a weird, car half-sleep. Not totally out of it-hnot really awake. My head leaned against the window, glass cool on my temple.

***

The gym was packed. Bright overhead lights. Roaring crowd and the sharp squeak of sneakers. I was locked in—ball in my hands. Shot clock winding down. I needed to make this play. I drove forward—fast, sharp, cutting left—

Whistle.

"Offensive foul! Pedersen, that's one."

What? That wasn't a foul. The defender barely moved. Reset. Shake it off. Focus. I got the ball again. Crossed, faked right, attacked the lane. I was making this shot.

Whistle.

"Charge. That's two."

Exhale. Okay. Play smarter. Another possession. Fast break. I passed, cut, got it back, rose for the shot—

Whistle.

"Illegal screen! That's three, Pedersen. Watch yourself."

This game had to be rigged. I turned to protest—but voices in the crowd cut through.

"Didn't say goodbye."

The words sliced through the noise like a perfectly placed pass. I blinked. The game kept going, but everything felt off.

"Didn't text."

The ball came to me, but it was like I wasn't in control anymore. My hands felt slow. Weighted. I pushed forward anyway. Pivoted, faked—

Whistle.

"Blocking foul! That's four, Pedersen."

"Didn't seem to care."

I shook my head, tried to block it out. This wasn't real. The scoreboard blurred. My teammates faded.

There was only one person I could see now. Someone in the stands. Small. Shoulders sagging.

I couldn't see her face—but I didn't need to.

My stomach twisted. I tried to call out—say something, anything—but my voice didn't work. She stood up. Turned. Started to walk away.

Whistle.

"Fifth foul. You're out."

Everything stopped. I walked to the bench. Defeated. he lights dimmed. The noise faded. A sneering smiley face emoji floated past.

Game over.

***

I jerked awake with a sharp inhale, pulse hammering. The car was still rolling down the highway. Nothing but rolling land outside the window. It was a dream, but more. I shifted, trying to shake it off.

The dream clung to me like sweat after a double-overtime game. I pressed a palm to my chest where weight still lingered. I'd fouled out. Not in dream basketball-in real life. I didn't even know if I'd get another quarter to make it right.

The highway stretched out—miles of open road and sky. I leaned my head against the window, watching the hills and buttes of western North Dakota roll by. I should've been rehashing camp. What I'd improved. What still needed work.

Josh Harlow gave me his number. Invited me to a pickup game. That should've filled my head. But my brain kept circling back. To her. That ridiculous dream a few nights ago. The dream I'd just had.

I sat up straighter, shaking my head. It wasn't real. But it felt real. And now I was sitting here, too many miles away, replaying all the things I didn't do.

Didn't say goodbye. Didn't text. Didn't check in. I rubbed my face, exhaling hard. How'd this freaking mess happen? I knew I'd let her down. Didn't know how to fix it. Didn't even know if we were still friends.

I squeezed my eyes shut, but that didn't help. I could see her—blonde curls catching the light, arms crossed, eyebrows raised in that unimpressed, tired-of-Aiden's-crap expression. I let out a breath, shaking my head. No clue where our friendship stood.

I grabbed onto something I knew for sure. The Josh Harlow was a Legend in the Making and he wanted my digits.

.

16

Whoa, Mom!

Aiden

Dad and I pulled into the driveway. I dropped my bag inside the door, expecting everything to feel the same. The familiar scent of Mom's cooking—garlic and something baking—drifted in from the kitchen. My stomach grumbled. Yeah. I was home.

I followed Dad into the kitchen, my mind already on the fridge, wondering if we had anything decent to eat. Before I reached it, Mom walked in. Her face lit up when she saw me.

"Aiden!" She pulled me in for a hug. Or tried to.

I stepped back, eyes wide. "Whoa, Mom! Did you swallow a basketball?"

I wasn't trying to be a smart mouthyyyhyhhhhh—it just came out. I had no frame of reference for how Mom looked. I'd been gone a few weeks. She was different. Dad pretended to give me a light whack on the back of the head.

"That's not how you talk to your mom, son. Even if—"

Mom laughed. "It's fine. I think he's in shock." She pointed a playful finger at me. "But listen up, buddy. That was your one and only free pass to comment on how big I'm getting."

I blinked, still trying to process everything. "I—wow. I wasn't expecting—."

She patted her stomach with a soft smile. "Well, inside this basketball, you've got two little WNBA stars growing and getting more and more anxious to meet their big brother."

I straightened. "Girls?"

Dad grinned. "Yep. We found out while you were at camp. Thought we'd surprise you when you got home."

I opened my mouth, then closed it. My throat felt weirdly tight. "Sisters," I said. The word felt strange—unreal—but kind of... cool. Mom pulled me in for a hug again, and for the first time in my life, there was something between us. The bump. It made everything real in a way it hadn't been before.

I swallowed, stepping back as I took her in. My parents had me young, so I'd only ever known her one way. She looked different. She'd always been happy, loving. Now she looked more. More like herself, more what she was supposed to be. She rested one hand on her stomach.

"It feels kind of wild, huh?"

I nodded. "Yeah."

Dad leaned back against the counter, crossing his arms. "Makes everything actually real, doesn't it?"

I glanced at Mom. Yeah, it sure did.

Mom smiled, her expression gentle. "You want to feel?"

I blinked. "What, already?"

She chuckled. "Can't feel kicking yet, but you can feel how firm my stomach is. It's weird, but kind of cool."

I hesitated. It felt too personal and unexpected. But then I stepped forward, pressing my palm gently against the curve of her stomach.

I paused. Then frowned. "Feels like a basketball."

Dad lost it. He doubled over, laughing. Mom rolled her eyes but smiled. "Of course you'd say that."

I grinned, rubbing the back of my neck. "I mean, seriously. The texture's kinda like the inside of a brand-new game ball."

Dad wheezed, still laughing. "Oh man, that's good. Hey, Lindy, the girls might come out dunking."

Mom shook her head, smiling. "You boys are hopeless. Things will be changing—soon you two will be outnumbered. Keep that in mind, boys."

I pulled my hand back, still a little stunned. "But seriously, Mom, you look amazing, and really happy."

Her expression softened. "I am."

Something in my chest tightened, not in a bad way, just a sense of change. Dad clapped me on the back. "There's going to be two little ones running around after there big brother."

I let out a breath, stepped back. "Yeah, okay, wow."

Mom patted my cheek, her smile turning teasing. "We missed you, honey. You doing okay?" She gasped. "Not sick of basketball, are you?"

I shook my head. "No, Mom. Not sick of basketball. Tired. Shocked there's a basketball in the middle of us when you hug me. Feeling, you know—glad to be home."

Dad leaned against the counter, arms crossed, watching me. His expression softened a little—not enough to be obvious, but I felt it. A quiet pause stretched between us. He knew there was more than I was letting on. Not about everything, but enough to tell that something was off.

It was the way I hadn't said much about camp on the drive home. How I kept shifting my weight, like I wasn't sure if I wanted to stand still or move. Maybe it was how my voice had caught, for a second, when I repeated the word *sisters*.

Or maybe it was the fact that the person I would have talked to about all of this, who would have listened while I tried to figure out what I was feeling—wasn't here. And maybe wasn't in my life anymore. Dad didn't say anything. Gave me one of those looks—steady, patient, knowing. And then, like that, he let it go.

His usual grin slipped back into place. "Get ready, it's happening. Diapers. Burping. Spit-up. Don't think little girl diapers are going to be any sweeter than little boy diapers."

I grimaced and grabbed my bag. "Okay, dad. You've convinced I'm not touching diapers. And on that lovely note, I'll head up. You didn't kick me out of my room, paint it pink while I was gone, did you?"

Mom laughed. "Of course not. You knew we were turning the spare bedroom into the nursery."

She reached up, patting my cheek. "Don't worry, Aiden. You'll always be my baby boy. My first baby. And my biggest baby, even after these two arrive."

I groaned. "Okay, Mom."

Dad snickered behind me.

I rolled my eyes and started toward the stairs, calling back over my shoulder, "Now, I'm off to shower and a shockingly early bedtime. And probably to dream about my sisters hatching out of a basketball-shaped egg."

Dad laughed again. "Wouldn't be the weirdest dream you've ever had."

"That's for sure." *If you only knew, Dad.*

Then came the thought—*sisters.* I wondered what kind of big brother I'd be to them. I showered and dumped my clothes in the laundry hamper. Not a good smell. I'd lug it down to the laundry tomorrow. There was a quiet knock on the open door. Dad. He didn't wait for me to invite him in—just leaned against the doorframe, arms crossed.

"Figured I'd check in before you crash."

I shrugged, keeping my focus on my phone, even though I wasn't really looking at anything. "I'm good."

"Aiden, you've always been a terrible liar. Glad that hasn't changed."

I huffed, running a hand through my hair. "Got back and was gob-smacked, I guess."

He nodded like he understood. No doubt he did. "I get that. Your mom looks different in just a few short weeks," he said, stepping into the room. "Change isn't easy. Even good change is hard. It's okay to feel unsettled. The only kid until fifteen, then twin sisters? That's a lot. But you're going to be a great big brother, Aiden. The babies are two lucky little girls."

I glanced at him as he sat next to me on the bed. "Thanks, Dad. I needed to hear that."

"And Aiden, I'm not going to ask for details unless you're ready to talk, but Mom and I noticed Ivy seemed to be missing from your life the last half of the school year. She's been your sounding board for years. Whatever's different there, you've got us."

"Okay, thanks." I sighed. "I know you're there for me. I do. Things are kind of a mess, but I... can't talk about it right now."

"You're still your mom's baby boy," he ruffled my hair like he used to when I was a kid. "And my little man, the Aidenator, my Little Dunker, my...."

I laughed and shoved him away. "Got it old man!" He squeezed my shoulder and got to eave.

"Nite, Aid."

110

The door clicked shut behind him. I flopped back, stared at the ceiling. Realizing how dumb I was to let what I'd had with Ivy possibly slip away.

AIDEN

HOME – NORTH RIVERBEND, ND

End of June to Early August

17

MISSING THE SOURCE OF RHYTHM

Aiden

The next couple of days passed in a blur. I fell into my usual routine—drills in the driveway, watching old game replays, practicing free throws until my arms ached. I told myself this was what I loved, what I'd always done. If nothing else, basketball still made sense. At least, it should have.

Something was off. The rhythm I'd always had—morning workouts, afternoon practice, evening drills—felt hollow. I sank shot after shot. I ran the same drills. But they didn't settle me. When I played, I wasn't really there. I missed easy shots—ones could make in my sleep.

My footwork was a half-step too slow, hands late on the release. The driveway hoop echoed with each bounce of the ball, but the rhythm—the steady, familiar rhythm that'd always been there—was gone.

I'd been really slow to understand. Doubt I really saw it clearly at all. Ivy was part of my rhythm. Even when I was too caught up in my own world, she was there—showing up, supporting, keeping things steady. I never thought about it, only expected it. Were we fixable? If not what would it to to me? Could I get a rhythm back without her?

***

I was stretched out on the couch, laptop balanced on my knees, eyes locked on the screen. The University of Minnesota's maroon and gold jerseys flashed across the court, Josh moving like he owned the place. I'd seen this game before—one of their big matchups against Purdue last season—but I still found myself rewinding certain plays, breaking down his movements.

Defense. Footwork. How he tracked the ball. But then I caught something. I scrubbed back and slowed the clip. Purdue's point guard didn't beat Josh with speed. He beat him with a hesitation. A half-second pause before changing direction, enough to make Josh commit too soon.

Huh.

I ran it back again, watching the subtle shift in Josh's weight, the fraction of a second where he bit too early. I could use that. Before I could rewind again, my phone buzzed in my hand.

Josh: Yo, Pedersen. I'm in Riverbend hanging out with my fam. One-on-one at Simmons Park? I won't tarnish your rep. Too much anyway. [smiley face blowing kisses]

I stared at the kissy-face emoji glaring back at me—somehow smug and mocking, like it knew something I didn't. He'd texted me a couple times before, and his phone always glitched like this. Randomly inserted yellow kissy emojis that sometimes morphed into other expressions. Once, they'd been glaring. Another time, looked like they were silently judging me.

Now, I swore one of them stuck its tongue out at me. Another flashed the L—loser sign—across its forehead. I shook my head. Watching too much game tape. Had to be the issue.

Me: My turf now, Harlow. Be afraid. Fifteen?

Josh: That works. No fear here. Gotta check on my little protégé. Don't let me down. [smiley face blowing kisses] [smiley face blowing kisses]

The late-afternoon heat pressed down on me as I stepped onto the court, sweat already gathering at the back of my neck. Josh was already there, spinning the ball lazily on his fingertips—that easy confidence of his making me grit my teeth a little.

"Pedersen," he greeted, tossing me the ball. "Was starting to think you weren't showing up."

I caught it, rolling my shoulders to shake out the stiffness. "Not a chance," I said. "Needed a real game. Not messing around in the park."

Josh smirked, nodding toward the hoop. "Alright then. Let's see if those weeks at camp actually did something for you."

I took my first shot—a clean jumper from the free-throw line. The ball arced perfectly, swishing through the net. I let out a slow breath. This. This was what I needed. A rhythm. A game. Something that made sense.

Josh nodded. "Not bad. Now let's see you keep up."

We played. Hard. For a while, I held my own—keeping pace, matching Josh move for move. But he had this way of reading the court like he'd already been here, had already seen the moves I would make. Every time I thought I had an opening, he was there, cutting me off, shifting into position before I could react.

"Good footwork," he noted after I faked right and managed to squeeze past him for a layup. "Use that more. Don't waste your first step."

I nodded, bouncing on my heels as he checked the ball back to me. We kept going, neither of us letting up. He rose for a mid-range jumper, and I reached high enough to contest it, but the shot was clean. Swish.

"Nice release," I admitted.

Josh smirked. "Be sure of your shot, Pedersen. You hesitate, you miss."

I took the ball at the top of the key, dribbled low, then stepped back and pulled up for a three. The ball kissed the rim before dropping through. Josh let out a short laugh, jogging after the rebound.

"There it is." He passed it back, motioning for me to go again. "Shoot like that every time."

The game settled into a rhythm—drive, defend, contest, shoot. A steady back-and-forth. Good plays on both sides. Not much talking beyond quick pointers and short jabs. Finally, after I clanked a mid-range shot off the back iron, Josh caught the rebound and dribbled out, slowing the pace.

"Solid work," he said, breathing steady. "You played sharp."

I let out a breath, bent slightly with my hands on my knees. "But?"

Josh gave a small shrug. "But nothing. You played sharp." He spun the ball in his hands before passing it back. "You seemed off rhythm for awhile there. You remind me of myself, Pedersen. When I'd too into myself. Anyway, just don't forget—you're a person first, baller second."

I caught the ball, turned it over in my hands. He didn't press. Didn't dig deeper. Just let the words stick like darts he'd thrown. I nodded once.

"Got it."

Josh clapped me on the shoulder before heading to the bench. "Good. Now let's run it back."

Later that night, I lay in bed, staring at the ceiling like it might give me answers. The window was cracked just enough to let the summer air drift in, still cool, not unbearably humid. My phone sat face-down beside me.

I didn't touch it. I'd avoided looking at Ivy's socials since she left. Guilt? Punishing myself? I wasn't sure. It felt easier not to—to pretend whatever was happening with her wasn't really happening.

But the words kept coming back, *Don't forget you're a person first, baller second.*

Yeah, well. I knew what grinding to be a baller looked like. Being a person first? That part was fuzzier. No playbook I'd ever seen addressed it. I rolled over and picked up my phone. Opened Instagram.

@ivy.celloforce stared back at me.

I hadn't looked. Not once. Told myself I was giving her space. Staying focused. Not getting distracted. But the truth was uglier. I didn't say goodbye. Didn't text. Didn't call. Let her leave. And I didn't look because some part of me already knew what I'd see—Her smiling. Having fun. Living without me. And that felt like getting dunked on from above and below at the same time. And it felt cowardly. But now I was scrolling.

***

First Post

Image: Ivy crossing her eyes behind her bow, expression pure chaos.

Caption: Facepalmed myself while holding my bow. Yes, it hurt. Facepalm incident triggered by a reminder that I once shared classical music as interpreted by kazoos and cats. And when I say shared, think big—like an airport. And inside a plane. Possibly gained one new member in my kazoo kult (aka: Jordan, bassist, fellow ND traveler. Still talking to me after hearing my Yoda voice).

#KazooForThePeople #BassistsAreChill
#FacepalmingWithABowHurts

***

Second Post

Image: Ivy holding a soccer ball, face pure disgust.

Caption: Facts, I am not an athlete, l somehow ended up at a soccer game, new friends = saved me from soccer. True heroes. Eternally grateful.

#MusicOverSports #StillWinning

***

Third Post

Image: Ivy mock-flexing with zero muscle.

Caption: Something about someone sharing the bow-facepalm story with everyone.

She'd used that move on me. I should've laughed. It was funny. It was Ivy. But the inside jokes weren't mine anymore. And there were names I didn't recognize. I used to be the one next to her in moments like that. Used to be part of the chaos. The cult. The caption.

***

Fourth Post

Image: Group hike. Ivy and someone—maybe that same guy?—mid-slide into a creek, both of them muddy and soaked.

Caption: *Cutest accidental slide into the creek I've ever seen.* @ellaenchantedbynotes @basslineandbaseball: Not my fault she trusts questionable shoes. @ivy.celloforce: Blame the hill. And gravity. And my tragic fashion sense.

She looked like she was having the time of her life. I locked my phone. Not because I was done scrolling. Because it hurt. I didn't say goodbye. Didn't check in. Didn't even try. Things had always come easy to me. School. Friends. Ivy.

A thought wormed through my mind, *you let the easy things slide.* Stupid not to realize that easy things still need effort. For years Ivy and I were easy, cruising along in our friendship without much effort. When had I last made an effort for her? No clue, so maybe she'd given up. I opened my phone again. Hit my contacts. Hovered over the message button.

Typed: Hey.

Deleted it.

Typed: I saw your posts.

Deleted that, too. Typed nothing. Stared. Then turned off my phone. She hadn't left me behind. I'd never tried to stay in step.

18

UPDATE MOB

Aiden

The local park—a sprawl of green with scattered picnic tables—was the designated hangout for the afternoon. Jenna and Emilia claimed the swings, their laughter ringing through the air as pumped themselves higher. Drew and Nate were locked in a mashup soccer game, competitive shouts echoing across the grass.

Tyler was sprawled on the lawn. I dropped my backpack and flopped down beside him, stretching out.

"Look who finally showed up," Maddie teased, her smirk full of mischief. "Get lost without any paint on the floor?"

"Yep. Got confused because I couldn't find the sidelines paint. Some guy in a ref shirt finally pointed me in the right direction," I said.

Tyler chuckled, shaking his head. "Guess that's one call a ref got right, huh? Bro, you might need someone walking in front of you to lay down paint, considering how much time you spend on the court."

"Most important place to get to, right?" I shot back, grinning.

Tyler was about to answer when Aria, who'd been lazily leaning on a picnic table, suddenly propped herself up on her elbows, her expression shifting.

"Who's got the latest Ivy update?"

Tyler turned toward me so fast it was almost comical. His gaze was sharp. Expectant. Like he was waiting for something—a name, a text, a status update. Which I didn't have. Because I hadn't put any effort into my friendship with Ivy before she left. Now I didn't know what to say or do.

"You're killing me, Aiden. You know that? Killing me."

Then he turned back to Aria and the rest of the group, the conversation moving on—even if I felt stuck right where I was. At the table, the group was buzzing. Phones passed around, laughter punctuating whatever they were looking at. Everyone suddenly seemed to have a connection to her. Inside jokes. Updates. Details I hadn't earned. I used to know all the Ivy things first.

Tyler nudged me. "Hey, you know why Nate and Drew are in the Ivy update mob?"

I shrugged. "Does it matter? You're gonna tell me anyway."

"Yep," he said easily. "They've both got a bit of a crush on our girl. And they've been texting her this summer."

I blinked, trying to keep my expression neutral. Texting Ivy? Drew and Nate?

"What are you talking about?" I asked, forcing a laugh.

Tyler sighed dramatically, like I was the greatest burden in his life. "Dude, really? You think it's your pretty face that keeps them coming back to the lunch table? For most people, there's actually a limit to the amount of basketball they can talk."

I let my gaze drift toward Nate and Drew. Good guys. Solid teammates. I never thought about them as competition for anything—least of all Ivy's attention.

"But wasn't that because of basketball? I mean..."

Tyler raised an eyebrow. "Sure, they talked hoops with you. But maybe they were also there for a different reason."

I curled my fingers into the grass beneath me. Since when had they been texting her?

"They got her number during the last couple of weeks of school. Hoping to hang with her this summer. Her music camp changed those plans. Texting will have to do for now, I guess."

Spending time with her this summer. The thought hit me like a sucker punch. Summer was always Ivy and me. Our time. Late nights sneaking into the park, biking to the creek, watching bad movies at her house. I hadn't even thought about making plans this summer. Hadn't asked if she wanted to do any of those things. Was I even surprised about Nate and Drew? Ivy made space for people who showed up. Something I hadn't done for too long.

Jenna's voice rang out from the table, carrying easily across the grass. "All of us girls got some pics yesterday. Looks like she's made some new friends—including that boy from Dickinson who's all about the bass."

My head snapped toward her so fast I heard a crack. Jenna grinned, eyes locked on me like she was testing for a reaction. "Mr. Bass Player and Ivy swing dancing. Looked like a great time."

I forced my expression to stay even, raising an eyebrow. "Bass player?"

"Yeah—double bass, not bass guitar," Emilia added. "Jordan, something, from Dickinson. Ivy sent a pic where he's practically cuddling his bass."

Drew, who'd been studying a picture on Jenna's phone, suddenly perked up. "Hey, I know this guy." He squinted at the photo again. "Oh yeah, I've played baseball against him."

Tyler snickered, tossing a handful of grass into the air. "So he's all about the bat, and sounds like he's got no treble with the ladies either."

The pun set off a round of laughter. I forced myself to join in. It was a joke. Teasing about Ivy having fun with a guy who wasn't me. But the thought hit me sideways—it had been simmering in the back of my mind, gathering steam, and now it was out.

I'd noticed when I scrolled her posts. I'd seen her smile with him. Read the jokes. The hashtags. The comments. Now it wasn't a rando from camp. Now he had a name. Jordan. Now he had context. And I was still stuck trying to act like I didn't care.

Maddie leaned back, smiling. "Ivy seems to be having a great time. It's cool she's meeting new people."

I nodded. My voice came out too flat. "Yeah. Good for her."

Aria leaned in. "We should plan something for when she gets back. Maybe meet this infamous bass master."

"Definitely," Tyler agreed. "Got to see if he lives up to the hype. See if he's worth all the treble."

I exhaled sharply, forcing a smirk. "Great idea. Let's do it."

They kept laughing, but the tightness in my chest didn't ease. I pulled at the grass again, fingers twitching. Maybe I'd text her. Not to say anything. Just to check in.

As I thought it, I already knew I wouldn't. Because it felt messy. And I didn't understand the rules.

19

WEIRDEST PICKUP GAME EVER

Aiden

Josh was hanging in Riverbend. He texted about getting a pickup game together. Not gonna lie, I fanboyed when he texted me. Even when the message showed up with those stupid blowing-kisses emojis the Josh effect was still strong.

The park, in late afternoon, was streaked with long, slanting tree shadows. The temperature bearable thanks to a light breeze. I dribbled absently, waiting for the rest of the guys to show. Tyler had arrived with me. He stretched his arms overhead, bouncing on his heels like he was warming up for a real game.

"Think we're about to get destroyed?" he asked, rolling his shoulders.

I snorted. "You worried, Ty?"

"Nah, just setting expectations low so it doesn't sting too much." He grinned, then nodded toward the group walking up.

Josh led the way, his usual effortless confidence making him easy to spot. Two guys I didn't know trailed behind him, school friends, I guessed, both tall, both built like they played. Off to the side, walking a little ahead was Drew. I'd texted him about playing and he was free—a rarity. Then I saw Whitney.

"Huh."

"Yeah," Tyler muttered, glancing over. "She's been here like ten seconds, and I already know she's plotting something."

I wasn't sure what to make of her showing up, even as Josh's cousin.

"Pedersen," Josh called, tossing me the ball.

I caught it and smacked it once against the pavement. "Harlow," I answered.

Josh smirked, his gaze flicking to Tyler. "This your guy?"

"Don't underestimate me," Tyler said, cracking his knuckles. "Or do. Makes it funnier when I score on you."

Josh laughed. "Fair enough."

"This is Tyler, and that's Drew over there."

Josh gave them the bro nod—the one that didn't work on Molly but definitely made guys think he was cool. The game started casually, the teams mixing up quick. It wasn't about proving anything—just playing. No refs, no official rules beyond calling our own fouls, and no one trying to dominate. Even Josh played like he was here to have fun.

I found myself slipping into rhythm. Fast breaks. Smooth passes. The occasional deep three when I had space. The hesitation move I'd picked up from watching Josh's game still worked—once.

Josh adjusted fast, cutting it off the next time I tried it. I shook my head.

"Already caught on, huh?" I muttered, grinning.

Josh gave me a knowing look. "Not bad, though."

I was about to pass to Ty when I heard, "Whoa, whoa, whoa...Time out."

Tennis shoes skidded on the blacktop. I tucked the ball under my arm. Then I saw why we'd stopped. A pink playground ball rolled onto the court, followed by a tiny girl sprinting after it. I stuck out my foot to stop it. The ball was bright pink—covered in yellow smiley-face emojis.

I yanked my foot back as soon as it stopped. Not at all because the emojis creeped me out. The girl skidded to a halt next to the ball but didn't grab it right away. She looked up at me with huge blue eyes, unblinking. Her blonde curls bounced as she stared.

"Hi! Tanks! Sohwwee."

An adult jogged after her, calling, "Eyyyyy..."

My heart jumped. For a second, I thought she'd say "Ivy."

"Isla, be careful. So sorry, boys."

She caught up and looked down. "Isla, my princess, you need to watch where you're running. You could've been hurt."

Isla's mouth turned down. "Sohwwee, Mommy." Then she perked up and pointed at me. "Dat pwetty boy stopped da ball. Tanks. Otie-dotie. Bye."

She walked off the court holding her mom's hand—but kept her eyes locked on me the entire way. The other guys started laughing, but Tyler and I exchanged spooked looks.

"Dude."

"Yeah, I know."

"Pedersen," Josh called, grinning. "Someone's got a little crush on you. The pwetty boy who stopped her ball."

Whitney, standing on the sideline, wore a puzzled look. She was still watching Isla and her mom.

I shook my head. "Play ball!"

Whitney stayed on the sidelines, arms crossed. She called out things like, "Nice shot, Aiden," but mostly stayed quiet.

It wasn't that I minded. I just didn't get her. Tyler did.

"Dude, she's trying so hard," he muttered as we switched sides.

"Trying what?" I asked, genuinely confused.

Tyler groaned. "You're killing me, Aiden. You're—never mind, man."

The game kept going until the sun dipped low, streaking the sky with orange and pink. Eventually, someone called last point, and after a few more plays, it was over. We all stretched, cooling down, tossing verbal jabs at each other about missed shots and dumb fouls. Josh fist-bumped me on his way out, promising a rematch.

Whitney lingered a little too long, but I was already focused on packing up my gear—and trying to shake the image of that little blonde-haired, blue-eyed face peering up at me.

Tyler shook his head. "Weirdest pickup game ever."

As we walked off the court I felt an absence. An absence shaped exactly like the person I usually talked to after stuff like this.

And it wasn't Whitney.

20

WHITNEY'S COVERT OPS

Aiden

It had been weeks since basketball camp ended. Summer felt like it was picking up speed—days and evenings filled with pickup games, hangouts with friends in all the usual spots around town. There was one new addition to the routine. One I would never have planned on: Whitney.

Everywhere I went, I found her. Or maybe—she found me. She had some freaky sixth sense about my location. I tried to brush it off, but I couldn't convince myself it was coincidence. I might be oblivious but not dumb enough to not see the way she acted. Not even I could misunderstand.

***

Messing around in the park with Tyler. And...there she was, strolling over with a casual wave and a knowing smile.

"Hey, boys," she called, leaning against the chain-link fence like she'd been invited. "Didn't think I'd see you here today."

Tyler gave me a look, eyebrows raised.

I shrugged, trying to act casual. "What's up, Whitney?"

"Oh, not much," she said, flipping her hair over her shoulder. "Thought I'd see what's happening around here." She pointed to the hoop, grinning. "You got room for one more?"

Tyler handed her the ball before I could answer, smirking. "Sure, why not?"

We ended up in a sort-of game, though it was obvious she was more interested in chatting than actually playing. I caught Tyler's amused glances and rolled my eyes. He was enjoying this way too much.

***

Later that week, a bunch of us were hanging out at Northbend Burgers, soaking up the AC and the last few weeks of summer. Ivy was still away, but Emilia, Jenna, Maddie, and Tyler were all there. It was a rare afternoon when I wasn't myself practice or hunting down a hoop. I decided to relax and I was relaxing. Until Whitney walked in.

She strode through the diner doors like everyone in the place should've been expecting her. I didn't have to look up to know it was her—something in the air shifted. I glanced at the girls, catching their expressions. Not one of them looked happy to see her.

"Hey, y'all!" she said, sliding into the last open seat—right next to me. Close. Too close.

Emilia muttered something under her breath—probably a creative insult in Spanish. Maddie rolled her eyes. Jenna, too sweet to do anything but look mildly distressed, pressed her lips together.

"Hope I'm not crashing the party," Whitney said, all smiles.

I forced a laugh. "Nah, it's cool."

. Except it wasn't. It really wasn't. The conversation limped along. I felt the tension in the way the girls glanced at each other. Whitney's presence changed the whole vibe. She was performing. Tyler cleared his throat, leaning back with a lazy grin.

"Whitney, are you a ninja? Because you have got high level shadowing skills."

She huffed, rolled her eyes. "If I am, I'm pretty choosy about who I shadow, Tyler. Don't get your hopes up."

Then she turned her smile on me—practiced, too bright, like she'd rehearsed it in the mirror hundreds of time.

"Anyway, maybe I enjoy the company. We high achievers will be spending a lot of time together when Aiden makes varsity basketball and I make varsity cheer."

Help me, inner cool guy squeaked out before he curled up into a ball. I was at least six inches taller, but I felt like a bunny about to be eaten by a snarling wolf. A wolf wearing a smiley-face emoji mask. She stood, tossed her hair. Not a strand moved out of place. The move was so perfectly choreographed there should have been backup dancers.

"Welp, wanted to say hey. Looking forward to seeing you at games. Can't wait to cheer for you, Aiden."

Then she was gone—leaving behind the faint scent of something expensive and the undeniable feeling that I'd been steamrolled. I dropped my head onto the table.

"Why me? Huh? Why me?"

The laughter around me was relieved, like we'd survived a natural disaster. Tyler clapped my back like I'd just lost a championship game.

"You see what she's up to now? Please tell me you get it."

"Yeah. I get it now." I scrubbed my face with both hands. "Almost makes it not worth getting to play pickup ball with Josh."

Tyler gasped. "The Josh Harlow is always worth it."

AUGUST

21

ON TIME-SEND SNACKS

Ivy

I dropped into a seat near my gate, stretching out my legs and adjusting my carry-on. The overhead screen flickered.

Seattle → Denver — ON TIME

I pulled out my phone. The girls would be expecting an update. Flying home felt different. I handed off my cello without a second thought. Okay—maybe not tenth through twenty-second thoughts. Still that's growth.

> **Me:** Camp van dumped me in Seattle. Hanging at Sea-Tac, waiting for my flight. Two flights til home. Send snacks. See you soon-ish.

> **Emilia:** YAY!! You're never leaving me again.

> **Jenna:** Here's a cheer for you! Hold the line, make it strong, Ivy get your butt home where you belong!

> **Me:** LOL. My butt's on the way.

Maddie: We need to catch you up. Did you know Whitney's basically Aiden's personal GPS tracker?

I paused.

Me: Personal GPS tracker??

Emilia: She's… there. Everywhere. Pickup games, the park, the diner—anywhere Aiden is.

Maddie: It's bad.

Emilia: Aiden looks like a hostage every day. But per uzhe, he's too nice to tell her to leave.

Emilia: She followed him into North Bend Burgers and slid up next to him at our table. No invite. No hesitation. Just plopped down like she belonged.

Maddie: Tyler asked her if she had a tracking device on him. "Do you materialize where Aiden is, or…?"

I laughed. Classic Tyler.

Me: Please tell me she looked embarrassed.

Emilia: Not even a little. She sneered at Ty and told him he had no worries from her.

Aria: Even Jenna looked cross.

Me: She made Jenna cross??

Jenna: More than cross. I had a small bubble of mad. LOL. Yeah, she's too much to take.

Emilia: Upside? Soooo easy to come up with nicknames for him now. Mr. Too Nice. Mr. Manners. Aiden-the-Ungetawayable.

Maddie: Don't forget his superhero powers!

Aria: Super Mean Girl Magnet Man.

Maddie: Super Yeah-No-Problem Man.

Jenna: Captain Courteous. She said with zero meanness.

I stared at the screen, feeling a twinge of something sharp. His chill, can't-rock-the-boat vibes—those wouldn't hold off Whitney. She looked right through me, but I'd been a fence. A short, fun-sized picket fence, but still. A boundary.

Was this karma? His obliviousness to me ramping up his Whitney-attracting pheromones? For a second, I felt sorry for him. Then the ache passed. Whitney was annoying. But his life still looked like it was on track. Mine had stalled. But not anymore.

Maddie: At this point, he needs a flare gun and a rescue whistle.

I exhaled, picturing Aiden's awkward half-smile. He wouldn't shove Whitney aside. He wouldn't even say no. But somehow, he still managed to ghost me. Not my business. Not anymore.

Me: C'est la vie.

Emilia: LOL! Ivy's pretending not to care.

The boarding announcement crackled overhead. I grabbed my carry-on and pulled up my boarding pass.

***

Sea-Tac → Denver

Little to no issue. (Unless you count me accidentally humming "Leaving on a Jet Plane" louder than necessary.)

Denver → Dickinson

Arrival

Touchdown in North Dakota. The terminal was quiet in that "is-it-a-federal-holiday" way. Not empty—just calm. Soft-spoken. Like the state itself.

I moved toward baggage claim, spotting my parents right away. Mom was waving like crazy. Dad smiled beside her, steady and warm. Relief settled into my bones. Home. Other airports make you walk forever to find your people. Here? They were right there, where the feeling began.

Mom pulled me into a tight hug—extra high squeeze ratio. "I missed you, honey."

"I missed you too," I mumbled into her shoulder. Lavender and sun.

Dad took my carry-on, kissed the top of my head. "How was the trip?"

"Flights? Easy, on time."

"Camp?" Mom asked.

"Fun. Tiring. Busy. Challenging."

"What about you?"

I caught myself mid-yawn. "Right now? Tired. But overall? Hyped. It was a really great summer."

Mom side-hugged me. "I'm glad to hear that."

As soon as we pulled out of the parking lot, my phone buzzed.

> **Emilia:** Welcome back to the Badlands. Where people are too nice and stuff their emotions. How's it feel?

I smirked, thumbs already moving.

> **Me:** Was I gone? Feels like I never left. Stuffing my feelings down as we speak.

> **Maddie:** Speaking of never leaving—we witnessed the worst escape attempt ever.

> **Me:** And??

Emilia: He literally walked in the opposite direction, and she followed. Hurt to watch.

Maddie: We need to launch an Aiden Extraction Plan.

Me: Sounds like a S.W.A.T. situation.

Emilia: Or S.W.A.P. — Separating Whitney from Aiden Permanently.

I chuckled. Sent a side-text to Emilia.

Me: Karma?

Emilia: ???

Me: Can't shake off Whitney, but had no problem ghosting me.

Emilia: Hmmm. Nope. Just his usual-Oblivious Polite Idiot™

Me: If you say so. Out to the farm day after tomorrow.

Emilia: Can't wait. For real. Never. Leaving. Me. Again.

Me: Ah, little mariposa. One day you'll grow wings and leave me behind.

Mom glanced over, smiled as I yawned again. Dad said, "We're glad you're home, kiddo."

"Me too."

The highway stretched out around us. Golden prairie. Big sky. Rolling hills of Theodore Roosevelt National Park at the edge of the horizon. I'd grown up with this view. I hadn't really seen it in a long time. My phone buzzed. I didn't check the group chat. Instead, I typed out a message to Jordan.

> **Me:** Almost home. Passing the national park. Resisting the call of the wild horses.

A few seconds later:

> **Jordan:** Stay strong, Preston. They can smell your indecision.

I huffed a small laugh, shaking my head.

> **Me:** If I disappear into the hills, tell Emilia she was right about everything.

> **Jordan:** Absolutely not. If you run off, I'm following. We'll start a horse-hair string ensemble.

I smiled and slipped my phone onto the seat. Glanced out the window again.

I knew exactly where I was. I knew how close we were to home.

But inside, everything felt just a shade off—washed in something gray. I wasn't sure if I'd truly made it home. It couldn't feel fully like home if Aiden was next door but not in my world.

22

FARM REUNION

Ivy

"Iveeeeeeeeee!"

I laughed, almost covering my ears as Emilia's squeal went higher. No matter how great my summer had been, I missed her. I was back at the Preston farm for cousin time.

"Ooof!" She wrapped me in a hug. My cousin was shorter than me, but her hugs felt like she'd been lifting with the football team.

"I missed you too. Ems, except you're about to break me."

Emilia let go with a pout. "You were gone too long. Never again, you hear me!"

We ran inside to her family and our Grandpa and Grandma Preston. Lots of hugs and catching up. Tía Mariella and Grandma fed us—stuffed us to the gills. Emilia and I escaped for some one-on-one cousin time.

Late afternoon sun stretched long shadows, casting a golden haze across the lawn. We were sprawled out on an old blanket. Hay, grass, and wildflowers scented the air. Leaves rustled in time with early cricket chirps warming up for the nighttime show. Cousin magic wrapped around us, taking us to a world of our own. A place to laugh and talk without holding back. It was so good to be back. This farm felt as much like home as the house I shared with Mom and Dad.

Emilia plucked at tall pieces of grass. "Tell me everything. How was music camp? No boring stuff—I want juicy details."

I laughed. "Juicy details and music camp might not belong in the same sentence."

"Come on, Ivy," Emilia teased, eyes mischievous. "What about that guy? What was his name again? Jake? James?"

She already knew his name.

"Julius," I said. "No, wait—Jasper? Jefferson?" I grinned. "You know it was Jordan, you goof. We got to be good friends. Hung out a lot."

Emilia gave me a knowing look, crossing her arms. "Okay. And? You can't stop there. You said he was cute. Are you going to see him more? Are you in lurve?"

I threw a handful of grass at her and shook my head. "Nothing happened, Ems. Except I made a great friend. I'm glad I met and got to know him."

Emilia raised an eyebrow, clearly not buying it. "Uh-huh. And what's the real story? Don't make me drag it out of you."

I sighed, laying back and stretching. "You're a pain, you know that?"

"Yep. It's supposed to be that way. *Yo soy tu familia.* Now spit it out!" She poked my ribs to emphasize her impatience.

She didn't poke hard, but she knew I was beyond ticklish there. "Fiiiiine, fiiine, stop poking me!" I stuck my tongue out and started talking.

"I had a great time getting to know him. He's cool, and we got each other. Anyway, he's hung up on someone. This girl, Sarah. They've known each other forever—live on the same block."

"Yikes," Emilia winced. "Did he talk about her the whole time?"

"No. But I could tell. He lit up whenever he mentioned her. She sounds amazing—kind, smart, super talented."

Emilia tilted her head, studying me. "Okay, but what about you? I thought maybe Jordan would be the one to... you know, help you move on."

I rolled my eyes, though I felt a slight ache at her words. "We're not talking about Aiden."

"Please, we're always talking about Aiden," Emilia laughed. "But fine. Jordan sounds great, but it didn't work out. So...what now?"

"Now I have another great friend who gets me," I said, lifting my chin. "And I get back to my life here. Besides, camp was about music, not romance. And nothing's going on with Aiden. Not in the way you mean."

"I've known for years that you feel more than just best friend feelings. Spill—what's different now?"

I sighed, twisting a piece of grass in my fingers. "One of my summer goals was to let go of any more-than-friendly feelings for him. To stop hoping he'll see me as more than his 'fun-sized' best friend."

Emilia's face softened, and she gave my shoulder a squeeze. "And?"

I nodded. "I thought maybe spending time with new people, new friends, would help. I thought maybe when I met Jordan, that would be it. And Jordan is great. But...we're really good friends. I think I knew that for sure after the 'Great Dandelion Massacre.'"

"Need details, chica."

I grinned, leaning back on my elbows. "I was walking to rehearsal. I knew I had time, so I took the longer path. It went through this mess of dandelions. Jordan came up a few minutes later and found me stomping and kicking them. Asked if I was 'massacring dandelions.' I told him—'Pick a side: me or the dandelions.' We ended up full-battle mode. He's tall. Guess who got totally covered in dandelion guts?

"We talked. He told me about Sarah. I told him about Aiden. I'd felt something early on, but by then, we were just... running around, goofing off. And it didn't feel the way it should've if he was the guy."

Emilia chuckled and shook her head. "Only you would have your heart swayed—or unswayed—by dandelions." She sobered. "Maybe that's how you'll know. When it's the real thing, it won't feel forced or figured out."

"I won the dandelion fight, though. I grabbed one and hid it. Blew it right in his face when we got to rehearsal."

Emilia laughed. "Short but sneaky—those tall people forget that about us."

"They do. After I blew the dandelion in his face, I said, 'Should've stayed on my side Jordan from Dickinson.'"

Emilia laughed harder. "Look at you going all Katniss on him."

"Yeah. Katniss in the friend zone."

"Fair enough," Emilia said, leaning back. "You deserve someone who's crazy about you. And not hung up on someone—or something—else."

I glanced at her, and we shared a small smile.

"Thanks, Em," I said quietly. "I'll figure it out. Eventually."

"Good. Until then, I'm here to remind you of your worth. And to tease you mercilessly whenever I can, obviously."

I laughed, the tension in my chest easing. There was a moment of quiet. I realized how much I'd missed her. No matter how complicated things felt, Emilia always grounded me. After a long pause, Emilia spoke again.

"No matter what's changed, you and Aiden have been besties forever. You'll always have good memories. Maybe hang on to the good that's been—not the frustration or disappointment of now."

"You mean make a list of my favorite memories with Aiden?"

"Sure. That, or whatever helps you remember and appreciate all the good."

I smiled, letting her words settle.

"Okay," I said softly. "I think I will."

The chapters of our past, present, and future were jumbled and out of order. I could still follow the story in them. It was a story that deserved to be reread.

I took Emilia's advice to heart. If Aiden and I never found our way back to what we'd had, I still wanted to hold onto the good. So I made a list. One memory at a time, I wrote it all down. And with each line that found its place in my journal, the ache dulled just a little. Friendships change. But knowing him had given me so much.

***

*Aiden, who knows what we'll be in couple months? But you've been my best friend since we were both in diapers. **You were one of the best parts of growing up. I hope you know and remember that, always.***

Thanks For...

Always waiting for me at the corner, even when I was running late.

Not laughing (too much) when I tripped over my own feet trying to keep up with you.

Letting me have first pick of the good snacks at your house.

Explaining basketball plays I never actually understood.

Saving me a seat—at lunch, on the bus, in class.

Making me laugh on days I didn't feel like laughing.

Knowing when to leave me alone and when not to.

Being my best friend.

I'm Glad We....

Built forts and fought over whose side was bigger.

Biked to the creek every summer, even though I always lagged behind.

Had our own inside jokes that no one else understood.

Made dandelion wishes—even when you said it was dumb.

Had the best (and worst) sleepovers, filled with stupid dares and too much junk food.

Played catch in your driveway, even though I was terrible at it.

Went to our first dance together—"as friends"—but still had the best time.

Stayed up late talking about everything and nothing.

Made it through middle school together.

Had a million little moments that made growing up better than it would've been without you.

I'll Always Remember....

The way your sneakers squeak on the court, that sound becoming familiar, almost comforting.

The day we buried a time capsule behind the school in fourth grade—do you have a clue what we put in that thing. I don't.

You trying to teach me a crossover dribble and failing spectacularly.

That time we got caught sneaking back from the park after dark, and you convinced my mom it was "for educational purposes."

Your ridiculous victory dances, even when they weren't deserved.

You standing outside in the rain when we got into a fight, refusing to leave until I forgave you.

The feeling that, no matter what, I could count on you.

The way everything felt easy—before it didn't.

And In Case It's Never the Same...

I hope you know you were the best part of growing up. And I wouldn't change any of it.

23

SAW A SIGHT

Ivy

The scent of roasted coffee beans and warm cinnamon curled through the air as Maddie and I settled into a corner booth at Brew & Bean. Conversation hummed around us, clinking mugs and espresso hisses providing the comforting soundtrack of home.

Maddie was deep into a story about a summer road trip with her parents, animated and smiling. I was trying to listen—I really was—my eyes drifted toward the window pulled by a streak of late afternoon sunlight. I saw them. Aiden. And Whitney. Outside, standing near the grocery store entrance, bathed in golden light like some poorly timed rom-com moment. Whitney was all animated gestures and wide smiles, practically glowing.

Aiden sat across from her, fingers tapping out an uneven rhythm against the table. He wasn't smiling. Wasn't leaning in. His eyes flicked to the clock on the store wall, then back to the table. Maddie followed my gaze.

"Oh." Her voice lost all warmth. "Yikes."

I said nothing, my grip on the coffee cup a little too tight.

She squinted. "You know, for a guy with fast reflexes, Aiden's terrible at escaping."

Still, I didn't respond. The ache in my chest wasn't going away. Whitney's laugh rang out—bright, familiar, and too close to the sound I used to make when we talked. She reached across the table and touched his arm, lightly, deliberately. He didn't lean in. But he didn't move away either.

Maddie exhaled. "Ivy. Look at him. That is not a guy having fun." She wasn't wrong. But he was still sitting there.

I turned back to Maddie and gave her a smile. Or tried to. "Let's go," I said quietly. "I'm ready to get out of here."

Maddie didn't push. She slid out of the booth and grabbed her drink. I followed, eyes forward. I didn't look back. I didn't have to. It didn't matter. Except it did.

***

Aiden

I was halfway through explaining—again—that I needed to get going when Whitney tapped my arm, her nails catching the light. And there they were. Kissy-face emojis. Painted across every single fingernail.

I flinched. The little puckered expressions winked at me with silent, mocking confidence. Every time she gestured—brushed her hair back, pointed to something, adjusted her sunglasses—they came at me. Like a cursed group chat made flesh. I tried not to stare.

I really did. But once I saw them, I couldn't unsee them. The tiny emoji faces haunted me.

"...so then I figured, why not?" Whitney was saying. "We should totally hang out more."

"Uh-huh," I said automatically, mind still screaming.

She smiled again. The emojis winked again. It felt like an ambush. I'd seen them before—on Josh's glitched texts, randomly invading my phone like digital graffiti, the creepy T-shirt from Mom. And now they were on fingernails. Cosmic punishment. That had to be it.

Her voice brightened. "Before I forget—"

Her hand lifted. *Closer.*

I snapped.

"Gotta go," I blurted, leaping to my feet. "I forgot—I need to grab something for my mom."

Whitney blinked. "Oh. Okay! Text me later!"

I nodded, already moving toward the store like my life depended on it. Which, honestly, it kind of did. If I saw one more winking face, I was going to lose it.

The sliding doors whooshed open. I stepped inside, dragging in a long breath.

Eggs. Milk. Sanity.

No more emoji nightmares.

Ivy

The scent of roasted coffee beans and warm cinnamon curled through the air as Maddie and I settled into a corner booth at Brew & Bean. Conversation hummed around us, clinking mugs and espresso hisses providing the comforting soundtrack of home.

Maddie was deep into a story about a summer road trip with her parents, animated and smiling. I was trying to listen—I really was—my eyes drifted toward the window pulled by a streak of late afternoon sunlight. I saw them. Aiden. And Whitney. Outside, standing near the grocery store entrance, bathed in golden light like some poorly timed rom-com moment. Whitney was all animated gestures and wide smiles, practically glowing.

Aiden sat across from her, fingers tapping out an uneven rhythm against the table. He wasn't smiling. Wasn't leaning in. His eyes flicked to the clock on the store wall, then back to the table. Maddie followed my gaze.

"Oh." Her voice lost all warmth. "Yikes."

I said nothing, my grip on the coffee cup a little too tight.

She squinted. "You know, for a guy with fast reflexes, Aiden's terrible at escaping."

Still, I didn't respond. The ache in my chest wasn't going away. Whitney's laugh rang out—bright, familiar, and too close to the sound I used to make when we talked. She reached across the table and touched his arm, lightly, deliberately. He didn't lean in. But he didn't move away either.

Maddie exhaled. "Ivy. Look at him. That is not a guy having fun." She wasn't wrong. But he was still sitting there.

I turned back to Maddie and gave her a smile. Or tried to. "Let's go," I said quietly. "I'm ready to get out of here."

Maddie didn't push. She slid out of the booth and grabbed her drink. I followed, eyes forward. I didn't look back. I didn't have to. It didn't matter. Except it did.

***

Aiden

I was halfway through explaining—again—that I needed to get going when Whitney tapped my arm, her nails catching the light. And there they were. Kissy-face emojis. Painted across every single fingernail.

I flinched. The little puckered expressions winked at me with silent, mocking confidence. Every time she gestured—brushed her hair back, pointed to something, adjusted her sunglasses—they came at me. Like a cursed group chat made flesh. I tried not to stare. I really did. But once I saw them, I couldn't unsee them. The tiny emoji faces haunted me.

"...so then I figured, why not?" Whitney was saying. "We should totally hang out more."

"Uh-huh," I said automatically, mind still screaming.

She smiled again. The emojis winked again. It felt like an ambush. I'd seen them before—on Josh's glitched texts, randomly invading my phone like digital graffiti, the creepy T-shirt from

Mom. And now they were on fingernails. Cosmic punishment. That had to be it.

Her voice brightened. "Before I forget—"

Her hand lifted. *Closer.*

I snapped.

"Gotta go," I blurted, leaping to my feet. "I forgot—I need to grab something for my mom."

Whitney blinked. "Oh. Okay! Text me later!"

I nodded, already moving toward the store like my life depended on it. Which, honestly, it kind of did. If I saw one more winking face, I was going to lose it.

The sliding doors whooshed open. I stepped inside, dragging in a long breath.

Eggs. Milk. Sanity.

No more emoji nightmares.

24

FARM SECURITY AND TINY NINJAS

Ivy

I couldn't wait to get to the farm again. I also wanted to skip it.

Emilia had invited us all over for a sleepover. My girls. My crew. I'd missed them so much this summer. But I knew what was coming: the Jordan vs. Aiden interrogation. Even without an actual Jordan vs. Aiden situation, they'd be nosy. So I arrived with my redirect reflex fully activated.

Emilia had warned me that her little brother, Miggy, had appointed himself farm security. I prepared to face his serious four-year-old stare without laughing. I'd just stepped one foot onto the gravel driveway when the front door swung open.

Miguel charged outside.

"STATE YOUR BUSINESS!" he declared.

I smiled and ruffled his hair. "Hello to you too, Miggy."

Miguel squinted. "Hmm. Looks like Sonidita. Sounds like Sonidita. But could be a clone."

Sofía appeared behind him, clutching her stuffed bunny and nodding gravely. "Cwone."

I gasped, pretending to be offended. "Fía, it's me—your cousin Ivy."

"Dita!" Sofía squealed and launched herself at my legs.

Tía Mariella had given me the nickname Sonidita—Little Note—as my cello skills grew. Miguel crossed his arms, still skeptical.

"Officer Fía, unhand the prisoner—uh, I mean the possible Sonidita clone. Now you." He pointed at me. "Prove it. What's your favorite kind of cake?"

"Chocolate."

Miguel tilted his head. "What's your second favorite?"

I hesitated. "Vanilla?"

Miguel sighed, shaking his head like I had disappointed all of farm security.

"That's wrong."

Emilia pushed past him, grabbing my wrist. "Stop being weird, Miggy. Come inside, Ivy."

I grinned at him as we passed. "I've been your cousin for almost ten years."

"Yeah but I'm farm security. And there's clones."

***

I was sinking comfortably into the couch, munching a cookie, when I noticed Miguel staring at me. Not just staring—assessing. I froze mid-bite.

"Can I help you?"

Miguel squinted. "Yeah. I have questions."

I looked at Emilia. She just shrugged. Typical.

"Okay?" I said. "Go for it."

Miguel crossed his arms. "One. Do you like baseball?"

I smirked. "Of course."

He nodded. "Good. Two. Do you still hate olives?"

I narrowed my eyes. "How do you even know that?"

"I listen."

He looked unbearably smug for someone under five.

"Three. How's the Bass Man?"

I choked. Emilia spit out the sip of water she'd just taken.

Miguel tilted his head. "Sooo?"

"Excuse me?" I said.

Miguel shrugged. "Ivy and the Bass Man, sitting in a tree—"

Emilia lunged, clapping a hand over his mouth. "Miguel!"

Miguel wiggled free. "What? She talked about him a lot." He pointed squarely at his sister.

"I did not —" Emilia began.

"You did too! I hear everything."

I crossed my arms. "He hears everything you talk about."

Emilia groaned. "Apparently, and unfortunately, yes."

Sofía gasped and turned to me. "Wike him?"

I pointed at her. "Don't start, little miss."

She lit up like a gossip columnist. "Ooooooh."

Miguel grinned. "That means yes."

"I didn't say anything!" I protested.

Miguel plowed ahead. "Okay, but what about the clueless basketball dude?"

I blinked. "What?"

He threw his arms out. "You gonna rescue him from the GPS that gots him captured?"

Emilia furrowed her brow. "What?"

Miguel sighed like we were all hopeless. "That dude never knows where he's going. GPS lies to him. He's totally lost right now."

I tried to keep myself from looking as clueless as I felt.

Miguel leaned in, solemn. "I'll help you plan a rescue. I'm Farm Security. I got it covered."

Then he paused. "Actually... it might be too late."

"What?" I asked.

Miguel shook his head. "The basketball dude got lost in Whitneyland."

Emilia yelled. "Miggy, what the heck!"

Miguel nodded gravely. "That's what I heard you say. He's trapped there."

Sofía gasped. "Twapped."

Miguel sighed. "Where the H-E-double hockey sticks is Whitneyland anyway?"

"WHO TAUGHT YOU THAT?" I shouted.

Miguel pointed at me. "You did."

"I DID NOT!"

He mimicked me perfectly: "'Where the H-E-double hockey sticks is my phone?' 'Where the H-E-double hockey sticks is my music?!'"

Emilia was wheezing now.

Naturally, I did what any mature cousin would: I scooped him up and spun him. Miguel shrieked. "AHHH! NO! SECURITY! HELP!"

Sofía flapped her arms in circles. "Heeeeelp! Heeeeelp!"

Emilia sighed dramatically. I set Miggy down. He fixed his sock headband and gave me a stare.

"I'm still watching you, possible clone."

Sofía nodded seriously. "Wawching."

***

When the girls arrived, Miggy was waiting.

Jenna stepped onto the porch first.

"Halt," he said. "State your business."

Jenna blinked. "Uh... I'm here for the sleepover?"

Miguel squinted. "Suspicious."

She sighed. "Are we doing this?"

"Yes."

"Fine. What's the question?"

Miguel straightened. "Do you like baseball?"

"It's okay?"

He sighed. "Strike one."

"Didn't know I was batting."

"Who's the greatest baseball player of all time?"

"Babe Ruth?"

Miguel nodded. "Acceptable."

Jenna smirked. "Glad I passed your rigorous check."

Then came Aria.

Miguel: "Do you like baseball?"

Aria: "Basketball."

Miguel: "That not what I asked."

Aria: "Basketball is my answer."

Miguel: "Fine. Who's the best basketball player ever?"

Aria: "MJ. Obviously."

Miguel nodded. "Acceptable."

And then Maddie.

The second she stepped up, his posture changed. He uncrossed his arms. Straightened. Stared.

"Hey, little dude," Maddie said.

Miguel gaped. Cleared his throat. "Do you like baseball?"

Maddie grinned. "Love it."

His eyes widened. "Do you *play* baseball?"

"I have."

Miguel whispered to Sofía, without breaking eye contact: "That's it. I'm gonna marry her when I'm twenty-eleven."

Sofía gasped. "Yeah."

The room exploded. Maddie tilted her head. "That right?"

Miguel nodded solemnly. "But we gotta play baseball first. And no kissing. Gross."

Maddie shook his hand. "Got it."

***

That night the girls were sprawled across Emilia's room. TikToks were watched. Gossiping occurred. We debated whether Maddie should be concerned about her new engagement. We'd fully settled into comfy when we heard it.

"SNACKAS ATTACK!"

The door flew open. Sofía burst in, tripped on a pillow, flopped to the floor, then bounced up again.

"NEE-NEE ATTACK!"

Miguel followed, peeking around the frame. "Shhh! Sofía! You're messing up the sneak!"

Sofía twirled. "NIN-NAPS ATTACK!"

Miguel rolled in like an action star and posed. "NINJAS SNACK ATTACK!"

The room lost it. Maddie was crying.

Miguel nodded at our snack pile. "We have come for—"

Sofía yelled, "SNACKS!"

He nodded. "Give the ninjas snacks."

He ignored them completely and walked straight to Maddie. In a whisper: "This is my future wife."

Maddie laughed. "We're already on snacks and marriage? That's fast."

Miguel shrugged. "I make plans."

Sofía nodded. Like always. Miguel grabbed popcorn, surveyed the room, then clapped.

"Okay. Mission successful. Sofía, we out."

Sofía saluted and toddled after him.

Jenna wiped fake tears. "Such a beautiful love story."

Maddie shook her head, smiling. "If he ends up marrying someone else when he's twenty-eleven I might cry."

Miguel's voice echoed from the hall. "Baseball-player ninjas make the best husbands. But no kissing."

***

I was in a deep sleep when I felt it.

Poke. Poke. Poke.

Poke. Poke.

Poke. Poke. Poke.

"Sonidita. Wake up. Hey."

It was Miguel.

"Miggy, what?"

His face was inches from mine.

"We gotta plan the basketball dude's rescue."

I squinted at the poker. "What?"

"Basketball-head dude need snacks."

"Pretty sure the Whitneys feed their captives."

"Yeah, but do they got *good* snacks? Like fruit snacks and string cheese?"

I groaned. "Miggy, go back to sleep."

"If he starves, it's your fault."

I fell back asleep dreaming about pelting Aiden with fruit snacks.

It was weirdly satisfying.

25

Driveway Awkwardness

Aiden

The hum of the Prestons' car pulling into the driveway snapped me out of my thoughts. I hadn't seen Ivy since the end of the school year. I never caught her before she left for camp. I didn't text all summer. Now she was steps away. Every choice I hadn't made pressed down making it difficult to take a first step towards her. I stepped out the kitchen door.

"Hey, Ivy," I called, my voice quieter than I meant as I walked to the invisible line where our driveways met.

She looked up sharply, surprised. "Aiden. Hi."

We stood there, caught in a silence that had never existed between us before.

"Good summer?" I asked, shoving my hands into my pockets. The words felt small. Useless.

She shifted the strap of her bag. "Yeah, it was... busy. You?"

I nodded. "Same."

I wanted to say more. I hadn't meant for things to be like this. I hadn't meant to disappear. But I did. And now, the apology sat in my chest, jammed somewhere between guilt and regret.

"I'm sorry I didn't text more," I blurted.

She hesitated. Her expression didn't shift. "It's okay," she said, voice flat. "I've been... busy, too."

We both gave a half-hearted laugh. Weak echoes of what used to come so easily.

"Yeah. Busy." The word tasted bitter. We both knew it was an excuse.

She looked down at the ground, her focus far from me. I searched her face, trying to read what I'd missed. I didn't know why I hadn't reached out. Why I let the days stack up like that. But I had. And I couldn't undo it now.

She hitched her bag up higher and stepped toward her door. "Okay, well... I guess I'll see you around," she said, quiet. Unsure.

"Yeah," I replied, my voice a whisper. "See you."

She didn't look back. I stood there, rooted to the driveway, the space between us stretching even wider than before.

***

Ivy

Aiden's voice cut through the quiet. "Hey, Ivy."

I looked up, startled to see him standing there.

"Aiden. Hi."

My heart twisted. I tightened my grip on my bag and hoped it would anchor me. When was the last time we'd really talked? May? Earlier?

"Good summer?" he asked, trying for casual.

"Yeah, it was... busy." I kept my tone even. "You?"

"Same," he said quickly, his eyes shifting. Then, more softly, "I'm sorry I didn't text more."

For a second, I wanted to believe it mattered to him. But I could still feel the empty space where his words should have been.

"It's okay," I said, steady. Frozen. "I've been...busy, too."

We both laughed. Hollow. Awkward. A placeholder for everything we weren't saying.

"Yeah. Busy," I echoed.

He shifted like he might say more. But nothing came. The silence stretched, thick with all the things we couldn't say aloud. I adjusted my bag and stepped toward the door. Before walking away completely, I glanced back.

"Okay, well... guess I'll see you."

"Yeah," he said, barely audible. "See you."

I didn't linger. Each step away grew heavier. We used to share everything. Now we couldn't even share a conversation. He used to be my best friend. My person.

Now he just felt like the boy next door. Impossibly far away.

26

Weather Report from the Diner

Aiden

After the awkward driveway talk, nothing really changed. A few polite smiles if we happened to walk out our front doors at the same time. Mostly, we stayed in orbit—close enough to see each other, far enough not to collide. Our friends didn't say much about it.

They pulled us both into things—group chats, movie nights, impromptu diner runs—like gravity doing its thing. Which is how we ended up here, packed into a booth at Northbend Fry and Dine, pretending everything was normal. Maybe it was our new normal. The awkwardness between Ivy and me was so real it could've been an extra person in the booth.

The place buzzed with clattering dishes, chattering customers, and the steady sizzle of the fryers. Our booth was crammed with bodies and noise—Ty making faces behind his milkshake, trying to get Emilia's attention; Aria and Jenna arguing over fries; Maddie clearly plotting something. Beside me, Ivy flicked through the menu like she didn't know it by heart.

I hated it. Hated our halting words in the driveway. How she looked at me before walking inside. I hated not knowing how to fix what I'd broken. Could I say something now? Make a joke and cut through the awkwardness. I nudged her arm lightly.

"Thinking of making a bold move?" I asked, nodding toward her menu. "Maybe this is the night you switch things up. Cheese fries instead of plain?"

Ivy

I kept myself from jumping when Aiden nudged me. Before I fully recovered, my phone buzzed. I glanced down and saw *Jordan* on the screen. I hesitated a second too long. Instead of going to voicemail or buzzing quietly on the table, my phone blasted *It's Raining Men* by The Weather Girls at full volume. Not just full volume—whatever volume breaks the sound barrier. The diner went dead silent as the dramatic horns blared, followed by the most enthusiastic "Hallelujah! It's raining men!" ever unleashed in public.

"Jordan must've changed my ringtone! I didn't pick THIS!" I stammered out, trying to sound calm. A full-on hysterical wail would've been the more fitting response. Jordan's name disappeared, but the song kept playing. I let out a garbled shout—which meant *I'm going to KILL him!*—snatched my phone, and sprinted out of the diner.

Behind me, Aiden laughed. Tyler shouted, "Watch for falling objects, Ivy!"

I paced outside and texted Jordan about my plans to drive to Dickinson and kill him. If this ended up as a crime of passion, I was leaving evidence of my guilt everywhere. Jordan called again. I answered, ready to send heart-stopping venom through the airwaves. Then I heard him. He was laughing. Laughing so hard I thought I might need to call 911 for him. So I started laughing too. Yeah, I was embarrassed—but it was funny. I laughed with Jordan, laughed so hard I cried.

"I'm so sorry, but not sorry, Ivy. I meant to fix that. Guess I didn't."

The laughter shifted and we started to talk, catching up as I paced back and forth in front of the diner.

Aiden

I tried not to grin idiotically as Ivy grabbed her phone and ran out. It was such an Ivy event; I couldn't help it. For a second, I almost went after her. I should have. But I didn't think I had the right to be the one to make sure she was okay.

Instead, I sat and watched her through the window. She was laughing with someone on the phone—Jordan. I bet it was Jordan. Odds were the ridiculous music on her phone was a Jordan thing too. Something different and unpleasant simmered inside me.

Ivy walked back into the diner, still laughing. She sat down and fanned her face. "I'm so embarrassed, but oh well. It's out there in the universe now." She took a sip of her shake, then leaned in with a wicked glint in her eye.

"Okay. I need ideas. Ruthless, creative, slightly chaotic payback ideas."

Aria perked up. "For what?"

"Jordan. Obviously. That ringtone was his fault."

"Wait, that was Jordan's doing?" Jenna asked, half-choking on a fry.

Ivy nodded. "And I'm still going to a concert with him next weekend, which gives me the perfect window for revenge."

Tyler side-eyed me like I had any control over the situation. My inner cool guy curled into a fetal position and quietly wept.

27

STUFF'S CHANGED WITH A SIDE OF FRICKLES

Ivy

The streets of Dickinson rolled by as our car headed toward the venue. My parents were chatting up front about Aunt Linda's Garden, clearly looking forward to spending a beautiful summer evening with one of my dad's brothers. But for me, tonight was about something else entirely—a chance to hear Lila Sandstrom live and finally spend some time with Jordan in his hometown.

We arrived and I scanned the growing crowd, and saw him—Jordan, standing near the entrance, talking and laughing with a girl. As I got closer, I recognized Sarah from the pictures Jordan had shown me. The Sarah he'd talked about—the one keeping him friend-zoned. The one keeping me from doing him bodily harm for leaving that ringtone on my phone.

Jordan spotted me and grinned, his face lighting up with his usual warmth. He pulled me into a hug, then stepped back, glancing between me and Sarah.

"Ivy, meet Sarah," he said, smiling. "You might remember I told you about her."

I nodded as I took Sarah's extended hand. She gave me an easy smile. "Jordan's told me a lot about you, Ivy. All good—and a lot of it funny," she laughed, her voice light and welcoming. I elbowed Jordan in the gut.

Sarah was lovely. Warm and funny. Her presence felt steady and drew a person in. Seeing them together felt right—like I'd found the missing piece and could finally complete a jigsaw puzzle I'd been working on. I felt a buzz of happiness for them. The three of us relaxed, falling into easy, laughing conversation as we headed into the concert.

When I got a chance, I glared at Jordan. "Stuff's changed? I was going to murder you, then hide the body for the ringtone stunt. Unfortunately, now there's a witness."

He smiled sheepishly. "It was funny in my mind. Sorry?"

"No, you're not. And it was funny. A tiny bit." I pretended to be angry. But really—I was happy for him. Some things, some stuff, could get worked out.

The crowd settled, and Lila Sandstrom took the stage. Her rich voice filled the air. She had a soulful sound that echoed the beautiful, gritty landscapes of Western ND. She sang about the prairie, the people who lived on it, and love that bound them together even through hardship. Her presence and performance felt deeply rooted here.

Sarah leaned over during a slower song, whispering, "I wasn't sure I'd enjoy her music, but I love it. There's something so... honest about it."

I nodded, feeling the music tug at my own heart.

***

During intermission, I got the full Jordan and Sarah story—straight from Sarah, while Jordan leaned back wearing his easy, content smile. Sarah was pretty in the pictures Jordan had shown. In person, she had a soft way that was best felt.

"Okay, so you know how Jordan is, right? Like, he could make taking out the recycling feel like an adventure?"

I nodded. "Yeah, he's basically a golden retriever with opposable thumbs for bowing his double bass."

Jordan made a low scoffing sound, but didn't argue. He knew it was true.

Sarah snickered. "Exactly. So, when he asked me on this road trip date down the Enchanted Highway, I figured, cool—scenic drive, some snacks, cute little roadside stops, right? Nope. He turned it into a full-blown immersive experience."

"Oh, this I gotta hear."

She grinned. "First stop, Geese in Flight. He rolls down the windows, cranks 'Free Bird' at full volume, and tells me we have to 'take off' before we can officially start the trip. Cue both of us sprinting through the gravel like lunatics, flapping our arms while a trucker passing by watches."

I pressed a hand over my mouth, trying not to choke on laughter. "Oh my gosh."

"Oh, it gets worse. At Deer Crossing, he pulls out a little box labeled 'Deer or Dare.' Every card is either a ridiculous dare—like 'prance in circles while calling yourself a majestic forest creature'—or a deep, weirdly philosophical question, like 'If you had to be an animal for a year, which one and why?'"

I groaned. "Please tell me he did some prancing for you."

Sarah smirked. "Oh, he did. And let me tell you—six-foot-tall prancing is not his strength."

Jordan, still lounging, shook his head. "It was elegantly masculine prancing."

"It was tragic," Sarah corrected.

I shook my head, laughing. "This sounds like absolute craziness."

"Oh, it was," she confirmed. "At Grasshoppers in the Field, he challenged me to a jumping contest. Got very offended when I gave his grasshopper jump a 6.5 out of 10."

I snorted. "I bet you were being generous too."

"Right?! Then at Fisherman's Dream, we had to make up ridiculous fishing stories. And I swear, I have never met a worse liar than Jordan. He tried to convince me he once caught a river shark in the Little Missouri."

I gasped dramatically. "A river shark? That's the best you had, Scott?"

Jordan held up his hands. "Hey, you don't know what's lurking in there."

Sarah shook her head. "And then—oh my god—we pull up to World's Largest Tin Family, and he goes, 'Hang on, I have something for this.' And this boy pulls out—" she paused for effect, "pre-made tin foil hats."

I nearly choked. "No. No way."

Jordan shrugged. "Look, if we were gonna pose with the tin family, we had to respect the aesthetic."

Sarah groaned, but her grin nearly outshone the lobby lights.

***

Lila came back on for the second half of her concert. Her covers were brilliant, but her original music gave me chills. The music and the company of two friends—one new and one new-adjacent—made my heart want to leap out of my chest and blow kisses to the world, or at least Dickinson, ND.

After the final encore, the three of us lingered in the lobby, reluctant to end the night. Dickinson's summer air outside was soft and warm, but the buzz of the concert still hummed under my skin.

"I'm starving," Jordan said, stretching like a golden retriever waking from a nap. "We skipping straight to milkshakes or detouring through savory first?"

Sarah looped her arm through his. "You already know the answer."

Jordan turned to me. "You've had Blue 42, right? Downtown?"

"Once, forever ago," I said. "I remember wood floors and maybe some kind of buffalo chicken thing?"

He gasped. "The buffalo chicken quesadilla. Life-altering. But tonight? I'm going all in on Zach's Mac Attack. It's got mac & cheese bites and jack cheese—on the burger. It's chaos. It's art."

Sarah rolled her eyes affectionately. "We don't take him to Blue 42 often. He gets emotional."

***

We ended up in a booth near the window, a spot we could sink into. The restaurant smelled like all the yummy fried things. There was a game of something on in the background, but none of us watched. Jordan lit up when the waitress came to our table.

"We'll start with the baked brie, fiesta fries, and—she needs to try the frickles."

"The what now?" I asked.

"Frickles," Sarah said, like it was obvious. "Fried pickles. With Havarti."

Jordan leaned in, eyes wide with mock gravity. "They will change your life."

"I'm sorry—cheese on pickles?"

"Cheese in pickles," he corrected. "Wrapped up in deep-fried glory and served with the world's best pepper jelly. You haven't lived until you've had a frickle."

"I feel like I've lived a pretty darn good life."

He waved me off. "Psssh, you know not what you're speaking of."

When the appetizers arrived, the baked brie looked refined, the fiesta fries looked dangerous, and the frickles... looked weird. Golden and puffy, like fried ravioli trying to jump into a different ethnic food category.

I used extreme caution and picked up a frickle. "If this ruins pickles for me forever, I'm blaming both of you."

"You're welcome in advance," Jordan said.

I took a bite. Crunch. Heat. Sharp pickle. Melty cheese. And then the pepper jelly—sweet and spicy and perfect.

I blinked. "Oh my gosh."

Jordan pumped his fist in victory. "YES. She's crossed over."

Sarah just nodded. "Another one converted."

I reached for a second. "I don't even understand what's happening in my mouth."

"It's called frickle enlightenment," Jordan said. "We're so proud of you."

I took another bite, closed my eyes, and let the flavors do whatever magic they were doing. "This is what Rossini was tasting when he wrote the end of the William Tell Overture," I announced.

Sarah blinked. "The—what now?"

"The finale," I said. "The galloping part. The one every commercial ever stole."

Jordan snapped his fingers. "YES. That tracks. He bit into one of these and just blacked out and wrote strings that sounded like a cavalry charge."

"Exactly," I said, pointing my fork at him. "It's chaotic. It's over the top. It wears the disguise of an appetizer, but it's somehow the main food on the table."

Sarah was laughing. "You two are unwell."

"Okay, but hear me out," Jordan said. "What if the frickle moment is less 'burst of energy' and more 'unhinged spooky joy'? Like... Danse Macabre."

I choked on my drink. "You think Saint-Saëns ate a fried pickle and went full skeletal violin?"

"Tell me the pizzicato part isn't the crunch," he said. "Tell me."

Sarah groaned. "I just wanted a peaceful snack and now I'm picturing skeletons doing jazz hands with dipping sauce."

"I'm still going with Rossini," I said, wiping my mouth. "But I'd accept Flight of the Bumblebee if someone ate a frickle and then immediately spiraled into a fugue state."

Jordan nodded. "Final offer: 1812 Overture, but only if the cannon blasts are replaced by extra-dimensional crunch sounds."

Sarah covered her face. Then she looked up slowly, like she was about to deliver a eulogy or a Grammy acceptance speech. "Okay. You know what? Fine. You want a frickle piece?"

Jordan leaned forward, eyes wide. I braced myself.

Sarah cleared her throat. "Queen of the Night aria. Mozart. Full soprano madness. High Fs. Ridiculous ornamentation. Entirely unnecessary drama. That's what a frickle sounds like in my soul."

We both stared at her.

"That... might be it," I said.

"She went full opera," Jordan whispered reverently. "We've been out-frickled."

Sarah sipped her drink like she hadn't just blown our minds as she trumped our classical rant with opera.

The food arrived and Jordan paused to admire his burger like it was a rare artifact. "I need a minute," he said. "It's so beautiful."

"You gonna write it a poem, or...?" I teased.

"I'm composing a haiku as we speak."

He actually did. He made us listen to *Ode to Cheese Knees*, and I wish I could pretend I hated it. We laughed until I forgot I was tired.

And I laughed when I saw Jordan's post the next day:

Image: The Zach's Mac Attack burger in full melty glory, frickles in the background.

Caption: Ode to Cheese Knees by yours truly

Mac bites on my bun

molten dreams and cheddar joy—

I kneel before thee.

Tagging my enablers and doubters: @ivy.celloforce — said it couldn't be done @sarahsoprano.nd — tried to stop me. They stayed on a lesser plain eating fries while I ascended.

#cheeseknees #burgerpoetry #blue42legend #macattackmagic #fricklesforever #eatingmylimitations #cheesedlines

28

FRICKLE DELIVERY

Ivy

I stood on the porch watching as Jordan and Sarah pulled in. He jumped out first, sunglasses in his hair, grinning like he had something to prove. Sarah climbed out on the passenger side, holding a paper bag aloft with great ceremony.

"We brought offerings," she said.

Jordan bowed slightly. "They're not fresh, but they were air-fried within the last hour. We present to you: frickles."

My eyes widened. "You brought me frickles?"

"Frickles," Jordan confirmed, handing over the bag like it was a newborn baby or sacred scroll. "Cheese-stuffed. Slightly soggy. But reheated with love and science."

Sarah nodded. "Still crunchy-ish if you eat them immediately. With haste."

I reached into the bag, pulled out a warm, golden pouch of pickled chaos, and took a bite. Crunch. Tang. Cheese. Jelly.

"Okay," I said, mouth full. "Still life-changing. Slightly less than fresh, but the magic lingers."

Jordan pumped his fist. "YES. We accomplished the frickle feat."

Sarah shook her head. "He insisted this was necessary."

"He was correct," I said, already reaching for another. "You've both earned your place in my favorite snack moments. If I write a memoir with recollections of food, you'll get a mention."

***

Six girls crammed into the booth at the diner with giggling reverence. It was a sacred moment—girl time only, no boy drama allowed. A time for connecting over everything, no need to be profound.

Jenna pointed a fry at Sarah. "We've only experienced Jordan's humor secondhand. Has he always been so...?"

Sarah laughed. "Sweetly unhinged? Yep. I heard his first haiku in first grade. About the joys of T-ball. I've got truly odd memories."

I grinned. "You have to show them the pictures from the Enchanted Highway."

Emilia started to protest. I shushed her. "We're not talking about boys. But we are allowed to laugh at them."

Emilia's eyes lit up. "Okay, Sarah, I've only heard it through Ivy. Give us the first-person account of Jordan's all-in Commit to the Enchanted Highway Experience."

"We committed to the experience," Sarah said. "Every stop. Every sculpture. Jordan made up some kind of challenge at each one."

"At Deer Crossing, it was Deer or Dare," I added. "Hence prancing."

"He spun in circles and called himself a majestic forest creature," Sarah said. "Honestly, though? The grasshopper jump contest was worse."

"Oh no," Aria said. "Please tell me there's documentation."

"There is," Sarah said, already unlocking her phone. "Behold: Jordan mid-jump. He claims it was athletic. I say it was... airborne panic."

She passed the phone around. The booth erupted in laughter. I'd seen the photos before, but watching the girls react made them even better. Whatever this was—it wasn't gossip. There was too much joy. I leaned back, smirking as Aria nearly dropped the phone laughing. "He wears a tinfoil hat well."

***

My backyard hummed as everyone gathered around the firepit. Jordan and Sarah followed me outside, and the group looked up as we approached. There were greetings and the group quickly pulled them in. Drew perked up when Jordan mentioned baseball, and within minutes they were deep in a debate about pitching techniques and the best stadiums in the league.

"Wait," Aria said suddenly. "The burger haiku master is among us."

Jordan grinned. "The one and only. It's an art form."

"Okay, haiku master—make the firepit memorable," Emilia challenged.

He held up an imaginary parchment. "Ashes and stories, / marshmallows melt the silence / and burns bright like truth."

After a ferocious fireside haiku poetry slam, the guys—no, the ballers (Aria played and was as good or better than the boys)—headed over to Aiden's driveway for a game. I sat on the porch, watching as Jordan proved he wasn't only a baseball guy. He was fast, sharp, and way too smooth for someone supposedly new to basketball.

"Wait, you can actually play?" Ty called, pretending to gasp as Jordan sank a clean layup.

Jordan grinned. "Never said I couldn't play. Bass, Baseball, Basketball—natural athlete/musician. What can I say?"

Ty rubbed his chin. "Point guard might not be your thing. But bass-ketball? You shine, man."

Groans all around.

"Did you actually say that?" Aiden asked, deadpan.

"Yup," Ty said, completely unfazed. "And there's more where that came from."

Jordan laughed, passing the ball. "I've got rhythm. I've got range. Don't expect me to carry the whole band."

***

The others drifted back to the firepit, but I stayed on the porch, needing a second. Watching Jordan out there—confident, effortless—shouldn't have hit so weird. He was a great guy. Sarah was great too. I liked them both. A lot.

But the way they moved together—laughing, teasing, getting each other—it was easy. Not effortless. Certainly not mired, stuck. Which was how I saw Aiden and me now.

It hadn't been that way for so much of our friendship before basketball. Before it was laughter and inside jokes and walking home even when it was snowing sideways. It was knowing we didn't have to say everything to understand each other.

I tried to forget that at camp. I tried to let it go. But I wanted the before back. And I wanted the kind of now I saw Jordan and Sarah have on the Enchanted Highway—with Aiden.

I watched him disappear into the shadows and firelight. How slim was the possibility of going back?

***

Aiden

I already knew about Jordan—social posts, group texts, friends talking. I'd been jealous without even knowing why. But now? He was with Sarah. And Ivy was happy for them. So what was I holding on to?

Jordan's a genuinely good guy. He fit here. People liked him. Sarah clearly did. And Ivy? She fit too—right into their rhythm. It wasn't him or even them. It was me.

I heard her laugh from the firepit. Bright. Effortless. I let it hit: I don't think I can fix us.

29

WALK TO SCHOOL?

Aiden

Ivy was perched on the edge of her front porch, her gaze lost in the quiet street. I took a deep breath to steady my nerves. It seemed like she was pondering the first day of school, same as I had been.

"Hey, Ivy," I called out gently, careful not to startle her.

She looked up, her expression softening at the sound of my voice. "Hey, Aiden," she replied, a hint of a smile playing at the corners of her lips.

Feeling suddenly unsure, I shuffled my feet. "Um, the first day of school is next Tuesday..." I trailed off, watching for her reaction.

"Yeah, it is," she said, eyeing me with curiosity.

I took another breath, rubbing the back of my neck awkwardly. "So, how about we walk together?" I asked, hoping the offer would bridge whatever gap had formed between us over the summer.

Ivy paused, considering it. The silence stretched, punctuated only by the gentle rustling of leaves in the breeze.

Finally, she nodded, her smile genuine this time. "Sure."

"Great!" I exclaimed—louder than intended. We figured out the time we'd need to leave, and I added, "Awesome. It's a date—uh, I mean, it's just walking," I quickly corrected myself, shutting my mouth before more words could tumble out.

Ivy laughed, the sound nearly as it should have been. "Okay, only walking. Got it," she teased, her eyes twinkling with amusement.

As I turned to walk away, Ivy called out, "Hey, want some fresh lemonade? My mom made some."

Surprised, I accepted. "Oh, sure. Yeah, sounds good."

While Ivy went inside to fetch the lemonade, I made myself comfortable on the porch, appreciating the unexpected warmth of the evening.

***

Ivy

"So," Aiden started, "Jordan seems like a pretty solid guy."

"He is," I said, my voice softening. "And he's a good friend, had my back from day one. You saw—he's dating Sarah now. Actually, we moved into just-friends pretty fast this summer. Just what we both needed, I guess."

"Oh," Aiden replied, his tone careful. An emotion I barely caught flickered and vanished. Relief?

"So, Aiden, did you bring Mr. Basketball to camp with you?" I asked, recalling the small stuffed basketball toy he'd gotten when he was eight.

Aiden groaned, laughing. "Mr. Basketball is near and dear to my heart, but no, he stayed at home."

"I distinctly remember you bringing Mr. Basketball to other basketball events with you," I teased.

He rolled his eyes but laughed. "And I thought we'd agreed that was a topic we were done with. Who knows though—I have tryouts coming up. Maybe I'll tuck him in my gym bag to be my secret weapon."

"Good luck charm, you mean?" I said, leaning back against a column. "But really, you've come a long way from those epic diaper slam dunks."

Aiden raised an eyebrow, smirking. "You still remember that, huh?"

"Of course I do! How could I forget? You used to brag about how you could dunk a basketball before you could even walk properly. And to be fair, you were dunking on a kiddie hoop that was, what, barely up to your waist?"

He laughed, shaking his head. "Hey, dunking is dunking. I was a prodigy."

"Oh, totally," I agreed, my tone dripping with sarcasm. "I still remember the day you missed your first shot on a real hoop. You were devastated."

Aiden groaned, running a hand through his hair. "Ugh, don't remind me. It was like a rude awakening. I went from king of the kiddie court to a guy who couldn't even reach the rim."

I grinned. "And then you were determined to be as tall as your dad, so you could dunk like a pro. You even used to make me measure you every summer."

Aiden laughed, his hazel eyes lighting up with the same playful energy I remembered from when we were kids. "I swear, I thought if I stretched every night, I'd grow faster."

"And I told you, 'Aiden, you're gonna grow. You just need patience.' But nope—every time I came over, you'd be hanging from the jungle gym bars in your yard, trying to 'stretch' yourself taller."

He leaned back, a nostalgic smile tugging at his lips. "I still haven't hit Dad's height. Guess I should've hung from that jungle gym more."

"Hey, you might still grow," I teased, glancing at his legs. "You've got a few years left."

"Ha, I'll take what I can get," he said, then his grin softened. "You've always believed in me, even back when I was just some dork with a basketball obsession."

I smiled, feeling a warmth spread in my chest. "That's because I knew you were gonna make it. I told you from the beginning—you were always going to do big things with basketball. You've just got that drive."

Aiden gave me a look, one that lingered a little longer than usual. "Thanks, Ivy. That means a lot, you know."

For a moment, everything felt easy—like we were back to being just us. No distance, no tension. It's funny how a stuffed basketball and some old memories brought us closer, even if just for a while.

"Besides," I added, trying to lighten the mood again, "you're still not the best basketball player I know. Aria's kinda got you beat there."

Aiden's jaw dropped in mock outrage. "Oh, no way! Aria's good, but I could totally take her one-on-one."

I raised an eyebrow, a grin tugging at my lips. "Shall I relay your challenge to Aria, Superstar?"

"Nah, hold off until we both make our varsity teams. Then we can school each other in a game of one-on-one," he replied with a wink.

I laughed, shaking my head. "You're impossible."

But even as we joked, there was an undercurrent between us. It was like we were almost back to where we used to be: teasing, laughing, comfortable. I held onto a sliver of hope that Aiden and I still existed.

30

601ST

"At least 600."

I wanted to interrupt him. Put a stop to the thunk, thunk, thunk of his dribbling. I threw the number out there for Aiden without any context.

"Oookay? 600?"

Long drawn-out okay. Okay, I'm humoring you, Ivy. Okay, I can still dribble. Okay, I might be able to jam this conversation into a tiny spot in my brain not occupied by beloved basketball.

"Actually, I said at least 600. And that's over about three and a half years." I sighed and kept on walking. He'd asked me to walk to school with him. Broke the silence between us. This morning though, it was like walking with a stranger.

"Okay, tell me what that means."

How compassionate was I feeling this morning? Not. At. All. Not following eight weeks of Summer Harmonies Music Camp in Washington. Two months with kids who got me and wore T-shirts with sarcastic musical puns. Kids who could describe and compliment my bowing. Kids who knew that the Star Wars theme is a riff on Wagner's Ride of the Valkyries.

"Ives, what are you talking about?"

Eight summer weeks of being seen, noticed by a cute boy. The boy and I remained in each other's friend zones. Still, he saw me, got me. Two months to ignore the sucking quicksand around Aiden. Forget about being stuck,unable to escape the killer sand. Forget about barely being a blip on his radar for months when all he recognized was basketball.

"Ivy, what's going on?"

Two months away. Two months that ended in a decision. I was done waiting. Done hoping he'd see more in me. See a girl first, convenient bestie second.

"Fun-size, you're being a brat. A teeny-tiny brat. But a brat!"

He'd stopped dribbling the basketball. It sat obediently motionless at his feet. I took a quick look at him over my shoulder. Felt his hands slide into my armpits — yikes-then he picked me and held at face level. Wow, he'd gotten strong and kind of muscley, not a scrawny middle schooler anymore. Not—*STOP IT IVY MARIE PRESTON!!!!* You're getting out of his quick sand. Do not lean into this weird moment.

"Ives, you're acting like a bratty four-year-old!"

"Put me down so I can kick you like a four-year-old too! Otherwise, I'll bite you!"

Listening to nonstop thunking had obliterated my cool, and I yelled at him.

"Ivy, really, what's up?"

I closed my eyes, breathed deep, sighed. A pause stretched between us.

"Every year we spend less time together. You started this year off, this walk to school, by bouncing Bertha the basketball without stop. Maybe it's pathetic to be mad at a basketball. It's our first day of high school. I hardly saw you the last few months of last school year. I didn't see you at all this summer. Didn't talk to you at all either. I was hoping we'd talk. Instead, you've been giving all your attention to your beloved orange sphere slash replacement bestie."

"I get it. Ives. I'm sorry."

I knew he was sorry at that very moment. How quickly would the moment be here when the bald orange girlfriend captured all his attention again? Crap! He was giving me his version of big eyes. And it worked. Such pretty hazel eyes. C'mere little puppy! I totally forgive you, let me pet you. *Stop, Ivy!!*

I needed to move on from being a sidekick, despite those pretty hazel puppy eyes. Stuck in Aiden's friend zone was painful. Being barely a radar blip hurt. I met his gaze and saw a flash of understanding, replaced by something less honest.

Sure enough, Aiden proved he didn't hear me when he said, "By the way, her name is Barbie."

"Aiden!" I grabbed Barbie and hurled a sharp chest pass — to nobody, actually. The ball sailed across the street. Anger at my clueless, idiotic best friend mounted. He'd proved he didn't hear me. I turned on my heel and started back up the sidewalk toward school, leaving Aiden to fish his precious Barbie out of a gross, mucky stream on the other side of the road.

"You make me so mad, Aiden. Like sic Miggy on you and fund his entire arsenal of pelting supplies kind of mad."

My voice got louder and louder. I was short, didn't mean I wasn't loud. I stirred up the noxious weed gods this summer. Hope I hadn't angered any basketball gods just now. Tossing a basketball into a murky stream had to violate some divine basketball mandate. Noxious weed gods, put in a good word with the basketball deities, please. Tell them I've got good intentions. I'm just sad and struggling. Don't let them zap me.

Couldn't dribbling have sounded like a Tibetan Singing Bowl? Peaceful? Soothing? Instead, thunk-thunk-thunk was the sound cracking my sanity into bits. I'd start a group, be the leader of T.H.U.D.— Thunk Haters United for Dignity. I didn't hate Aiden playing basketball. He was a wonder the court. I'd supported him for so long. I wanted him to succeed, even if every dribble or drill took him farther away and we kept shrinking. It just hurt.

He caught up to me of course, with his giraffe legs, grabbed my elbow to stop me.

"I'm listening Ivy, what's up. Huh?"

A petty, mean part of me wanted to ignore him. I pushed that part away.

"Six hundred. It's, uh... it's the number of times we've done this."

He frowned, trying to figure it out. "What, walked to school?"

"Yes. Walked to school. Roughly 600 times. I mean, it's a mental estimate, not a science fair project or anything."

He was quiet. No laugh, no snickers, no smirk. No dumb boy slip-up like "way to obsess, Ivy." He looked at me seriously for the first time in forever. "Six hundred?" he repeated, his voice softer now — deeper and quieter.

I saw we were at the cracked stretch of cement that meant we were almost at school. I didn't think Aiden would feel it the way I did — the weight of this plain old sidewalk. The spot we'd crossed together so many times.

"Yeah," I said. "Six hundred or something. Every time like this time — but different. We made each walk different. Filled it with something new. When's the last time we really talked to each other two days in a row?"

He pushed his hair back, the inky black strands shifting into that permanent cowlick he never bothered to fix.

"You didn't say goodbye to me this summer. I tried but you weren't around. You left me waiting or forgot me. Aiden, did you even notice I was gone for two months?"

"I'm sorry, Ives." He was quieter than usual.

Sorry for what Aiden? I wanted to ask, I really didn't want the answer.

Instead I said, "Let's get going don't want to be late on our first day of high school, right hotshot."

As we made it the rest of the way I thought about the number again. That number was about how many times we'd trekked this way to school since second grade, when we officially became big kids. I did the math — sketchy math, sure. I didn't need exact numbers to know the importance of these walks.

Six hundred walks. Six hundred times we'd passed this way together. I was exhausted. Not from the walk. It was my heart that was worn out. Six hundred times and counting, and I wondered if a concrete sidewalk would be the only thing still connecting us.

And I decided to stop trying to keep our paths close.

31

A Basketball Musical

Ivy

We reached the walk leading up to the school doors, Aiden bouncing beside me with every step. The basketball under his arm thudded against his hip like it was trying to get inside faster than he was.

I heard something. Not the usual noise—cars idling, kids chattering—something steady underneath it all. First—ba-da-da-da-da, ba-da-da-da-da—hammering. Then guitar—bah-chh-chh, bah-chh-chh—sharp and fast. Then keyboard—bright bursts flashing over the beat. A chorus of whoa-oh-ohh rolled in, rough and loud.

Aiden glanced at me, grinned, and said, "Catch you later, okay?"

He flipped the basketball into one hand, caught it against his hip, and shoved the door open wide. Then he threw his head back and shouted, "YEAH!"

The music poured out the door as he stepped in. Aiden slid forward like the floor had been waiting for him. He stomped twice, kicked out his heel, and spun. His basketball bounced up to perch on one shoulder, rolled down his back, and popped back onto his other shoulder.

Students caught the rhythm without missing a beat—heels sliding, palms slapping, sneakers pounding. The singing broke free. "Loose, stay loose, get on those basketball shoes!"

The chant bounced from side to side, fists punching, sneakers stomping in time. Aiden spun, grinned, and sang out:

"Owhee, my team, shoot it, shoot it!"

He flung an invisible basketball high into the air, spinning under it like he already knew it would fall through the net. The hallway roared back, the beat snapping sharper.

"Loose, stay loose, get on those basketball shoes!"

The crowd danced basketball drills down the hall. Aiden danced deeper into the crush, his ball flipping shoulder to shoulder, spinning like it belonged to the music.

Then I heard him over it all: "I've practiced—so hard!"

He launched another invisible shot—and the hallway erupted.

He moved into the crowd—and kept going. The music bled away. The stomps faded into squeaking sneakers. The claps into slamming lockers. The hallway was just... a hallway.

I stood there, the sound of *everybody get, everybody get* still echoing in my mind. I think the basketball gods figured out how to punish me. But hadn't the whole basketball musical thing already been done?

For a second, I just blinked. And then—an arm slung around my shoulders. Maddie.

"Morning, Ivy. What's going on with the weather today? Anything worth catching?"

"Good morning, Miggy's fiancée," I shot back.

Maddie had a way of knocking me out of my own head with just the right balance of sarcasm and X-ray vision. I'd be needing that today.

"So, was it good weather walking to school with..." She trailed off, eyebrow raised.

I rolled my eyes. "Yes, I walked with Aiden."

"And...?" Maddie pressed, her grin widening.

"It was sleety and nasty," I said flatly. "Dropping clueless jocks the whole way."

Maddie tilted her head, her teasing fading into something more serious. "Okay, give me two songs—ones I actually know, not from your crazy playlists—that tell me what's going on."

I thought for a second. "Okay. Song one: *The Story of Us* by Taylor Swift. Because Aiden and I? We've got this long history, but I feel like I'm stuck in the past while he's moving on. Song two: *Back to December*. Because it's like I'm wishing we could turn back time, even though I know we can't."

I looked at her, "And I sound like the queen of Swiftian heartache."

Maddie rolled her eyes. "I get it though, she gives us the words we need for our feels. How'd any teen survive before Tay was around to interpret their angst? So you want to rewind. But you also don't want to lose how much you've grown. Been there, Ives."

"Yeah. It's like I'm stuck wanting to keep the old but knowing I don't want to go back to it. It's confusing."

Maddie met my eyes, "Everyone who knows you two probably figured you'd be in a different place by now."

She paused. "Don't tell anyone, but Miggy was all about a double wedding with you two—except, you know, no kissing. 'Cause that's gross."

"I'm not even sure how good of friends Aiden and I are anymore. I didn't talk to him this summer at all."

Maddie sighed dramatically. "So, no double wedding. Darn. Would've been a fun reception with juice boxes."

I grinned despite myself. "Let him down gently, Maddie. Don't crush his sweet little farm security heart. You'll need a lot of fruit snacks and a brand-new baseball."

Maddie's expression turned soft again. "It might be time to figure out what you want—not just what fits into Aiden's world. Just think about it, okay?"

I sighed, my shoulders slumping. "It might be time. It's just... he's always been there. As far back as I can remember."

Maddie nodded. "I know, Ives. It's a big change."

She patted my shoulder. "Okay, we've both got important things to do. I've got to let my four-year-old husband-to-be down gently. And you?" She gave me a look. "You might need to figure out what you want to be different this year."

Then she turned, heading toward the office. "I was looking forward to being some kind of in-law to you."

She glanced back with a wink. "Family-in-law or not—love you, Ivy."

"Love you too," I said, just loud enough for her to hear.

She was right. I've been orbiting Aiden for so long, I don't even know what should be at the center of my life. I can think about it. But breaking free of his orbit? I had no idea how I'll manage that.

32

COSMOS CURRENTLY CLOSED

Ivy

With Maddie's wisdom furrowing into my brain, I wove in and out of the crowd, wondering where the heck all these high schoolers had come from. It was like some farmer grew a crop of teens, harvested the chaos, and sold it on the black market of confusion.

I reached my locker. Jenna and Aria were already there, leaning against the metal like they were posing for a back-to-school ad. I forced myself to smile back even though the day already felt overwhelming.

Jenna squealed like Christmas, her sixteenth birthday, an Easter egg hunt, and the state football championship game were all on the syllabus for day one of ninth grade English. She immediately linked arms with me.

"Can you believe we're finally in high school?"

I glanced at her shoes. Laced up tight. Good—less chance she'd bounce straight out of them.

"I've seen most of these faces every day for years. It shouldn't feel different... but it does," I admitted.

Aria grinned. "High school, finally. Time to pretend we're reinventing ourselves."

"Pretend?" I asked.

"Yep. Imaginary reinvention. I've chased basketball for years. Jenna's been jumping and flipping since birth. You've become cello queen. No way we're ditching all that now. We're waving goodbye to middle school angst. Clean slate. So, juicier high school drama? I'd be open."

I nodded, trying to soak up some of Aria's confidence.

But in my head, everything came crashing at once—Aiden starring in some high school musical, a double wedding, a made-up future—smashed to pieces. Maddie's challenge identified the real problem: finding what fit me, not him. That truth was gnawing at my brain.Walking together hadn't changed a thing. I said words. He heard them. Filed them away somewhere. How was I supposed to let go of years of history?

"Hey, chicas!" Emilia called, wrapping her arms around my middle from behind. I smiled before I even turned. She had that effect.

"Hey, cuz," I said, shifting to hug her back.

As we broke apart, Tyler strolled over, his too-cool swagger still perfectly intact from third grade.

"Look at us, big bad high schoolers now, huh?" he said, nudging Emilia. "Ready to break some hearts, Emmy?"

Emilia rolled her eyes, pink rising in her cheeks. "Pfft. Nope. I am interested in dissecting them in biology."

She gave me one last squeeze. "And that's where I'm off to. Byeeee!"

She tossed her hair and walked away, leaving behind her usual whirlwind of energy.

I looked up at Tyler. "You have biology too, don't you?"

He sighed like he'd just been assigned to the fifth-grade junior varsity basketball team. "Yep."

I leaned in and whispered, "Stay out of reach of Emilia's scalpel. Protect your vital organs."

"Too late," Tyler muttered. Yeah. That's what I thought. Jenna and Aria were watching the whole thing with laser focus.

"What do you two know that I don't?" I asked, narrowing my eyes.

They grinned in unison. I widened my eyes and mouthed *wow*. They immediately sandwiched me between them as we peeled off toward our English class. Tyler was headed after Emilia, looking a lot less high school cool than he had five minutes ago.

"So... a Tyler-Emilia thing just failed to launch," I said, shaking my head.

"Girl, we've been watching that mess all summer," Jenna groaned. "It's been painful. He gets two steps closer, and Emilia runs ten blocks in the opposite direction."

I could imagine it. "So basically, Ty's stuck in the desert, chasing after a vanishing mirage?"

"Exactly," Jenna said. "One moment he's gearing up to say something deep—probably something ridiculous—the next, Emilia's suddenly fascinated by a pencil sharpener across the room."

I laughed. "Oh man, I don't think I can watch this in real life."

"No kidding," Aria added dramatically. "It's like *Groundhog Day*, and no one's getting a clue they're supposed to change, but the audience has to sit through every repeat."

I shook my head. "You two must have some plan cooked up. I can't imagine either of you just reliving the same day over and over."

Aria's eyes gleamed. "Oh, Jenna and I have plans. Big plans. Operation 'Get-Ty-and-Emilia-to-Stop-Being-Idiots' is officially in motion."

"Please tell me that's not the actual name," I said, half-laughing, half-cringing.

"It's a working title," Aria said with a smirk. "But first, there's Operation Baskets and Cello Bows—"

"Nope. Back it up, sister. I don't want to hear it."

"But seriously," Aria pushed, "we can't just sit back and let this keep happening. Maybe the cosmos needs you and—"

I slapped my hand over her mouth. "Ah, ah, ah. Stay out of my cosmos. I love you and Jenna, but no."

They both gave me matching pouts. Ridiculous. I loved these girls, but in their good intentions they didn't see how much easier it was to push for a relationship from the outside. From the inside?

It wasn't simple desert and mirages. It was murky. Complicated. So much harder to pin down.

33

SIX WORDS FROM THE
WELLS OF CREATIVITY

Ivy

The bell rang, and Jenna, Aria, and I made a beeline for Creative Writing—what I already knew was going to be my favorite class.

It wasn't just the subject that excited me. It was the fact that I'd be sharing it with Aria, Jenna, Maddie, Emilia, and—surprise bonus—even Tyler.

When I walked in, Emilia and Tyler were already camped out at a round table in the back—the best spot in the room. Emilia was clearly trying to ignore Ty, who sat there smugly, his arm draped across the back of her chair.

"Interesting," Jenna sang under her breath.

"Oh yeah. Mirage girl's gonna have a hard time running from desert boy," I snickered.

"Hey, cuz! Saved you a seat," Emilia called, patting the chair next to her.

"Thanks," I said, sliding in and dropping my notebook onto the table.

I looked at my crew filling up the table. It kind of felt like we needed a team name or matching jackets. Almost perfect. Just missing one idiot dribbling a basketball down the hall.

Mr. Henderson was young. And whoa, he was enthusiastic. But everyone said he was one of the coolest teachers at school. He clapped his hands—loud, like he was starting a parade—and beamed at all of us.

"Welcome, writers!" he said, like we were already crushing it just by showing up.

Mr. Henderson kicked things off with some icebreakers, starting with a six-word memoir.

"Six words to tell us something about you," he said, bouncing a little on his toes. "Big or small, serious or funny—just own it."

The class flew by—icebreakers, quick story games, enough momentum to make me wish the period was twice as long. When the bell rang, I wasn't ready for it to end. I was already excited to see what we'd be doing next. I grabbed my stuff and headed out with the girls, our laughter bouncing down the hallway.

"Six words: Jenna can not stop giggling already," Aria teased.

"Hey!" Jenna protested, laughing even harder.

Emilia and Ty were walking ahead of us looking too casual.

"Six words: Emilia's letting the desert inch closer."

Emilia must've heard her name because she turned and stuck out her tongue at us. I grinned, already feeling that itch to dig into the creativity Mr. Henderson wanted us to find.

***

Six-Word Memoirs

    Tyler: Court king, guard close, play hard

    Ivy: Music grounds me, while notes soar

    Emilia: Farm roots deep, *corazón leal*

    Aria: Driven to win, heart beats strong

    Maddie: Brains and mischief, wit sharp as steel

    Jenna: Bubbly spirit, kindness spreads like sunshine

34

Face Down a Cold Front

Ivy

I was still riding the Creative Writing high—and totally not ready for the fifty-below windchill blasting down the hallway with Whitney. The glow from my friends didn't stand a chance against the ice storm heading straight for me.

Her presence swelled in the hallway, her entourage pausing like vultures, ready to pick at whatever might be left behind by her sharp, frozen words. Whitney locked eyes with me, her popular-girl shine flashing like sunlight off a frozen lake.

"Still clinging to Aiden and his friends, Ivy? Can't find your own?"

Of course. In Whitney's world, my friendships didn't count. Like I'd lucked into them instead of actually belonging. I sucked in a breath and made myself focus. Don't snap. Don't let her win. My friends are real. *She's just trying to mess with your head*.

Whitney stepped closer, her smile glacier-cold. "What about your little music hobby? Think you're gonna play your way into everyone's hearts?"

Her jab stung, but I wasn't giving her the satisfaction. Music wasn't some trick for popularity points. It was mine. Way bigger than whatever game she was playing.

"Actually, Whitney," I said, calm even though my heart buzzed, "my friends are real. They actually care about me. And my music? It makes me happy. Way more than any popularity contest ever could."

A flicker of surprise crossed her face—just for a second. She hadn't expected me to clap back. She recovered fast, letting out a sharp, hollow laugh. "Keep dreaming, Ivy. High school's not your concert hall."

Just then, Aiden rounded the corner, catching the tail end of her ice queen monologue.

"Everything okay?" he asked, stepping closer.

Whitney shrugged, her voice sweet with a chill beneath. "Nothing. Just making sure Ivy knows she's lucky."

I nodded, forcing a small smile. "Yeah, I'm fine. Not worth talking about."

Whitney gave her usual designer-brand huff, her mini-me army trailing behind giving their knockoff imitations.

"Okay, just checking." Aiden gave my arm a quick squeeze. Of course he had to show up right then. And be so perfect. Definitely not helping with my getting-out-of-his-orbit plan. Before I could respond, Whitney, still lingering, let out a too-light laugh.

"Oh, Aiden, always the protector. Ivy can handle herself, can't she?"

"Of course she can," Aiden said, his eyes still on me. "Doesn't mean she has to."

Whitney's smile wobbled. Her eyes narrowed—just barely—as she processed his words. That wasn't the ending she was after. With a final huff, she flipped her hair and sauntered off, her dark entourage pulled in her wake.

And just like that, the hallway warmed. The sting of icy shards melted off. Aiden watched her leave, then turned back to me, his expression softening. "I know I've been oblivious lately, but...."

I cut him off, squeezing his arm lightly. "I know you've got my back. But I handled it."

Aiden chuckled—soft, genuine, and gravitational. "Okay, fun size—I know you're tough. Just remember you've got a lot of friends behind you. Not just me."

"I know," I said, fighting the hope his presence kept lighting up in me.

Six words to myself: *Find your own orbit, just friends.* I let the words anchor me—heavy enough to keep my feelings from rocketing.

35

FULL BODY EXHALE

Ivy

Home at last. The quiet of my room was a full-body exhale after the chaos of the first day of high school. I dropped my backpack by the door and collapsed onto my bed, the softness a total contrast to the stiff chairs I'd been trapped in all day.

So...the 601st walk to school? I opened up to Aiden. Said some things. He appeared to listen—then flipped right back to full-on basketball brain. I got so frustrated I tossed his basketball into a muddy stream. Definitely on the bad side of the basketball gods now. Oh, and I might've imagined a choreographed musical starring Aiden in a *Footloose*-style dance scene—but with a basketball. Totally normal, right?

Maddie teased me about a double wedding—her and Miggy, me and Aiden. It's not weird enough that my four-year-old cousin considers Maddie his fiancée. I actually felt a little sad it couldn't happen because I don't even know where Aiden and I stand. At least I clapped back at Whitney today.

Jenna and Aria can meddle all they want, but my cosmos is staying intact. For now. Oh, and Emilia-Tyler? Definitely a thing. Mirage-ish, but a thing. And now I'm worried about Ty's vital organs. To deal with it all, I tapped into my wells of creativity and thought in pithy six-word phrases.

I pulled out my journal—a battered spiral notebook that had basically become my therapist. Flipping to a fresh page, I scribbled a title:

First Day Ninth Grade – Highs/Lows

I looked at what I'd written. Yep, that had come out as six words.

Highs:

Seeing My Friends – Laughing with Jenna, Aria, Maddie, and Emilia felt like air after being underwater. Just... easy. Like, okay, I'm not doing this whole ninth-grade thing alone.

New Start – Aria's right... this is our chance to hit reset. Be braver. Weirder. More ourselves. I'm not as into high school drama as Aria is, but a clean slate? Kinda appealing.

Lows:

Just Overload – People. Feelings. Flashbacks. Possible hallucination. But hey, at least Aiden stayed on beat while he danced.

Flash-Freeze Mean Girl Encounter – Definitely a low. She came in hot (cold?) for max damage. But... kind of a high, too? I didn't flinch. I clapped back. Loud.

Things That Helped:

Emilia's Hug – She squeezed me like she meant it. Like she knew exactly what I needed.

My Girls + Tyler in Creative Writing – One class with each of them. And all of us together in Creative Writing? YES.

Tossing Aiden's Basketball into the Mud – Just hoping the basketball gods have a short memory.

And Now Aiden:

We talked today. It wasn't awful. For a second, I thought he heard me. Really saw me. Felt a flicker of possibility—like we could be us again. Ivy and Aiden.

Then it slipped away. A flash of change... gone just as fast. I drew a line under everything and wrote the question that wouldn't leave me alone.

Do I even want things to go back to how they were... or am I hoping for something different now?

That line took up more space in my head than the rest of the page combined. I didn't have an answer.

But I knew pretending we could go back would only make it worse. I leaned back against my pillows, leaving the page open beside me. My eyes drifted to the little cello charm hanging from my lampshade. It shimmered softly in the light. It reminded me why I do hard things.

Music is still mine. Even when everything else feels off-balance, it stays. I sat up and added one last line.

Tomorrow's Goal: *Figure out my own orbit.*

Okay... but that'll take a bit. I closed the notebook.

I still didn't have a plan, but writing it down made the mess in my head feel less like chaos and more like something I could work through. I changed into pajamas and crawled into bed early. Wiped. I tugged the covers up, stretched out, and buried my face in my pillow.

Thunk. Thunk. Thunk. Then—bam. Swish. Aiden. Shooting hoops next door. I sighed. I wanted to be annoyed. Or angry. Or anything simple. Instead, my chest just tightened. That sound—his rhythm, his focus, that whole Aiden-ness—used to mean he was right there.

Now it just reminded me of the space between us. Like we're on opposite sides of something neither of us knows how to cross.

I wasn't even sure we should try.

36

WATCHERS AT THE END OF THE DRIVEWAY

Aiden

I felt the grainy surface of the ball, the spring and give with each press and release. The sound of it on cement—thwup, thwup, thwump—shifted in tone as I moved around the driveway. The feel, the sound, the motion—usually a calming rhythm.

Tonight, it was scrambled. Off. The loss of rhythm threw everything out of whack. My shots arced toward a net tangled with everything—school, basketball tryouts, Ivy.

Every thought clanked off the rim or thudded against the backboard. Nothing swished through. Nothing was on point. Nothing was clean. Her words from that morning ricocheted in my head—the sound of them, the weight behind them.

"I don't think you even noticed I was gone."

That hit hard. A blow sharp enough to bruise my ribs. And it stuck—deep, piercing. And now? Ivy was different. In a good way I couldn't quite name. She'd changed. And I hadn't been there for it.

She'd been gone all summer. Whatever had changed—it had nothing to do with me.

Jordan. New friend. Camp buddy. Music guy. Cute, according to literally everyone. Jordan probably knew exactly how she'd changed—after knowing her for less than three months.

Why did that bother me so much? I'd been chasing basketball—tryouts, stats, reps. So focused on what I wanted... I didn't even check in. She remembered the stuff I forgot. The walks. The little things. Like they mattered.

The ball slipped from my hands and rolled to the edge of the driveway. I stood there, staring up at the sky, thoughts knotted tight—like I was missing something obvious, but it stayed out of reach.

I sighed, rubbed the back of my neck, and walked over to grab the ball. Then I saw them. Chalked across the pavement, a messy row of smiley faces.

Bright, uneven circles with curved mouths and round eyes—some winking, some sticking out their tongues. And two, right in the center, blowing kisses. I froze.

No. Nope. Not this again. Just sidewalk chalk. Some neighborhood kid messing around. But I swore those kissy faces were staring straight at me. Mocking. Winking. Blowing smug little kisses like they knew something I didn't. I shook my head, forcing out a breath of laughter.

"Great. Now I'm hallucinating chalk."

Still, my grip tightened on the basketball as I stepped over them, deliberately not looking down again. Just a coincidence. That's all it was. As I headed back up the driveway, the unease stuck with me.

No matter how much I tried to shake it off, I couldn't stop feeling like those stupid faces knew exactly what was on my mind.

37

Only Listening Required

Ivy

We didn't walk to school together this morning. I told myself it was fine—no big deal—but deep down, I knew better. I'd unloaded on him yesterday, and now it felt like he was avoiding me. Maybe I deserved it.

Now, standing at my locker, I pretended to be captivated by the disaster inside. But my eyes had other plans—drifting across the hallway to where Aiden was surrounded by a flock of girls. They were all smiles, their laughter high-pitched and grating. He flashed one of his trademark grins, the kind that could make a toothpaste commercial jealous.

"Focus, Ivy," I muttered, trying to sort through the chaos of books and papers.

I stole another glance. Aiden—effortlessly charming as always. He looked relaxed, like he didn't have a care in the world. Meanwhile, I was over here, insides tied in knots.

"Hey."

The word was soft. Hesitant. I nearly jumped. Aiden was suddenly right next to me. His voice pulled me out of my spiral, and I turned toward him, my heart doing a little somersault. He wasn't wearing that easy grin anymore—his expression was serious. Almost nervous.

"Sorry," he said, shoving his hands into his pockets. "I had to get to school early for practice. Tryouts are coming up, and..." He trailed off, scratching the back of his neck. "But I heard you yesterday. I just—"

His words hung there, unfinished. Like he didn't know how to bridge the space between us. For a second, I wanted to make it easy. Say something light. Sweep away the awkwardness. But I couldn't. Not yet.

"It's fine," I said, sharper than I meant to.

I turned back to my locker, pretending to rummage, even though I wasn't really looking for anything. "Hope practice went well."

He hesitated. I thought he might leave. But then he shifted closer.

"It wasn't just about practice," he said quietly. "You were right. I've been stuck in my own world... thinking mostly about myself."

That got my attention. I looked up at him, my heart pounding. His face was open. Vulnerable in a way I didn't see often.

"I didn't mean to make you feel like I wasn't there," he said, voice low but steady. "I should've been better."

I blinked. "You didn't check on me once. I was gone two months," I said before I could stop myself.

He flinched. And for a second, I regretted saying it. But he nodded—like he knew he deserved it.

"I know," he said. "And I'm sorry, Ivy. I didn't mean to—I just got so caught up in everything else. It's not an excuse, but...."

He didn't finish. The silence stretched between us.

Part of me wanted to tell him it was okay. That I understood. Another part wanted to stay mad a little longer—to let him feel just a fraction of the frustration and hurt I'd been carrying. Finally, he sighed, his shoulders sagging a little.

"I don't know how to fix this," he said, barely above a whisper. "But I want to try. Can we... can we start there?"

I didn't answer right away. Instead, I took a deep breath and closed my locker with a soft click. He looked at me then, a small, tentative smile tugging at the corners of his mouth.

I folded my arms. "I just want you to listen. Pay attention, okay? I'm not asking you to give up your basketball kingdom."

He nodded silently. The tension between eased slightly.

"And Ivy, I did notice you where gone. I noticed all summer long."

For a moment, we stood there. The hallway noise faded into the background. We weren't close to fixed, but it was a small start.

SEPTEMBER

38

Emotional Interrogator

Ivy

I dropped a stack of books in my locker, then flipped through my assignment notebook. I scanned the spines of my textbooks, making sure I had what I'd need. History paper due next Friday. Math? Definitely a pop quiz this week, maybe a test next week. Creative Writing? A couple of small journaling exercises.

I slid the right books into my backpack and bent to zip it up—

"¡Hola, mi sonidita loca!"

Emilia grinned as she dropped her backpack next to mine. I turned to lean coolly against my locker and promptly fell inside. I forgot the door was still open.

Emilia laugh-snorted, grabbed my arm, and yanked me upright.

"Ivy, you're such a *friki*. A cute little dork."

"So you're calling me a weirdo... but with love?" I said, brushing myself off.

"With extreme love," she replied, giving my arm a dramatic shake.

"By the way, you laugh-snorted."

Emilia gasped and dropped my arm. Her best glare locked onto me—sweet and deadly.

"I do not and never have laugh-snorted."

"Sorry, what? You'll have to speak louder so I can hear all the way over here in reality."

I slammed my locker shut. "I meant to do that. Reflex test for cousin instincts."

"You're lucky I love you."

"True facts."

She rolled her eyes and looped her arm through mine.

"Grab your backpack. I'm walking home with you. Mom or Dad'll pick me up later."

"A high school play date! Let me cross the bridge to your alternate reality and we can go. On the way home you can tell me the deal with you and Tyler—as it exists in your reality."

"There's no deal with us," she huffed. Then muttered something in Spanish that definitely translated to *I'm related to an idiot.* I just grinned.

The walk home was perfect. Crisp but not cold air. Big blue sky. Perfect weather for cousin confessions. Except Emilia didn't do confessions. I swung my backpack lazily.

"So... anything interesting happen this summer while I was off fighting mosquitoes at music camp?"

Emilia side-eyed me. "Define interesting."

I grinned. "Oh, I don't know. Lots of texting. Group hangouts? Suspicious amounts of texting. Hanging out at the diner? Flirty texting? Texting and more texting?"

She rolled her eyes. "Psshh. *¡Cállate, loca!*"

"Right," I said, like I totally believed her. "Because no one possibly texted you every day just to remind you of his presence?"

Her foot caught on a sidewalk crack. She stumbled. Recovered fast. "Maybe. Sometimes. Not like—on purpose."

"On purpose is exactly how texting works, Emmy."

She made a strangled noise and sped up. I matched her easily.

"So," I said, swinging my backpack again. "Just putting this out there—were you texting a boy whose heart became yours in third grade when you called him Prince Butthead? Señor Show-Off? Captain Annoying? Duke of Dumb?"

Emilia covered her face. "I hate you."

"I love you too," I said brightly. "Now spill."

She peeked through her fingers. "He just... texted sometimes. Jokes. Stupid stuff."

"Stupid stuff like what?"

She shrugged helplessly. "Fishing. Popcorn. Farm animals."

I clutched my chest. "The classic language of love."

"It wasn't like that," she said quickly. "We were just... talking."

"Talking," I echoed. "With emojis or no emojis?"

She blushed. "Sometimes."

"Confirmation!" I shouted.

Emilia tried to shush me. I wasn't done.

"And movie nights?" I asked innocently. "Any suspiciously-close-adjacent seating arrangements?"

Her face turned redder. "We were in a group."

"Uh-huh. Were you sitting group-adjacent or almost-couple-adjacent-but-pretending-it's-not-what-it-looks-like?"

She shoved me. "I'm not talking about this."

I laughed, skipping ahead. "It's fine. You don't have to. Your face is saying everything."

"I'm never walking home with you again."

"And yet here you are." I grinned. "Which means I get to ask a question. On a scale of one to Tyler's smile, how much are you into him?"

Emilia groaned into her hands. "*Madre mía!* You are literally the worst."

"That's not a number, Ems."

"Maybe like... an itty-bitty amount?"

"Even more Confirmation!" I shouted. "Somebody call the feelings police!"

"You're not normal," Emilia said, dragging me along faster.

"But you love me anyway," I sang.

"Yeah, yeah. Even if you're an evil interrogator poking into all the feels."

"Well, the interrogator has evidence."

I pulled out my phone, flipped to a screenshot, and handed it over.

Tyler: Don't worry, Meela. You're still my favorite red M&M thief. (winking emoji)

Tyler: WAIT NO NOT FOR YOU ABORT ABORT

Emilia froze. Mouth open. Then shut. Then open again.

"THAT—That was supposed to— I—"

"I'm listening," I said smugly.

She muttered in rapid Spanish, face flaming.

"I rest my case," I said sweetly.

"You're impossible."

"And yet! Still your favorite cousin."

She groaned and stomped ahead. I jogged to catch up, grinning the whole way.

"And just when you thought you were safe," I said cheerfully, "there's more."

"Noooo," she moaned.

"Oh yes," I said, unlocking my phone. "Miggy intel."

Miggy: Sonidita, this is your cousin Miguel Cabrera.

Ivy: Hi Miggy! I miss you.

Miggy: ok

Ivy: You're supposed to say you miss me back.

Miggy: ok

Ivy: What's up? Baseball question?

Miggy: no you just got your head filled up with music and the basketball head guy

Ivy: I've got more in my head than that! My head's stuffed full!

Miggy: but you got a bassman guy in your head now too

Miggy: so you can't fit more in your head

Ivy: WHOA WHOA WHOA. Bassman?? Miguel Ángel Preston, EXPLAIN.

Miggy: Meela was bossing and talking. I listen.

Ivy: Wait. Meela was bossing WHO?

Miggy: I don't know the guy she's texting. I heard her laugh and say "Ooookay I'll probably see you there."

Miggy: That's why I texted you. Who's Meela talking to? Can you make sure they don't start kissing?

> **Ivy:** MIGGY. This is now a critical mission. Operation No Kissing is officially active.

I looked at Emilia. She was face-palming.

"How does Miggy text like this?" I asked.

She groaned. "I have no idea. And I don't want to know."

"At least I convinced him I'm smart."

"Oh yeah. Real convincing. 'Stuff. I know a lot of stuff.'"

"Exactly. I'm officially qualified to advise him and Sofi about stuff when they take over the world."

We reached my house. I grabbed her arm, towing her upstairs to my room. She flopped across my bed. I flopped beside her.

"So then, Emmy."

She groaned.

"Stuff," I said.

39

News from Next Door

Ivy

I'd managed to get Emilia to fess up to a few things. She liked Tyler—a little bit. Tyler was smarter than he seems. They were still texting. And most importantly—there was no kissing.

If Miggy asked, I could officially report, "Sir, no kissing, Sir."

We grabbed snacks, did homework, and chattered like always. Then, Emilia unknowingly detonated a bomb.

"Oh, I meant to ask you, Ivy. What's the latest on how Mrs. Pedersen is doing?"

I froze mid–page flip. The question sent a chill down my spine. Like I was about to turn a metaphorical page—and I wasn't going to like the story being told on the other side.

"What do you mean, how's Mrs. Pedersen doing?" The words tumbled out of my mouth.

"Waiting for the b—" Emilia started, then stopped. She looked at me fully now, her playful expression gone. Her face was serious—no twinkle, no teasing.

"Uh...wow. Okay. There's some news I thought you already knew."

***

Stunned.

I sat completely still, like I'd been carved from stone. Was my heart still beating? Were my lungs still pulling in air? Everything felt muffled and heavy. My mind was stuck in a loop- he never told me, never told me. Emilia sat next to me, leaning in. She gently rested her head on my shoulder. I half-expected her to pull away—like the cold, heavy weight I'd become would be too much to bear.

"I'm so sorry, Ivy," she whispered. "I won't make excuses for him. At this point... there really isn't anything to make it better."

Somehow, my granite lungs still found the air for a deep breath. I tilted my head to rest against hers.

"It was getting better," I murmured. "We were finally starting to connect again. But this? This hurts. And I think... maybe the hurt isn't going to stop. I can't keep waiting here—wide open—just to get hurt by him again."

"I know," Emilia said softly. "I'm glad you heard it from me, even if it should've come from Aiden. It hurts watching you wait around, hoping to be seen by him. You deserve better, Ivy. I don't know if that's Aiden anymore."

Neither did I.

40

REMEMBER ME?

Ivy

Long, afternoon shadows crossed the driveway. I stood there, arms crossed, watching him go through his drills. He hadn't noticed me yet—too wrapped up in dribbling, shooting, and whatever endless cycle of basketball moves kept his brain occupied. I waited, frustration coiling tighter and tighter in my chest. Finally, I couldn't take it anymore.

"Aiden!"

He stopped mid-dribble, turning around with that easy grin. "Ives! Didn't see you there." He walked over, still casually bouncing the ball, like nothing had changed between us. "What's up?"

I stared at him, the heat rising in my face. "I heard about your mom. About you being a big brother. Twins."

The basketball slipped from his hands, rolling into the grass. His expression shifted—surprised, guilty. "Oh... right. I... I meant to tell you. It's just been so chaotic with everything going on."

I clenched my fists, holding back the sting of tears.

"Too chaotic to tell your best friend?" My voice cracked, but I pushed on. "I was gone all summer, and I come back wondering why everything feels so... so weird, and then Emilia mentions your mom is pregnant like it's old news. Like I'm the last person to find out."

His face flushed, and he glanced down. "I know, Ivy. I should've told you. I just... with basketball, and camp, and everything, it slipped my mind."

"Basketball!," I snapped, my voice tight and trembling. "That's all you ever think about, isn't it? Don't you get it, Aiden? This isn't just about some news you forgot to mention. It's about you forgetting me."

He opened his mouth, but I wasn't done.

"Your mom and dad are like family to me." My voice wavered, but I kept going. "They must think I'm awful—I haven't congratulated them, haven't checked in, haven't said anything because I didn't know. Because you didn't tell me."

I took a shaky breath, swallowing past the lump in my throat. "Did you even think about how that would make me feel? How it would make them feel?"

He ran a hand through his hair, looking frustrated—maybe at himself, maybe at me for calling him out. "I wasn't trying to shut you out, Ivy."

"But you did," I said quietly. "You pushed me out. You pushed your mom and baby sisters to the background, too. It's like you decided if something wasn't about basketball, it wasn't worth your time."

Aiden stiffened, the hurt flickering across his face, but I didn't care.

"I waited, Aiden," I whispered. "I waited for you to text me. To care. To remember me. And you didn't."

His eyes locked onto mine then, something breaking in them, but I was already shaking my head.

"You know what? Forget it. Just... forget it. I really hope everything goes okay for your mom and the babies. I hope they're okay. But right now, I don't want to talk to you. Not now... and maybe not for a while."

His eyes widened, like he hadn't expected that. Like he thought he could just say "sorry" and I'd brush it off. Before he could open his mouth, I turned around and walked away.

I had to walk away. I didn't look back. I didn't want to see the regret on his face or hear whatever excuse he'd try to give. As I left his driveway, the weight of everything I hadn't said sat heavy in my chest. The anger, the hurt—it was all bubbling over, and I didn't know if I could forgive him for this. At least not anytime soon.

For now, I needed distance. Space to feel everything I'd been holding in. Space to figure out if Aiden was even the friend I thought he was.

41

Call 1-800-Tyler to Get the Hard Truth

Aiden

I lay flat on my bed, one arm draped across my forehead, my phone resting on my chest. I scrolled through my contacts. Ivy's name was right there. I ignored it. I exhaled sharply and hit dial.

It rang twice before Tyler picked up, the sound of a game blaring in the background.

"Yo," he said. "Didn't think I'd hear from you today. Something wrong?"

I hesitated. *Yeah. Everything.*

"Nah," I muttered, rubbing my forehead. "Just... needed to talk."

Tyler let out a low whistle. "Huh. Must be serious if you're actually calling about something that's not basketball or needing a ride."

I frowned. "What's that supposed to mean?"

"It means," he said, still mashing buttons, "you don't make phone calls unless it involves a hoop or your transportation plan."

I opened my mouth to argue but shut it again. He wasn't wrong.

"So?" Tyler continued, his tone easy. "What is it? You bomb a test? Finally realize Whitney's the worst?"

I exhaled. "It's about Ivy."

Tyler's controller clicking stopped.

"Oh," he said after a beat. "What about Ivy?"

I rolled onto my side. The words felt too big. Too heavy. "She's pissed at me."

Another pause. "Okay... What did you do?"

I rubbed my face. "I—I didn't tell her about my mom."

"What about your mom?"

"The pregnancy," I said. "The twins."

Silence.

"You mean Ivy just found out?" Tyler asked slowly. "Like... today?"

"Yeah."

"And not from you."

"No."

Tyler let out a low breath, like he needed to physically exhale the stupidity of my actions. Then gave a short laugh. Disbelieving. "Oh, man. Aiden. Are you serious?"

"I meant to tell her."

He didn't answer right away. When he did, the humor was gone.

"Ivy's basically family. How do you forget to tell her something like that?"

"I don't know!" I snapped, sitting up. The room suddenly felt too hot. "I was busy. Basketball, camp, everything…"

"Everything else," Tyler echoed. "Let me guess—did you even talk to her this summer?"

"I mean… we texted."

"How many times?"

I hesitated. "A couple?"

"A couple." His voice went flat. My stomach twisted.

Tyler sighed. "Let me get this straight. You didn't say goodbye before she left. You barely texted. And she finds out from someone else that your mom's pregnant—with twins—and you're wondering why she's mad?"

Hearing it laid out like that made my chest tighten. "I didn't think it would matter this much."

Tyler let out a humorless laugh. "Wow. You really don't get it, do you?"

I grabbed the basketball beside my bed and tossed it toward the ceiling. "I know, okay? She already yelled at me about it."

"And let me guess—you got defensive."

I caught the ball, squeezing it. "I didn't think it was that big of a deal."

"Aiden," Tyler said, exasperated. "You've had Ivy in your life forever. You've never had to try to keep her there. But guess what? She's done waiting for you to notice her."

My jaw tightened. "That's not what's happening."

"Then why are you calling me? Why does this feel like the end of the world?"

I didn't answer. Couldn't. The silence stretched between us.

Tyler's voice dropped. "You keep acting like Ivy will always be there. But what if she's not? What if she stops trying?"

I exhaled through my teeth, pressing a fist to my forehead. "Yeah, you keep saying that."

"Because it's a possibility."

Silence again. Then, quieter. "If she stops showing up—can you live with that?"

I gritted my teeth. Could I? My fingers dug into the seams of the basketball. No. But I wasn't ready to admit it out loud.

Tyler sighed. "Man, you are unbelievable."

I sat up. "What now?"

"You act like she's just your friend—but she's not *just* a friend. And you know it."

My pulse kicked up. "That's not—"

"Oh, shut up," he cut in. "If it was just about friendship, you wouldn't be calling me like this. You wouldn't be this messed up. So stop pretending."

I swallowed hard. My voice cracked. "I—." But the rest of the sentence never came.

Tyler let out a breath. "Fine. Whatever helps you sleep at night."

We sat in silence for a long beat.

"You still playing tomorrow?" I asked finally, reaching for anything else.

"Yeah. And you're gonna show up, and I'm gonna kick your ass."

I snorted. "We'll see."

"Oh, we will."

I ended the call. My brain spun in circles trying to figure out how to think about everything Ivy and Tyler had said.

42

BEING AVOIDED

Aiden

I didn't expect Ivy to be happy to see me. But I guess I thought... something would be the same. It wasn't. I spotted her at the lockers between classes, tucking a book under her arm, her hair in a loose braid. My first instinct was to walk up to her. I stopped myself before I moved. Would she even want me to?

I hesitated, waiting for some kind of sign. But before I could decide, she shut her locker and walked away. No hesitation. No glance in my direction. I let out a breath and turned the other way. Maybe she hadn't seen me.

But the second time? No way that was an accident. I was standing by the vending machines when she came around the corner, laughing at something Emilia said. For a second, it felt familiar—her laughter, the way she crinkled her nose. And then—she saw me. Her expression shut down. The laughter vanished. She didn't glare. Didn't roll her eyes. She just turned on her heel and walked the other way.

Something twisted in my stomach.

The third time? Worse.

I was already at our usual lunch table, half-listening to Tyler and Drew argue over some ridiculous football stat, when Ivy walked into the cafeteria. I didn't mean to look for her. She had her tray, scanning the room—pointedly not looking my way. She sat at a different table. She'd never done that before. Emilia, Jenna, and a few others were with her—but it didn't matter. We were always at the same table. Even if we weren't in the same conversation, we shared the space.

Tyler must've noticed. He stopped mid-sentence and followed my gaze. "Huh."

I grabbed a fry off my tray and tore it in half for no reason. "She's just—" I started. But I couldn't explain it away.

I had taken her for granted. I'd shut her out. Now she was shutting me out. Crap. It didn't feel good to be left behind. Ivy not wanting to sit with me? Just a taste. I'd dished out so much more. I pushed my tray away. I wasn't hungry anymore.

43

YOU NEEDED TO HEAR IT

Aiden

Basketball practice was rough. Not because of the drills. Not because Coach was harder on us than usual. Because my head wasn't in it. I ran the plays. Took the shots. Pushed through conditioning. But everything felt off. The ball didn't feel right in my hands. My timing sucked and I knew it.

Tyler must've noticed too, because as I grabbed my water bottle and slung my bag over my shoulder, he gave me a look.

"You good, man?"

I shrugged. "Just tired."

"If that's your story." Of course he didn't buy it, but he let it go.

Everyone else filtered out of the gym, heading toward the locker rooms. I adjusted the strap of my bag, ready to follow. And I saw Emilia, leaning against the far wall of the gym, arms crossed, backpack slung over one shoulder. Waiting for me.

I froze mid-step. A second passed. Two. Then I sighed, wiped the sweat off my face with my T-shirt, and crossed the gym toward her.

"You're waiting for me, aren't you?"

She tilted her head slightly. "What gave it away?"

I jerked my thumb at the empty gym around us. "Can we not do this here? I'd rather not have an audience."

Her mouth quirked. "Fair. Let's walk."

We pushed through the gym doors into the hallway, the cooler air brushing against my overheated skin. Our footsteps echoed against the lockers, sharp and loud in the quiet. Emilia stayed silent for a few beats, hands shoved deep in her sweatshirt pockets. Finally, she glanced over, voice low.

"I'm not here just to tear you apart, you know. I'm mad... but I care. About both of you."

I blinked, thrown off for a second. "Yeah?" My voice cracked before I caught it.

She gave a half-shrug. "Yeah. Doesn't mean you're off the hook, though."

I huffed a breath, kicking lightly at a crack in the hallway tile as we walked.

After a moment, she said, "You don't even know how bad you hurt her."

I pressed my fingers against my temples. "I know, okay?"

"Do you?" Emilia's voice sharpened, but not cruelly. "Because I don't think you do."

"It's not like I did it on purpose," I muttered.

She stopped walking. I did too.

"That's the problem, Aiden," she said, folding her arms. "You don't do anything on purpose. You don't show up for her on purpose. Even as a friend—you're supposed to show up."

I opened my mouth. Closed it again. She studied me for a beat longer.

"You don't realize how much she waited for you. How many excuses she made for you. Until she finally stopped."

Her words cut deeper than anything I'd let myself admit until now. I let out a slow breath, rubbing the back of my neck.

"Yeah," I said quietly. "You're right."

Emilia blinked like she hadn't expected me to admit it.

"I know I screwed up. I just... don't know how to fix it."

She sighed, softer now. "This isn't a basketball game where I can draw up a play for you. Ivy doesn't need a grand gesture. She needs to know you actually care."

I nodded, the truth of her words sitting on my shoulders.

"I'm not the enemy," she added, heading for the parking lot. "You needed to hear it. What you do with it—that's up to you."

44

MOM, I MESSED UP BAD

Aiden

Practice had been craptastic. Every shot clanged off the rim; every play felt forced. It was like my body was there, but my mind was miles away, tangled up in everything except basketball.

Then Emilia. Everything she said was true. It was almost worse that she came at me not hating my guts but as my friend. I walked home, the crunch of leaves, gravel, and my sneakers hitting the sidewalk louder than usual. Good, because I didn't want to hear what was in my head.

The hoop over the garage came into view as I approached the house. Normally, it would've been my escape to work through whatever was bothering me, to dribble and shoot until my arms ached and the world faded away. Now that hoop felt ominous.

I didn't want to pick up the ball, even though I craved the distraction. For the first time, I was afraid of what it might mean if I did. What if I kept using basketball to push everything else away? To avoid the things I didn't want to face—like how much

I'd hurt Ivy, or how I barely recognized myself outside of the game anymore?

The house was quiet as I opened the door and stepped inside. I heard a quiet call, "In the living room, Aiden."

Mom was resting on the sofa, leaning back on a pile of pillows. She sipped tea and paged through a magazine. The curtains were open, letting in light. The whole house felt hushed, waiting. She looked up and gave me a smile.

"Aiden. Hey sweetie. How was practice?"

I managed a small smile as I settled into an armchair. "It was fine. But... I actually wanted to talk about something else."

Mom lowered the magazine, her eyebrows knitting together in that way that told me she was listening intently. "Of course. What's on your mind?"

I swallowed hard, trying to organize everything I was feeling. "It's about Ivy. I've been so stuck in my own head, thinking about myself.

"I didn't say goodbye to her before she left for her music camp this summer. I messed up even worse though, Mom. She found out about... you, the twins... from someone else. I never bothered to make sure she knew."

Mom's face softened, and she reached out, her hand resting gently on top of mine. "Oh, honey."

The warmth of her touch made something in my chest tighten.

"I was just... so focused on basketball, and on everything going for me, I didn't stop to think that Ivy should've heard it from me. I forgot. And now… she's really hurt. She doesn't feel like I'm there for her. And I get it. I haven't been."

Mom squeezed my hand, her voice soft and steady. "Aiden, do you think maybe you've taken Ivy for granted? When you two were younger, you were in the biggest support role. Even then, though, she always believed in you—that you could accomplish what you wanted to."

I sighed, leaning my head back and looking up at the ceiling. "I'm a selfish jerk. I don't think I can fix this. Fix us. I don't know what to do."

Mom reached for my hand and gave it a squeeze. "First, you're not a selfish jerk. That's not who you are as a person. Ivy knows that. But yes, your actions, or inaction toward Ivy, were selfish for the past few months. And now you're seeing that reality."

I nodded, looking down at our hands. "But what if… what if I've messed things up too much already? She said she's tired of me saying I'm here for her when I'm really not."

Mom let out a small sigh, her gaze warm and understanding. "Aiden, Ivy knows you care about her, but she needs to see it—really see it. It's not enough to tell someone you're there for them if your actions don't match. Words are important, but they have to be backed up by what you do."

The truth of her words wrapped around me. "So… what do I do? How do I make it right with her?"

"Start by being honest," Mom said, her voice gentle but firm. "Don't try to explain it all away. Just tell her you're sorry and that you understand why she's hurt. And Aiden, you can't fix what's happened in the past, but you can change what you do now. Ivy needs to know you've learned from the past and that you want to change. You'll need to show her. Be consistent. Be the friend she needs you to be—the one who's really there."

I looked up, meeting her gaze, feeling a flicker of hope. "I want to, but... I feel like I've let her down so much already."

Mom's hand tightened on mine, her eyes kind. "Aiden, everyone makes mistakes. What matters is how you move forward. If Ivy means as much to you as I think she does, then show her. Show her with your actions that you care."

I nodded, taking a steadying breath. "I need to talk to her."

She smiled, reaching up to gently touch my cheek. "You do, but you'll have to be okay with her timeline. You can't force it. Remember, we're here for you too. You don't have to figure this all out alone."

Dad walked in just then, with a snack for Mom. He glanced between us, his face softening as he took in the scene. "You okay, son?"

"Yeah," I said, giving him a small, grateful smile. "Just... trying to figure some things out."

Dad nodded and sat at the end of the sofa. He picked up Mom's feet and placed them in his lap. "Ivy stuff?"

"Yeah, I guess I've basically ignored her for a few months, thinking only about myself, about being a great basketball player. I don't understand why I got so deep into basketball. I let it take me over. I love it, but sometimes it felt like the only thing."

Mom looked at me. "Honey, I think at first basketball became your outlet. You've got so much energy, so much drive, and the game gave you a way to channel that."

Dad added, "It started as something fun, something to challenge you. We discovered—you discovered—that you're good at it. Really good."

"But Aiden, you're not only a basketball player. It's not the one thing that defines you," Mom added. "Maybe that's part of what's happened. It started being the only way you saw yourself—the only thing that truly mattered."

"Do you think it's too much now? Like... maybe I'm letting it take over everything?"

My voice wavered, and I felt the heaviness of the question sink in the space between us.

"I think it's okay to love something and to be good at it. Basketball isn't bad for you."

Dad nodded. "You need to add balance and perspective. I don't think you'll need to give up basketball—but we need to pull back from being about it 24/7."

Mom gave me a reassuring look. "And remember, just because you see faster results in your basketball skills doesn't mean it's the only part of you, you should work on. Relationships, friendships—they all take work. What you put in doesn't always show right away. People aren't easy, but they're worth it. You and

Ivy have had a special friendship. Any work you do now to show her you see what happened will be worth the effort."

I heard their words, letting them settle into the parts of me feeling agitated and confused. I realized this is what Josh had meant about being a person first and a baller second. I couldn't keep saying I was there for Ivy—I had to actually be ere.

I was determined to prove to her that she could count on me. No more empty promises. This time, I was going to show her with everything I had. I was getting up to go, but Mom stopped me with a gesture.

"Aiden, before you go, let's figure out the specifics—how we can help you find balance. What boundaries do we need to put in place?"

I sat back down, ready to deal with it. Dad was massaging Mom's feet, swollen as usual now.

Dad started, "I want you to limit your practice time on weekdays. Keep it to team practices and anything coach-scheduled. Cut back on the extra hours you've been putting in after dinner."

Mom nodded in agreement. "And maybe no basketball at all on one day during the weekend. Save a day for family activities, make plans with Ivy and your other friends."

I mulled it over. Cutting my practice time felt uncomfortable. At the same time, part of me felt relieved.

"Okay, yeah. That's fine."

"We're proud of you for recognizing you need a change, Aiden. Let's start this plan tomorrow," Mom said. "No basketball after dinner and spend time with people one day this weekend."

I nodded, feeling apprehensive but light. "I hope Ivy will talk to me."

Dad clapped me on the shoulder as he stood up. "She will. She might not want to hear you out right away. Respect that."

I left the room with determination. This was the right step—not just for my relationship with Ivy, but for myself. I was more than just basketball, and now I needed to figure out who else I was.

***

In my room, I dropped my backpack and sat on the edge of my bed, staring at the scuffed toes of my sneakers.

A few weeks ago, everyone had been hyped about this big creative writing assignment Mr. Henderson gave out—digging deep into their "wells of creativity," or whatever. Write a letter from your fifteen-year-old self to your younger self.

I remembered hearing my friends talk about it at lunch, all dramatic like it was some life-changing moment. At the time, I thought it sounded dumb. Now? I wasn't so sure. I bet ten-year-old me knew more about what mattered than fifteen-year-old me.

I grabbed a battered notebook off my desk and flipped it open. Clicked my pen. Stared at the blank page for a second. And then I started to write.

***

Dear Fifteen-Year-Old Me,

Remember Ivy? You used to think she was the best part of every day. You used to wait at the sidewalk until you saw her coming so you could walk together. You used to listen when she talked about music, even when you didn't get it. You used to know that friends are more important than winning.

You forgot.

You got busy trying to be the best at basketball. You started thinking about yourself first, second, and third. You stopped noticing when she needed you. You let her stand alone.

If you're reading this—If you still care—Fix it. Not with words. With showing up. She's still there. But she won't wait forever. You shouldn't make her.

***

I stared at the page when I finished, my hand cramping around the pen.

Ten-year-old me would be disappointed. Not because I wasn't a good basketball player. But because I forgot what mattered. Forgot who mattered.

I ripped the page carefully out of the notebook, folded it twice, and slid it into the worn copy of *How to Shoot Like a Pro*—the one I was always picking up and flipping through whenever I got restless. The one that usually told me to work harder, hustle more, focus only on the game.

Maybe now, when I cracked it open again, I'd have something else to think about too.

I flipped to a clean notebook page.

Things Only I Know About Ivy.

45

OPERATION CINNAMON ROLL COMMENCES

Aiden

I stared at the list I'd started—*Things Only I Know About You.* The list was done. The work? I'd barely scratched the surface. If I was actually going to do this, I needed help. And unfortunately, I knew exactly who that help had to be.

It couldn't be Aria. She'd say yes, sure, but not without a full Q&A session, complete with follow-up commentary, sports metaphors, and a narrowed-eye read-through of every sentence I wrote. I wasn't ready to be emotionally out-rebounded.

Jenna was worse. She'd decorate the locker. Probably add sparkle tape and a second note signed *Love, Team Redemption.* Ivy would know immediately—and so would the entire school.

Emilia? No. Too close. Too family. And something about the way she looked at me lately—quiet, calm, like she knows the whole story even when I haven't said a word—makes it feel like I haven't earned the right to ask her for anything.

Which left one person.

Maddie.

Still terrifying. But if she said yes, she'd get it done. No drama, no glitter, no pep squad announcement over the loudspeaker. Just quiet precision and a decent chance Ivy would actually read the notes before throwing them away.

I opened my phone and typed the message before I could talk myself out of it.

***

Maddie was waiting the next morning—leaning against the lockers, one ankle crossed over the other, arms folded like she had all the time in the world. Her body language said, *"Nothing happening here move on."*

"Don't worry, Maddie. I'm not going to ask for your help burying a body."

"You'd better be asking for help designing the best grovel in the history of YA romantic fiction."

I wasn't totally sure what that meant, but I was about 90% certain it involved public humiliation and at least one tearful monologue.

"There's probably some groveling involved somewhere. First—I need a favor."

"It had better be at least groveling-adjacent and romantically oriented. Otherwise I'm walking."

"I need you to drop something in Ivy's locker for me." I pulled a folded paper from my jacket pocket and held it out to her.

"A note," she said, frowning. I'd never heard her sound that disappointed. "*Check yes if you forgive me?* That doesn't fly, Aiden. We are not in a reboot of middle school."

"Look, Maddie, I get how much I've screwed up. It's not a stupid middle school note." I sighed and rattled it off in one breath. "I've-been-making-lists-to-give-Ivy-about-the-good-stuff-I-remember."

"You've been making..."

She waited.

"Lists."

She waited.

"Of?"

She waited.

"Good memories."

"About?"

She waited. I could feel my ears turning red. Maddie's smile was getting bigger with every pause.

"How I did pay attention to the details about her."

Then Maddie gave me a slow blink.

"Aw! Aiden, you're using Ivy's love language. I'm in. Operation Cinnamon Roll is a go."

I groaned. "Please don't call it that."

She plucked the note from my hand. "Too late. Operation Cinnamon Roll already has momentum."

I exhaled. "Can you get them into her locker every morning this week without anyone seeing you?"

Her voice softened. "She misses you. She won't admit it, but she does."

She gave me a very pointed look. "But listen. If you mess this up again—if you even think in her direction like you're gonna disappear again—I will personally use an ax on the school's basketball court chop open an Aiden-sized grave."

46

A Discovery of Notes

Ivy

Right, left, right. I spun my combination not expecting anything new. But there was a folded piece of paper, wedged between my books like it had been placed there on purpose. The handwriting stopped me cold. Aiden. I swallowed and picked it up before I could talk myself out of it.

***

Monday – Things Only I Know About You

- You have a tiny scar on your right hand from when we tried to build a treehouse and you slipped on a nail.

- You don't like melted cheese on sandwiches, but you'll eat it on pizza.

- You always count the number of steps when you walk up or down a flight of stairs.

- You hate the sound of Styrofoam squeaking.

- You never drink the last sip of a water bottle because you say it tastes weird.

- You always crack your knuckles before you play but pretend you don't.

- You hum in your sleep after a recital or concert.

- You bite your lip when you're thinking really hard, but only when your thoughts are about music.

- You always stop to pick up litter.

- You always wait until the very last second to make a wish when you blow out candles.

I pressed my lips together, gripping the paper tightly.

No signature. No explanation. Just the list.

I folded it carefully and slipped it into my backpack, pretending my hands weren't shaking.

***

I told myself I wouldn't expect another one. A note didn't mean anything. When I opened my locker, there it was. I hesitated, then unfolded it.

Tuesday – Things Only You Know About Me

- I love milk, but only if it's ice cold, even a tiny bit warm and it makes me want to barf.

- I talk to myself when I'm doing homework.

- I don't like sitting with my back to a door.

- I never remember song lyrics, but I always remember movie quotes.

- I still have the lucky rock you gave me in second grade even though I fell and broke a finger after you gave it to me.

- I can tell the difference between your "I'm fine" and your *real* "I'm fine."

- I don't like wearing socks to bed, but if I don't, my feet get too cold.

- I like doing macrame though I haven't done it I awhile.

- I can tell when you're about to cry, even before you can.

- I don't mind big hairy spiders, but I'm terrified of wasps and bees.

I shut my locker, pressing my forehead against the cool metal for just a second. I wasn't ready for this.

***

I wasn't looking for it. I wasn't. But the second I opened my locker and saw the paper tucked inside, my heart kicked up. Another list. This one hit differently.

Wednesday – Times I Should Have Listened Harder &
Appreciated You More

- When you showed up at my games even when I never asked you to.

- That time you stayed up texting me after I missed that free throw and thought I ruined everything.

- Every time you let me complain about practice even though I never really listened when you talked about music.

- When you made me a playlist after my first basketball camp so I wouldn't feel weird on the trip home.

- That summer we sat in your driveway every night just talking about random things.

- The time you saved me from getting detention by "accidentally" dropping your music folder so the teacher wouldn't notice me sneaking in late.

- Every time you called me out when I deserved it. (Like now.)

- When you asked me to be your duet partner for that one performance, and I said no without even thinking. Later I found out you only needed someone to turn pages. You got Emilia to do it. I should have said yes as soon as you asked.

- Every time you told me I was more than just basketball. I should have believed you.

- Every time I thought we had all the time in the world.

I folded the paper my hands unsteady. Why was he doing this? I shoved the note into my bag and walked away before I could let myself think too hard about it.

***

I didn't want to expect anything. Still I had a bubble of anticipation inside as I opened my locker. The list was waiting for me, just like the others. I told myself I could ignore it. But my hands had already unfolded the paper.

Thursday – Stuff I Should Have Told You
- I always noticed when you were at any game I played

in—even when our fourth-grade team lost every game that season.

- I can hear your voice in a crowd.

- I actually did like the books you told me to read—I just pretended I didn't because it was fun to hear you hype up the books.

- I started recognizing songs just from hearing you practice, and now I miss it.

- Sometimes, when I heard you talk about music, I wished basketball had as much beauty as the music you played.

- I always assumed you would be there, and I never thought about what it would feel like if you weren't.

- I don't think I ever really said thank you for all the ways you showed up for me.

- I don't like this version of us. Mostly it's the version of me I don't like.

- I should have told you about my mom. I should have told you everything.

- I know I don't deserve another chance, but I want to fix this.

- I miss my best friend.

I pressed my lips together, my fingers gripping the edge of the paper. He wasn't asking for anything. He wasn't waiting for me to talk to him. He was just leaving these. I wasn't sure how I felt about it all.

***

I opened my locker and found the last list. At least, I thought it was the last one. I stood there longer than I needed to, staring at the paper before picking it up. I didn't even have to open it to feel the lump in my throat.

Friday – My Favorite Memories of You
- The time we made a fort in your living room with every blanke and pillow we could find, and your parents let us sleep there the whole night.

- When we got caught in the rain walking home, and you dared me to dance in the middle of the street. I was too embarrassed, but you did it anyway, spinning in circles like you didn't care who was watching.

- The night we stayed up late on your front porch, counting fireflies until we lost track, and you fell asleep with your head on my shoulder.

- The first time you ever played your cello for me, really played.

- The day we skipped rocks at the lake for hours, and you made me keep every single smooth one we found, because you said they were lucky. I still have some of them.

- When I was sick, and you left a bag of cough drops and a note on my porch, even though you hate being around people who are contagious.

- The way you always made up ridiculous stories about strangers at the diner, like we were inside some kind of secret world that only we understood.

- The day we tried to bake cookies and ended up with an entire tray of burned, melted disaster—but we still ate them anyway because we refused to admit failure.

- That time you told me I was more than just basketball. I didn't get what you meant then, but I do now.

- Every single one of our 600 walks to school.

47

A FEW OF YOUR FAVORITE THINGS

Ivy

Friday night my phone buzzed beside me on my bed. I ignored it for a few seconds, staring at the ceiling, willing myself not to care. But when I glanced at the screen and saw Aiden's name, my stomach twisted. I could have ignored it. I didn't. I tapped the message, my pulse kicking up before I even read it.

> **Aiden:** Are these all still your favorite snacks? – Lemon bars – Strawberry licorice, but only the brand from that one gas station – Those weird kettle chips you made me try and I almost threw up – Peanut butter pretzels (but not the ones with too much salt) – Gummy bears, but only the red and white ones – The iced tea that's impossible to find but you always manage to find it anyway?

Of all the things I expected from him, this wasn't it. Not another apology. Not another deep memory. Just... a question. I hesitated, my thumb hovering over the keyboard. For a week,

Aiden had been slipping lists into my locker, proving—without saying it outright—that he hadn't forgotten our friendship. That he actually remembered the things that mattered. But this? This was different.

I could have ignored it. Pretended I never saw it. Instead, my fingers moved before I could stop them.

> **Me:** LOL, I found that tea at the convenience store the day you tripped over your own feet and took down an entire display of granola bars.

A few seconds later, the typing bubble appeared.

> **Aiden:** Yeah, I was showing off for you before I tripped. And I know I'd rather be a clumsy idiot than the stupid jerk I have been to you.

I stared at the message, my smile fading just slightly. For the first time, Aiden wasn't just joking. And I wasn't sure what to do with that.

The typing bubble popped up again.

> **Aiden:** Nite, Princess.

48

SNACK DELIVERY

Ivy

I padded into the kitchen in mismatched pajamas expecting the usual—quiet house, maybe a pancake smell trail from the griddle if I was lucky. Instead, I stopped cold at a bag sitting smack in the middle of the kitchen table. A note from my dad was next to the bag.

Ivy,
Think this is meant for you. Found it when I grabbed the Sunday paper off the front steps. We're going to the late church service this morning.
Dad xox

I'd always loved that my dad was a big burly guy who signed off with Xs and Os. This morning I didn't stop to reflect on it. I was curious about the the bag. The paper crinkled in my hands as I opened it.

Inside it I found:

a lemon bar, wrapped in wax paper

a small bag of kettle chips—my kind

a pack of strawberry licorice with the gas station label still stuck to the side

a mini container of peanut butter pretzels—light on the salt

a baggie with just the red and white gummy bears

and tucked against the side, a chilled bottle of iced tea—the impossible to find kind

I stared at it for a long moment. He wasn't waiting for me to talk to him. He was just leaving these. No expectations. No text follow-up. No knocking on the door. Just this. A bag full of memory. A quiet offering.

I set the bag back down, unsure whether I wanted to cry or scream or laugh. Maybe all three. Maybe none of the above. I sat down and pulled out the lemon bar first. Took a bite and sat there chewing. I was uncertain how I felt.

Uncertainty felt okay for now.

49

Notes Week Two

Ivy

I didn't find a note in my locker Monday morning. Which would be easier, right? Without a conversation Aiden had shown me something. He remembered. He noticed. He cared enough not to say anything when he could've said too much. If there were no more notes, I could hold back more. Not everything, but take a longer time to figure it out.

When I walked into the cafeteria at lunch, I didn't veer off toward the end table near the windows. I didn't pretend to text while hovering near the vending machines. I just walked back to our usual table. I didn't sit next to him. I sat down right between Emilia and Jenna. No one said a word. I still felt the shift. Noticed the space I'd stepped back into, even if I wasn't sure how to stay there.

When I opened my locker after school—just before orchestra rehearsal—I found another folded piece of paper. Same kind of notebook paper. Same fold. No name. Now familiar.

I unfolded it carefully.

One Thing I Never Told You

When we were younger, I used to get jealous of how much time you spent practicing. I thought maybe your cello would take you away. But it didn't. You didn't change—you just got better. And I got proud. I wished I could be that good at something. Then I found basketball. I thought I'd finally caught up. But now? I wish I'd been as good at remembering what matters—like you always have been.

Do you still have that little rabbit book that always made you cry (but you swore it was a happy cry)? Text me just a YES or NO, Y or N. Please?

I texted *Y.* Figured I wouldn't give him those two extra letters yet. One was enough.

I sat through rehearsal with the note folded in the pocket of my jeans. I didn't pull it out again. No need to. I had it memorized.

***

Tuesday's note was already waiting when I got to school. Same spot. Same paper. I pulled it out slowly, unfolding it like it might turn to dust.

I Thought You Knew

Do you remember when you found Mr. Basketball tucked under your pillow? You thought I'd forgotten him. I didn't lie—but I didn't correct you either. I put him there on purpose. You were so sad that day. I just wanted him to be close to you. I always thought the luck he gave me came from all the hugs he got from you. So I hugged him—and hoped maybe he'd help you too.

Do you still have the adventure book with the torn cover because we read it so many times? YES or NO, or Y or N, same as before, okay?

I had forgotten about Mr. Basketball under my pillow. Aiden was always leaving a trail of his stuff behind him. Jackets, school papers, earbuds, basketball socks in weird places. I figured it was just another thing he forgot. Now I saw the careful placement of Mr. Basketball under my pillow—like Aiden had hoped my sad feelings would swish away. Kind of a stuffed basketball dream catcher.

I texted him *Y.* One letter was enough.

***

Wednesday came with another note. I opened it before my first class pretending I was double checking homework.

Something I Miss

I liked making you laugh when I missed dumb basketball shots. So the summer after seventh grade—I started missing on purpose. Just to hear you laugh. When I stopped missing, I stopped hearing you laugh. That's why I started practicing when you weren't around, so I wouldn't stop your laugh. And I just realized—even the best shot I've ever made never felt as good as hearing you laugh.

Do you still have that stuffed lion you named after a composer I can never remember? Just let me know, OK? Y or N?

My eyes stung, just for a second. He used to do that—try to distract me with ridiculous layups and exaggerated fake-outs. Using his driveway like an improv stage. I thought he was just goofing around. I didn't realize he was aiming for something else entirely.

I only sent a *Y* though.

***

Thursday's note made me laugh out loud. Quietly. But still. It was tucked into the edge of my music folder again.

Something I Still Don't Know

I still can't pronounce this dude's name when I read it. Dvořák. You were playing his music, and you didn't make me feel dumb for asking. We spent an hour coming up with fake pronunciations. Divorce Yak. Dumb Snacks. DoortotheShack. My favorite was Divorce Yak. Do you remember yours?

The tiny bear you used to carry everywhere until one of your cousins tried to take it. You still have it? Text me just a YES or NO, Y or N.

I covered my mouth in the hallway. Of course, I remembered mine. It was *Drawer Shock*. And I'd made a whole voice for it. That memory had been folded away somewhere in the back of my brain. He pulled it out like it was easily found. Like it still mattered.

I gave him three letters. *YES.*

***

Friday's note was waiting in the exact same spot as Monday's. I didn't open it right away. I carried it around all day, tucked into my sleeve. I didn't know why. Except maybe I did.

If You Read This One....

If you read this one—I hope you know I'd do anything to change the past. And I hope you know I'm trying to change myself for the future.

Do you still have that ridiculous stuffed dinosaur I said was creepy, but you swore had "personality?" Text me just a YES or NO, Y or N.

***

I held the note in my hands for a long time after the final bell. Then I folded it slowly, pressed it flat, and slid it into the same zipper pocket as the others.

It wasn't some big moment. No dramatic music, no racing pulse, no glowing light from the inside of my backpack. Just me, sitting on my bed, rereading Friday's note one more time. And the question at the bottom. Text me just a YES or NO, okay.

The answer was yes. Of course it was yes.

Leonardo the Slightly Lopsided lived in my closet, tucked between two old notebooks and a rolled-up hoodie I hadn't worn in a year. I picked up my phone. Stared at the screen for a long second. Then typed:

> **Me:** Yes, but excuse you, Leonardo is not ridiculous. He is a distinguished dinosaur with an excellent track record of keeping nightmares away.

> **Me:** And yes, I still have the tiny bear. No one is allowed to touch it.

> Me: The rabbit book is on my shelf. I haven't read it in years, but I'm pretty sure it would still make me cry. A happy cry, obviously.

> **Me:** The adventure book… I think it's somewhere in my closet. The cover is barely holding on.

> **Me:** And I'm not telling you the composer's name. My lion deserves for you to remember or figure it out.

I hit send. And then I just sat there, waiting for the part where I felt like I'd made a mistake. That part never came.

50

THROUGH THE LOST BUNNY FOG

Aiden

I'd never stood in the stuffed animal aisle for more than five minutes. I'd been here a while now and I was starting to itch. Finding what I needed was harder than I thought. I stood holding two tiny bears up to my face like they were whispering sacred three pointer tips to me.

Each was a different color brown. Neither matched Ivy's bear. How hard could it be to find a matching bear? In my mind: easy. In reality: impossible. I grabbed the one that looked closest and turned to look at stuffed dinosaurs. One of them looked like it could be related to Leonardo—though it was from the good-looking side of the family.

I added it to the basket. The tag said its name was Spike. Good-looking, sure—but possibly a high school dropout. Could I rename it? Was there stuffed animal etiquette? I groaned, dropped it in the basket. I'd figure it out later.

Stuffed animal aisle—painful.

Children's book section—worse.

Why did every author insist on writing stories about a lost baby bunny? It felt like emotional sabotage and possibly the root cause of teenage angst. I shook off lost-bunny paralysis and grabbed *The Rabbit Listened.* The bunny didn't get lost and was a role model for good listening.

I googled the adventure book after scanning every shelf of "classic adventures." Of course it was out of print. I'd try another play. I jogged over to the library and stood awkwardly in the children's section, waiting for help.

The librarian was as nice as I remembered when I asked how to repair a book. She didn't hesitate, just printed out instructions and recommended archival book tape.

That night, I did the hardest thing yet: I listened to hours of classical music playlists. I couldn't remember the name of the stuffed lion. Ivy deserved me putting in the work to figure it out. I didn't know the name but I knew the sound. One of Ivy's favorite composers. She played his music on the cello and listened to it.

So I listened. Listened more. Listened even more and finally heard something familiar. I checked the screen: *Tchaikovsky.* Or, as I once called him, *Chai-Iced-Coffee-Ski.* Relieved, I flopped back on my pillow. Remembering wasn't enough. I wanted to show her I cared. So I started building a playlist.

Finally, needed to rename Spike, a name that would keep him in school. I Googled "Leonardo?" Google said *Da Vinci.* Yeah, I probably should've known that. But I'd just spent hours listening to classical music.

The dino became Da Vinci, Vince when he was hanging out with his MMA buddies. Da Vinci when he was getting his PHD in Musical Paleontology. I googled Musical Paleontology and found out it's a real thing.

***

Ivy,

Did you know that Musical Paleontology is a real thing? Ask Da Vinci about it (you'll meet him in a minute). Anyway, I know stuff won't fix how I messed up. But I want you to see that I've paid attention. That I know you and I miss you.

Here's why I put together this assortment of random things.

-The Rabbit Listened book because I wish listened better. No bunny gets separated from its mommy in this one so you shouldn't need to cry.

-Our adventure book is out of print. I talked to the children's librarian, and she gave me instructions for fixing a book which is where archival tape comes in.

-Tiny Bear #2 wants to hang with TB #1. If a bear has to live on a shelf it should have a best friend there too. TBT #2 is also one of the best point guards in the TBBA (you can figure that out Ives).

-Da Vinci, is the dinosaur formerly know as Spike. He's in need of a distinguished best friend. (Two best friend dinosaurs=double nightmare protection). Da Vinci is known as Vince to his MMA buddies. His fellow PHD candidates know him as Da Vinci. He's studying Musical Paleontology. Google tells me it's a real thing. Crazy huh?

-Tchaikovsky – Ivy really digs your stuff. I think you're her favorite composer. Listen with her to what people are doing with some of your music.

-Also, Chai-Iced-Coffee-Ski, dude your name is long and hard to remember. Since I figured it out do me a favor and ask Ivy if she'd be okay meeting me Tuesday on her porch.

Aiden

51

NEW FRIENDS IN IVY'S ROOM

Ivy

Emilia was curled up on the end of my bed, flipping through one of my old cello magazines like it might turn into celebrity gossip. I was lying next to her with my face halfway buried in a pillow, not doing homework.

The tiny stuffed bear from Aiden sat on my shelf next to Tiny Bear 1. Leonardo and Da Vinci were slouched together like they'd just survived a long road trip. The adventure book was back on my nightstand. The fresh tape holding the cover made it look like someone had cared about it.

Emilia finally looked up. "Soooo?"

That was all she said. Just *so*. But she said it in a way that meant: *Let's talk about the thing you don't want to talk about but also can't stop thinking about.*

I rolled onto my back. "It's just stuff," I said. "A stuffed bear. A bunny book. A playlist."

"You forgot the taped-up adventure book," Emilia said. "And the dinosaur sidekick. Also the note. And the fact that you've been looking at that bag like it's sacred."

I didn't answer.

She nudged my foot with hers. "You're allowed let it to mean something, you know."

"It's just... I don't want to fall for a nice gesture and forget everything else."

"You're not falling for anything." Emilia sat up straighter. "You're taking it all in, thinking. Despite the past few months is Aiden the kind of guy who thinks stuff is all you want? Does he want you to fall for something?"

I sighed. "No, that's not how he's ever been. This has all felt real, like he's present and sees me. Not just past me. Not just music me. *Me*-me."

Emilia gave a soft shrug. "Then maybe you're allowed to let that matter. Even just a little."

I didn't say anything as I reached over and straightened Leonardo's ear.

52

STUFFED ANIMAL JUSTICE

Aiden

We sat on her porch steps, not quite side by side. Ivy's knees were pulled tight to her chest, arms wrapped around them. She didn't look at me when she spoke.

"It didn't start this summer," she said. "It started in March. Maybe earlier. You stopped seeing me. And I kept trying—trying to catch your attention, trying to get back in sync with you, but you didn't give me a chance. You didn't notice."

I swallowed. "I didn't. I thought we were just busy. I thought we were fine."

"You were fine," she said. "I wasn't."

Silence stretched between us. I let it be there for a moment.

"I wasn't fine, but I didn't understand why. I missed you, I think, without even realizing it. Everything felt off. I really felt it at camp. Like I couldn't settle. I didn't recognize it was a result of having lost my connection with you."

She glanced over, just barely. "You didn't lose it. You stopped making space for it. I kept walking beside you for so long. Tried to be there even when you didn't see me anymore."

I nodded. "I took you for granted. I know that. I didn't appreciate everything your friendship means. I've been thinking about this a lot. About us. About how I let everything fall apart and didn't even try to fix it."

I rubbed my hands together, bracing for how this would sound. "I had this dream. On the way home from camp. I was in a game—loud crowd, bright lights, everything moving fast. But every time I made a move, the ref called a foul. 'Didn't text.' 'Didn't say goodbye.' 'Didn't even notice.'"

Ivy didn't say anything. I kept going. "And you were there. In the stands. Not yelling. Just... watching. And then walking away. I couldn't stop you. Couldn't even call your name. When I woke up, it felt like I'd fouled out of something way more important than a game. Like I'd used up all my chances."

I let the words settle before adding, "And the worst part? I knew something was wrong awhile ago. But I didn't do anything. I didn't know how. No playbook. No rules. I told myself I'd figure it out eventually. And then...I didn't."

I let a long breath. "I was scared of messing up worse. So instead I just...didn't show up at all. And that hurt you more than anything I said or didn't say."

She didn't speak, but her arms relaxed slightly.

"I talked to my parents," I said. "About how I got so deep into basketball that I forgot who else I was. And they helped me figure some things out."

I glanced over at her.

"They told me I needed to rebalance. That if I wanted to be more than just a basketball player, I had to live like it. So I've cut back. No more extra practices after dinner. One weekend day off, every week. Space for other things. Space for people."

She exhaled slowly. "You didn't tell me all that in your notes."

"I know. I wanted to tell you face to face."

A pause.

"I meant what I wrote. All of it," I said. "The stuff I remembered. The things I never said before. I wasn't trying to fix everything with a bag and a playlist and a lemon bar. I just wanted you to know that you matter to me. That I still know you. Maybe not like before. But enough to want to earn more."

She finally turned to look at me.

"I didn't know how to feel about everything you did," she said. "It was like...every part of it was something I'd forgotten about myself until I saw it again. I knew you telling me you were still there. That I meant something."

I nodded, but stayed quiet.

"What you've done in the last two weeks helped. A lot. I know putting all that down on paper wasn't easy. I'm not ready to say we're back to where we were," she said. "But I believe you mean everything you're saying."

"I do."

"It's going to take time."

"I know."

"And don't act like Leonardo's cool just because I am."

That startled a laugh out of me. "He's not?"

"No. He was deeply offended for several years. and he's grudge holder."

I reached into my hoodie pocket and pulled out a folded page. "Good thing I brought a formal apology."

Her eyes narrowed in amused suspicion as I unfolded the note: "Leonardo. I deeply regret calling you a lumpy frog in front other kids on the school playground. I was too young and foolish to appreciate your creaturely nobility. Your arms are delightfully stubby. Your tail has presence. Your fabric patterning evokes prehistoric confidence. Your vibe is 'I'm prehistoric and I rock.' I'm totally here for that with you. Peace out."

I looked at Ivy. "Is he accepting my apology?"

"He's considering it," Ivy said. "But there's a process."

I followed her gaze—and only then realized Leonardo was seated on the porch behind her, propped up against the step railing like a small, stern judge. Next to him sat Da Vinci, one ear flopped dramatically forward like he was over it already.

"Oh," I said. "We're live."

"Yep," Ivy confirmed, clearly relishing this. "The Court for Stuffies' Grievances is ready to hand down your sentence. Even though Leonardo pushed for you to be fed to a pterodactyl, you are to serve community service volunteer hours. The honorable judge Ivy Preston saw your potential and has sentenced you to be a Big Brother to Dinosaurs. Your duties include modeling and teaching them how to be better best friends."

I blinked. "That's... specific."

"Justice demands detail. And your first act of community service is to read *The Rabbit Listened* to the dinos gathered here."

She handed me the book I gave her.

"Lean in. Hold the book so I can see it. Don't block anyone." She reached into her pocket and pulled out her phone. "Smile."

I didn't have time to protest. Click. Photo taken. "For the records," she said. "In case the parole board needs evidence of remorse."

I cracked the book open and cleared my throat. Leonardo stared me down. DaVinci tilted slightly to the left, as if to say *carry on, peasant.* For the next ten minutes, I read *The Rabbit Listened* to two stuffed dinosaurs and the girl next door.

When I finished, Ivy didn't say anything for a moment. Then she murmured, "That helped."

"Leonardo? Or us?"

She gave a small smile. "Yes."

53

Thanks for Sticking Around

Aiden

Tyler and I sat on the gym floor, backs against the padded wall, the faint echo of basketballs during practice hanging in the air. The rest of the team had already cleared out after practice, but neither of us had moved. My legs were sore, my shirt was damp with sweat, but my mind was too tangled to leave.

Tyler tossed a water bottle in my direction. "So, you gonna sit there all night, or are you gonna tell me what's up?"

I sighed, cracking the bottle open. "Give me a sec, man. It takes a minute to find my softer side."

Tyler smirked. "I figured. Didn't think you had one, honestly. Thought it was just basketball drills and bad decisions in there."

I scoffed. "You wound me."

"Naw, I'm already one with my softer side. I'm shooting soft puffy darts of wisdom at you."

I rolled my eyes. "Appreciate that."

Tyler grinned. "I got you, man. But seriously, spill."

I exhaled, shaking my head. "I talked to Ivy."

Tyler raised an eyebrow. "Yeah? And?"

I leaned my head back against the wall. "It wasn't some big fix. We didn't magically go back to how things were. But it felt...real. Like we actually saw each other for the first time in a while."

Tyler nodded, waiting for me to continue.

"She told me she needs time," I admitted. "She's not ready to just go back to how things were, and for the first time... I get it."

Tyler let out a low chuckle. "Wow. Actual personal growth. Someone alert the very tiny slice of media representation in North Riverbend."

I rolled my eyes, but I couldn't help the smirk tugging at my lips. "Shut up."

"Nah, seriously," Tyler said, leaning his head back against the wall. "That sounds like real progress, man. Not easy, but real."

I nodded, staring down at the scuffed gym floor. "I was so focused on trying to fix things, I didn't stop to think that maybe she wasn't ready for that yet. I just assumed... I don't know. That wanting things to be okay was enough."

"It's not," Tyler said simply. "Wanting it doesn't mean anything unless you back it up."

I let out a slow breath. "I know. And it's not just Ivy."

Tyler gave me a questioning look.

I rubbed a hand over my face. "I should've talked to you earlier. Instead of just expecting you to wait around like Ivy did."

Tyler shrugged. "I knew you'd get there eventually. Took you long enough, though."

I huffed a quiet laugh. "Yeah. I guess I'm finally seeing all the ways I've taken people for granted."

"Welcome to self-awareness, my dude," Tyler said, clapping a hand on my shoulder. "It's about time."

We sat in silence for a while, the gym lights casting long shadows on the floor. Tyler's words lingered, heavy but necessary. I had been so caught up in my own world, in my own wants, that I never stopped to think about what everyone else had been giving.

"So, what now?" Tyler asked. "You gonna stop waiting for stuff to fix itself?"

"Yeah. She told me trust doesn't just come back because I want it to. I have to prove it. So that's what I'm gonna do."

Tyler smirked. "Good answer. Now let's just hope that's enough for Emilia and the rest of the girl squad to cancel their plans."

"Plans?"

Tyler snorted. "Dude. Emilia has a detailed revenge plan. I've seen the blueprint."

I narrowed my eyes. "You're exaggerating."

"Am I?" Tyler raised an eyebrow. "Aria's in charge of psychological warfare. Maddie has resources I don't even want to ask about. Jenna? She plays innocent, but she's terrifying when she wants to be."

I rubbed a hand over my face and laughed. "You're telling me I'm doomed."

Tyler laughed. "Eh, we'll see. Maybe you'll live if you don't screw this up again."

I shook my head, letting out a breath. "You know, I don't say it enough, but... thanks for sticking around."

Tyler shot me a look. "Yeah, yeah, I get it. You're having feelings. Let's get out of here before tears fall."

I chuckled, shoving his shoulder. I felt lighter than I had in months, even with a possible death threat hanging over my head.

54

Lunchroom Bops

Ivy

I watched from a distance as most of my friends got wrapped up in tryouts for various sports. Aiden, Ty, and Aria in basketball tryouts. Jenna and Maddie in their own worlds. Jenna was spinning through cheer routines, chasing that varsity badge. And Maddie was out at the softball diamond—not trying out, just participating in fall training. Everyone was caught up in this swirl of hopes and nerves.

Emilia and I were the only two of our friends not trying out. Even the friends we didn't see all the time had tryouts.

There were three topics of conversation all week.

1. Tryouts, tryouts, tryouts.

2. I wonder how I did?

3. I can't wait for this to be done.

We tried the supportive friend route. After a few days, we didn't give anyone the cold shoulder, but aside from wishing good luck, we left them to their conversations. It was just Emilia and me. Every day at lunch, in between classes, while our friends were preoccupied, we discussed crucial topics like:

What would it take to snap them all out of
their tryout trances?

- A School-Wide Curse – Someone (Tyler) accidentally awakened Phantom Phil, the vengeful spirit of a 1963 varsity benchwarmer who never got playing time. Now, all varsity hopefuls must participate in a high-stakes trash-talking contest to keep Phil entertained, while the best free-throw shooter must defeat him in a cursed game of GHOST—like HORSE, but every missed shot makes the gym lights flicker, a mysterious basketball roll across the court, and, if you lose, Phil curses you to airball forever.

- Miggy's No That's Gross Campaign: Miggy is appointed the official Anti-PDA faculty member. He's given a bullhorn, a whistle, and a chicken assistant. He patrols the halls and blows his whistle at any hint of PDA. He is heard shouting, "Uggh, kissing's gross.!" "Aren't your hands sweaty and gross?" and generally railing against the slightest show of romantic feelings.

- Willy Wonka Lands a Golden Deal with Professional Sports:—Let the Games (& Snacks) Begin: The freshman class inexplicably turned purple and burst into song about

Golden Tickets hidden in the cafeteria. The tickets grant entry to every professional championship game for the next century. There was no catch—except you had to remain in the cafeteria for 12 straight hours to claim your prize. (Good luck surviving the mystery meat fumes that long.

*Eventually, the entire freshman class was nominated for a Grammy Award, causing mass confusion among actual musicians. A major record label signed them under the name The Cafeteria Collective, and their debut album, "Golden Bops & Lunchroom Drops," went platinum in a week. No one knew how it happened.

What would be the easiest varsity sport to try out for?
- Dramatic Door Holding – Competitive kindness but make it passive-aggressive. Athletes must hold the door for an ever-growing line of students while maintaining a "This is my life now" expression.

- Competitive Lunch Line Strategy – Who can calculate the shortest possible line and still get the last chocolate chip cookie? Requires speed, stealth, and a willingness to elbow Tyler out of the way.

- Power Napping – If you can fall asleep between second and third period and still wake up before the bell rings, you've got what it takes.

- Varsity Locker Slamming – Points awarded for dramatic door swings, speed of access, and ability to intimidate underclassmen without actually meaning to.

- Synchronized Eye Rolling – A team event in which participants must execute perfect, in-sync eye rolls whenever a teacher says, "You won't always have a calculator in your pocket."

And most importantly—

I'd Rather Do This Than Try Out for a Varsity Sport
- Memorize every Taylor Swift song in chronological order.

- Babysit Tyler and Aiden in a room with a single basketball and a floor made of lava.

- Read a 600-page dialogue-free historical fiction novel about the invention of toothpaste.

- Eat a whole bowl of kale with no dressing.

***

Ivy

That evening, I bent down, gently picking a handful of dandelions from the edge of the field by my house. The white puffballs were so delicate, like little wishes waiting to float into the universe. I remembered all the times Aiden and I blew those things to make silly wishes, the way we'd laugh and race to see whose seeds flew higher.

The bouquet grew as I gathered more, making sure to pick the biggest, fluffiest dandelions I could find. It was a small gesture—one that felt both silly and meaningful.

I filled a mason jar with water and dropped the dandelions in. I tucked a note in the weedy bouquet and placed it on his front porch as the sun dipped low, casting long shadows across the sidewalk.

I stepped back, taking a final look at the jar with the bouquet of dandelions, feeling a strange mix of pride and vulnerability. I didn't know if he'd understand, but I hoped he would.

***

Aiden

I spotted it on the front step as I grabbed my shoes—a mason jar packed with dandelions, each one perfectly gone to seed. There was a note tucked into the bouquet. I recognized Ivy's handwriting: You've got this. You don't need it but you can blow these for a little extra luck.

I stood there for a second too long, just looking at it. The jar was warm from the morning sun. Her handwriting was messy and tilted, like always. I could practically hear her voice—half-teasing, half-hopeful. Even when we weren't talking much, she still got me.

I carried it all the way to school, tucked under one arm like something fragile. Slid it carefully into my locker, between a crumpled hoodie and my stats notebook. Before tryouts, I grabbed it again and found a safe corner of the gym floor to set it down—out of the way, but close enough to feel like it was there with me.

The gym smelled like floor polish and adrenaline—like the whole place knew today mattered. Coach's whistle sliced through the air. Last day. Ty jogged up beside me and clocked the jar. "That your new pregame ritual?"

"Guess so," I said, rolling out my shoulders. "Let's make it count."

We went hard—one-on-ones, defensive slides, shooting under pressure. Everything felt sharper, faster, heavier. But I stayed locked in. Every second mattered. After the final drill, I sank to the floor, chest heaving. My legs were dead. My heart was still racing. But it was done.

I grabbed the jar on my way out, holding it carefully as I stepped into the late afternoon light. A breeze tugged at the edges of the day, just enough to carry something away.

I tilted the jar and blew.

The seeds lifted and scattered, floating in every direction.

I didn't make a specific wish. And maybe it wasn't even about varsity basketball. But I hoped—quietly, fiercely—that maybe this was a new kind of start. Not all the way back. But maybe far enough forward to matter.

***

Golden Ticket, Gotta Win
    (Verse 1)
Watch too much TV
    ESPN on always
No time for studying, uh, uh
Skip the studying, uh huh
    Missed my English quiz,
Didn't study, watched the game,
I'll just wing it now, who cares,
Just gotta pass the class, not flunk
    Did I just start dreaming,
    Dream that, wish that, Wonka had a ticket just for me,
    In his hand, to get into every game for free.
    (Chorus)
The QB needs to pass, pass, pass, pass, pass
And the coach is gonna yell, yell, yell, yell, yell,
Baby, I just wanna win, win, win, win, win,
Gotta get that pass, get that pass!
    And the linemen gonna block, block, block, block, block,
And the refs are gonna call, call, call, call, call,

But I just want that prize, prize, prize, prize, prize,

Win a golden pass, golden pass!

(Verse 2)

Tryouts start today,

But I'd rather stay inside,

Varsity is tough, mm-mm,

This is way too much, mm-mm.

Could I pick a sport,

Where I don't have to run?

Pencil rolls or naps, mm-mm,

Count me in for that, mm-mm.

(Pre-Chorus)

But then I heard that Wonka was hiding tickets,

Tickets in the lunch line, chance to make me lifelong VIP

Lifelong VIP!

(Chorus)

'Cause point guards gonna block, block, block, block, block

And the coach is gonna yell, yell, yell, yell, yell,

Baby, I just wanna win, win, win, win, win,

Gotta get that pass, get that pass!

And the linemen gonna block, block, block, block, block,

And the refs are gonna call, call, call, call, call,

But I just want that prize, prize, prize, prize, prize,

Win a golden pass, golden pass!

(Bridge)

Golden tickets, let's go!

Every game, front row!

Wonka's rules are wild,

Twelve hours in the caf? Oh no!

But I'd rather sit here,

Than run laps and sweat,

If it's varsity or lunchroom,

You know what choice I get!

(Final Chorus)

The fans are gonna cheer, cheer, cheer, cheer,

And the coach is gonna yell, yell, yell, yell, yell,

Baby, I just wanna win, win, win, win, win,

Gotta get that pass, get that pass!

And the linemen gonna block, block, block, block, block,

And the refs are gonna call, call, call, call, call,

But I just want that prize, prize, prize, prize, prize,

Win a golden pass, golden pass!

(Outro)

I'll just win it all, win it all,

I, I, I'll win it all, win it all,

I, I, I'll win it all, win it all,

Gotta get that pass, get that pass!

55

Varsity Boa-taoshi

Ivy

Our table in the cafeteria buzzed with strange combination of exhaustion and pure happiness. Everyone was still a little bleary-eyed from the weekend tryouts, but the energy was contagious.

Aiden sat across from me, grinning like he'd just won the lottery, his tray piled high with pizza and fries. Ty leaned back in his chair, looking almost as smug, arms folded behind his head. Jenna was beaming, her ponytail bouncing as she laughed, and even Maddie managed a grin despite her usual sarcastic eye-rolls.

Aria, though, might've been the most elated. She was still in shock over making varsity as a freshman, her cheeks flushed pink.

"I mean, I knew I had a shot," she said, practically vibrating in her seat, "but actually making it? It still feels unreal."

"You totally deserve it, Ari," Jenna said, lifting her water bottle for a toast. "And cheers to Aiden and Ty for making the varsity squad, too! Freshman power, am I right?"

They tapped water bottles, the metallic clink filling the air. I lifted mine a little slower, watching everyone's happy faces, feeling a mix of pride and affection. It's hard not to feel proud, even though I hadn't been part of the tryouts. I felt lucky just to be part of this crew.

Emilia leaned in, grinning like she'd been waiting all lunch for this. "So," she said, tapping her chin with mock seriousness, "have you been working on your Bo-taoshi moves?"

I raised an eyebrow. "Obviously. I've been perfecting the art of pole defense. It's all in the elbows."

"Please," Emilia scoffed. "You're definitely an offense girl. Chaos energy all the way."

Ty lowered his slice of pizza mid-bite, eyes narrowing. "Bo-taoshi? That sounds like a battle cry. Are we talking war games? I'm in. Do I need armor? Because I have armor."

Aiden laughed. "You do not have armor."

Ty shrugged. "I emotionally purchased things after watching *Gladiator*. Don't worry about it."

Maddie leaned in, amused. "Can someone explain what this even is?"

Emilia was already on it. "Two teams. One pole. A hundred and fifty people per side. No rules except mayhem."

"Basically capture the flag meets *Mad Max*, if your flag was a giant wooden pole and everyone lost their minds."

Jenna's eyes went wide. "And this is your plan B?"

"Just one of many," I said.

"We had a whole debate about it," I continued, sitting up straighter. "So, in honor of your real athletic accomplishments, I made a list."

I cleared my throat and held up an invisible scroll. "Presenting: Ivy and Emilia's Official Guide to Totally Legit Varsity Alternatives."

"First up, Wife Carrying. It's a Finnish race where you carry your spouse through an obstacle course. Prize? The wife's weight in beer."

Ty pointed at Emilia, eyes sparkling. "We're gonna need to bulk you up. No offense, but I want more than a six-pack when we win."

Emilia arched a brow. "You did hear it's called *wife* carrying, right?"

Ty winked. "Yeah, just preparing. Got my future all mapped out."

Emilia blushed, then smirked. "Miggy's going to have something to say about that."

Ty spread his hands. "Miggy and I are working out terms. If this were the Middle Ages, he'd be happy to get a llama for you."

Emilia didn't miss a beat. "Hopefully it would be a llama that likes to spit on you."

Jenna groaned. "This is why we can't take you anywhere."

I pressed on, grinning. "Next, Cheese Rolling. You chase a wheel of cheese down a hill and try not to die on the way."

"Ty's dream," Aiden said. "Chaos and snacks."

"Extreme Ironing," I continued. "For those who want to press their button-downs while rock climbing or hang gliding."

Jenna made a face. "Who are these people?"

"And finally," I said with dramatic flair, "Bo-taoshi. A Japanese sport where 150 people try to knock over a pole. Total chaos. Like... gym class meets battlefield."

Everyone was laughing now, and for a second the cafeteria disappeared—it was just us, ridiculous and alive, somewhere between childhood and whatever comes next.

56

THE RHYTHM &
INTERRUPTION

Aiden

School and life had found a rhythm. Morning rush. Classes. Practice. Homework. Repeat. But this year, those ordinary things didn't feel so ordinary. Not with Ivy drifting back into my orbit. She still kept a little space between us, like she was testing the ground before stepping forward. But we were talking again. Not every second. Not about everything. But it was something.

She sat by me at lunch more often than not. Asked about practice. Rolled her eyes at Ty's latest antics. She laughed at my bad impressions again, even if it came with that tiny, hesitant pause—like she was still deciding how much she could trust the moment.

Once, I found a bag of gummy worms in my locker. No note, just the exact brand I used to swipe from her during movie nights. I didn't say anything. Neither did she. But the next day, I brought her a mini bottle of her favorite lemonade and set it on the table at lunch like it was nothing.

She didn't thank me out loud. But she drank every drop. I didn't push. And she didn't run. That's how it started to feel—like something we were rebuilding, carefully, one moment at a time. And then I'd go home. To worry about about my mom and the little sisters I hadn't met yet.

***

Mom had been on bedrest for weeks now, and by the time she hit her third trimester, the whole house felt like it was holding its breath. One afternoon, I came in from practice, shoulders sore and head still full of plays Coach wanted us to run. I dropped my bag by the door. The kitchen smelled like soup, but Dad's back was stiff as he stirred the pot, like whatever he was holding in had nowhere left to go.

"How's Mom?" I asked, bracing myself.

He sighed, shoulders slumping. "She's struggling, Aiden. They diagnosed her with preeclampsia. It's... serious. Dangerous for her and the babies."

I nodded, but my chest felt like it was caving in. My gaze drifted toward her bedroom door, the weight of it all pressing down hard.

***

"Aiden, get dressed quickly," Dad said. "We're taking your mom to the hospital."

I jolted awake. The urgency in his voice was sharper than any alarm clock. I was dressed in minutes, my heart hammering as I watched Dad help Mom into the car. Her face was pale, her breathing fast, and every part of me wanted to shout, to ask what was happening—but I kept quiet.

Dad pulled up to the ER entrance and jumped out. Seconds later, he returned, following a nurse pushing a wheelchair toward the car. He darted around and opened Mom's door.

"Okay, Linds... let's get you into the wheelchair, love. They're waiting for you, you're expected."

Mom groaned—not from pain, but at Dad's bad pun. "You're not any funnier at the ER than you are at home, you doofus."

She was sweating. Her skin was too pale. Not just parking-lot-light pale—something scarier.

"Hi, mama, I'm Janice. I'll be one of your nurses helping you get these baby girls into the world." The nurse moved quickly but calmly—a strange combination. She gently took over from Dad without making it obvious.

Dad turned back to me. "Aiden, sorry bud. My mind's not firing on all cylinders. Can you park the car? Just take it over to an emptier part of the lot. Don't worry about parking straight."

He tossed me the keys.

"Come in through the same door. Stop at the desk. Give them Mom's name, and someone will point you in the right direction."

I blew out a breath. "Okay, Dad. I've got it. Get in there. I'll see you in a minute. Longer if I clip a few cars in the lot."

He pulled me into a quick, tight hug. "That's less funny than a dad joke. See you inside."

Behind the wheel, my hands shook just enough to make me grip tighter. I had my permit. Dad and I had been practicing. I could do this. I got the car parked. The ER entrance swallowed me and spit me out into bright lights and echoing voices. At the desk, I gave Mom's name. They pointed me toward a hallway. Dad was waiting, hovering near a bank of chairs, clearly torn.

"Hang in there, bud. She's in good hands. I'll be back—just want to check in—"

"Dad, go. I'll be right here."

Relief flickered across his face as he turned and headed toward her. And I was alone. I dropped into one of the plastic waiting room chairs, my knee bouncing, fingers gripping the edge of the seat like that would keep me from unraveling. The lights hummed above me. Then I saw it. A smiley face sticker. Half-stuck to the tile. Worn at the edges, stepped on a hundred times. I stared at it, breath uneven.

Seriously, not now. But this one wasn't mocking me. Not like the chalk. Not like Whitney's cursed glitter. It was just there. Watching.

I rubbed my hands over my face. This is ridiculous. It's a sticker. Some kid must've dropped it. It didn't mean anything. And yet... I couldn't look away. It looked... expectant. Waiting for me to do something. I exhaled, leaned back, tilted my head toward the ceiling. My thoughts wouldn't stop. My mom was behind those doors. My dad too. And me? I was stuck here, spiraling. Alone. Except—no. I wasn't. I could be talking to someone.

Ivy.

The thought pressed against my ribs. Why hadn't I already? I glanced at the sticker again. Still there. I pulled out my phone. My fingers fumbled on the screen. My heart pounded as it rang. Once. Twice. Then—

"Hello. Aiden?"

"Ivy?"

"Aiden, are you okay?"

Her voice was soft but alert—like she already knew something was wrong.

"I...I'm sorry," I managed. "I know things haven't been right between us, but I just... I needed to hear your voice."

She didn't hesitate. "What's going on?"

And the words broke loose.

"It's my mom. They took her in for an emergency C-section. She's got preeclampsia, and it's bad, Ivy. Really bad."

Her breath caught. "Aiden... that must be terrifying. What do you know? Are you with her?"

I shook my head, even though she couldn't see me. "Not yet. She's with the doctors. I don't know what to do. I can't lose her, Ivy. I can't."

"I know," she murmured. "It's okay to be scared. Anyone would be. But she's in good hands, Aiden. They'll take care of her. And the babies."

I closed my eyes, letting her voice anchor me.

"I've been such a jerk lately," I whispered. "So focused on basketball. I didn't even check in on her. I didn't see this coming."

"I know you," Ivy said quietly. "And I know how much you love her."

The tears I'd been holding back threatened to fall.

"I want to be better," I said. "For her. For my dad. For you."

"You can," she said. "Start now. Be there. That's enough."

"Thank you," I breathed. "For answering. For being there."

"Always," she said. "Call me when you know more. I'll answer."

She repeated it, like she meant it. "Call if you need me."

I couldn't respond. Maybe I made a noise, because she said it one more time.

"I'll answer."

By the time I hung up, my hands weren't shaking as much. My breathing had slowed. I didn't feel like I was drowning. I glanced back at the sticker. It didn't look like it was waiting anymore. It looked... satisfied. Not smirking. Not mocking. Just...knowing.

"Yeah," it seemed to say. "That's what you needed to do."

I closed my eyes..

57

OF COURSE I'M HERE

Ivy

I collapsed onto my bed, my phone still warm in my hand, like holding onto it might somehow keep Aiden close. My heart thudded, each beat echoing the fear in his voice. Worry gnawed at me—images of the hospital, of Aiden, of his parents—all spinning through my mind like a Ferris wheel at night. Lights on. Going around and around.

My room felt too still. The silence was too sharp against the chaos inside me.

I sat up, my pulse a steady drumbeat of urgency. The longer I stayed there, the worse the ache in my chest grew.

I couldn't just lie there.

Aiden needed me.

I tiptoed to my parents' room and knocked softly before easing the door open. The glow from the hallway spilled over them, tangled in sleep.

"Mom? Dad?" I whispered, my voice shaking but urgent.

Mom stirred, her eyes fluttering open. "Ivy? What's wrong, honey? It's the middle of the night."

"It's Aiden's mom," I said quickly, the words tumbling out. "She's in the hospital. Emergency C-section. He's scared—they're all scared. I need to go to them."

Dad sat up, rubbing his eyes. "Now? Ivy, it's past midnight."

Mom looked more awake now, concern lining her features. "It's a half-hour drive to Dickinson. And you have school tomorrow."

"I know," I said. "But I have to go. Aiden needs me."

They looked at each other, silent. And in that look, the decision was made.

Dad exhaled, then nodded. "Grab a jacket. I'll get dressed."

Minutes later, we were in the car, the engine purring in the quiet as we headed toward Dickinson. The roads were nearly empty, the world outside wrapped in darkness. Dad glanced over at me, his face lit by the dashboard.

"You care about him a lot, don't you?"

I nodded, staring out the window. "I do. It's been complicated, but yeah—I care. And right now, he's hurting. I can't be anywhere else."

He reached over and squeezed my hand. "Then that's where we'll go."

As the lights of Dickinson approached, something protective stirred in me. Whatever was waiting at the hospital, I'd face it—for Aiden. For his family. For the bond that had always tethered us, even when we'd drifted. The bond that tugged me toward him tonight. Because he called. And I came.

We pulled into the hospital parking lot. The ER lights cut through the night. Dad walked in with me and helped me figure out where to go. My stomach churned with nervous energy. Every step forward made the knot in my chest tighter. Then—we found him.

Aiden was hunched in a corner of the waiting area, elbows on his knees, fingers laced together like he was holding himself together by force. His head snapped up at the sound of our steps. And just for a second, something lifted from his shoulders.

"Aiden," I breathed.

He was on his feet in a heartbeat, arms wrapping around me like I was the only thing anchoring him. His hug was desperate. Fierce.

"Ivy, you came."

"Of course I came," I said, pulling back to look at him. His eyes were red. His face pale. Tight.

"How's your mom? The twins?"

"They're still in surgery," he said, voice thick. "I haven't heard anything more. Dad's trying to get updates."

He pulled me into another hug. Tighter this time.

"I don't deserve you," he whispered. "Ivy, I don't. But I'm so glad you're here. I didn't think I'd make it. But now you're here."

I squeezed his hand. Tried to pour strength into my voice.

"Of course you deserve me to come, Aiden. Mistakes don't cancel that. Not when we really need each other."

We sat down together. His hand found mine and didn't let go. We waited. In silence. In fear. In hope. And despite the uncertainty pressing in from all sides, I was wholly glad to be there. Not because of what was happening, because I could be there for him—when it counted.

When it mattered most, we didn't hesitate. He called. And I came.

58

Hey There Little Ones

Aiden

They hadn't let Dad stay once things escalated. Mom's doctor told him he'd have to move to the waiting area. She was only three doors down, but it felt like light years. Dad's face looked gray in the hospital lights, and he'd been pacing for the last thirty minutes—though it felt like hours.

Ivy sat beside me, her hand still wrapped in mine. She hadn't let go since she arrived. Every time Dad passed in front of us on another lap, he gave her a faint, grateful nod.

Then—finally—the doctor stepped into the waiting area, his scrubs wrinkled, his voice calm but tired.

"Mr. Pedersen," he said, looking right at Dad. "Your wife and the babies are stable. It was a difficult delivery, but they're here. Two little girls. They're strong and quite healthy. Little fighters too."

Relief crashed over me like a wave. My breath hitched as I stood and hugged Dad, gripping him tighter than I meant to. I glanced at Ivy, and she was already on her feet too, eyes wide and shining. She didn't say anything—just reached for my other hand.

Lyric and Luna. My sisters.

Somehow, they were here. Somehow, we'd made it through.

***

Mom was in a room, the girls in the NICU. We stopped by her room before heading in to see them. She couldn't sit up, not really—propped halfway with pillows, her hospital gown wrinkled, an IV taped to her hand. Her skin looked pale, her hair damp at the temples, but her eyes were steady. Fierce, even. When she saw Ivy, a soft smile broke through the exhaustion.

"Ivy," she said, her voice scratchy but warm. "You came."

Ivy nodded and stepped closer. "I'm so glad you're okay."

Mom reached for her hand and gave it a brief, gentle squeeze. "Thanks for being here...for Aiden. It means a lot."

"I wouldn't be anywhere else," Ivy said softly.

Mom's gaze shifted to me. "They're beautiful. Strong. Tell them I love them, okay? Tell them I'll be there soon."

"I will," I said, leaning down to kiss her forehead. "Close your eyes, Mom. Rest."

***

A nurse met us just outside the NICU doors.

"Twins are in Bay Two," she said kindly. "You'll need to wash your hands up to the elbows, then gown and glove. No jewelry. Phones stay out here."

I nodded, barely hearing her over the buzz in my ears. Ivy gave my hand one more squeeze before we stepped to the sink. The water ran warm. I scrubbed like they showed us, over and over, even after the timer stopped. I wasn't sure I'd ever feel clean enough to be near them.

Ivy didn't rush either. She was careful, methodical—like it mattered. Like they mattered to her too. We slipped into yellow gowns, tied at the neck and waist, then pulled on gloves that snapped tight at the wrists. The nurse led us in.

The NICU was quiet, but not silent—monitors beeped softly in a rhythm that felt like a heartbeat for the whole room. Overhead lights were dimmed. A few nurses moved between stations, their footsteps hushed. Then I saw them. Lyric and Luna.

Curled together in a shared isolette, tucked side by side. Each wore a tiny knitted cap—one deep purple, one pale yellow. Their legs touched. One had her arm flung across the other's belly, like even now, even here, they knew they belonged together.

So small it hurt. So alive it took my breath. Their chests rose and fell with determined little breaths, their fists curled near their faces. Wires trailed from their bodies to blinking machines. I hated those wires and I needed them more than anything.

The nurse beside me gestured. "You can reach through here. Just your finger. No stroking—just let them feel your presence."

I nodded, throat tight. Slowly, I slipped my gloved hand through the opening and hovered my finger near Lyric's hand. Lyric was wearing the purple hat. For a moment—nothing. Then, gently, her fingers curled. A whisper of a grip.

I turned slightly and reached my pinky toward Luna's fist. She didn't grab hold, not exactly—but her fingers shifted, brushing against mine before settling again. My chest clenched. Fierce. Fiercer than anything.

"Hey there, little ones," I whispered. "I'm your big brother. I'm here now. Mommy loves you—she'll be here soon." I chuckled, fighting back tears. "I haven't called her Mommy in a while. But...we've got a good one. A good daddy too."

I felt Ivy step up beside me. She didn't speak at first—just stared at them both, her hands clasped in front of her like she didn't want to break the moment.

"They're beautiful."

"Yeah," I said, still watching their faces. "They really are."

Lyric stirred, shifting just enough that Luna's hand slipped more fully into hers. Ivy let out the tiniest gasp. And I knew—we weren't alone in this. None of us.

59

SISTERS COME HOME

Aiden

Ivy must've been watching for us, because she showed up at our door less than fifteen minutes after Mom and Dad brought the twins home. No fanfare—just Ivy being Ivy. Practical. Steady. With that soft look in her eyes, like she saw the gap I felt between me and the kind of big brother I wanted to be—and was too kind to point it out.

Two baby sisters wasn't just a schedule shift. It was a full-on Final Four upset. The tiny tyrant team pulled off the impossible: toppling the number one seeds of order and routine. My parents tried to shield me from the worst of it. Told me to focus on sleep, school, basketball. But with two newborns in the house? Didn't matter. Chaos had home-court advantage.

Ten days after the twins came home, I wandered into the living room sometime after midnight. Dad was slumped on the couch, the baby monitor sliding off his knee. Mom swayed in the armchair, holding Luna, her eyes barely open.

I stepped in without a word and gently took Luna from her arms. She yawned, then melted into my chest like she'd been waiting for me all along.

"You're doing amazing, Mom," I whispered.

She gave me a tired smile. "I couldn't do this without you, Aiden. You're a great big brother."

The words settled somewhere deep. Pride. Responsibility. I felt the gap narrowing between who I was and who I wanted to be—for them.

The first few weeks were a blur—and Ivy was there. Not with fanfare. Not with speeches. Just... there. Slipping back into our lives like she'd never left.

She came over most evenings after school, always bringing something—dinner, snacks, energy. She'd fold laundry, rock a baby, unload the dishwasher. Somehow, without ever making a fuss, she calmed the chaos just by walking in.

One afternoon, while Mom napped and Dad had to go into his office, Ivy sat cross-legged on the floor with the twins. Lyric was curled against her chest, wide-eyed and calm as Ivy rocked her gently.

I stood in the doorway, just watching.

For a second, it felt like no time had passed. Like this was just another version of the hundred afternoons she'd spent in our living room growing up.

Lyric's tiny fist wrapped around Ivy's finger, and something inside me let go a little.

"They really like you," I said, settling beside her.

Ivy glanced down, her cheeks pinkening slightly. "I'm just... I'm really glad I get to be here with them."

She brushed a thumb along Lyric's downy hair. "They're tiny miracles."

We sat in silence for a while. The distance between us—everything we hadn't said or fixed—was still there. My little sisters were helping to close the gap.

60

CELLO EMERGENCY

Aiden

Both twins were screaming their heads off. They had been fed, diapered, burped—everything we could think of—but nothing was working. Mom bounced Lyric while Dad tried rocking Luna, but the crying just kept going, filling every inch of the house.

Then, almost too low to notice at first, the sound of Ivy's cello floated through the air. A slow, gentle melody slipped into the chaos, threading through the noise. And like magic, both babies settled.

Their cries softened into whimpers, then quieted altogether. Wide-eyed, they stayed awake but calm, blinking like they were trying to figure out where the music was coming from—and if it was safe to keep breathing. Mom's head snapped up, eyes wide with something between relief and amazement. She shot me a look that was half-panicked, half-demanding.

"Aiden—go. Get Ivy. Get the cello. Here. Now."

I didn't waste a second.

I tore out the door, sprinting across the yard and up Ivy's front steps. I pounded hard, and when she opened the door, I barely gave her a chance to say hello.

"Grab your cello. Emergency."

Her eyes flew wide. "What kind of emergency?"

"Twin meltdown. Your playing stopped it, but then you stopped and they lost it again. Mom is about to lose it too. Just—please, Ivy."

Ivy didn't ask more questions. She grabbed her cello case, slung it over her shoulder, and jogged beside me back to the house. Inside, she set up, tuned quickly and started playing something lullaby-ish, something soothing, something classical. The twins screamed even louder.

Ivy winced, adjusting her bow. "Okay, okay, not a Brahms kind of night." She pivoted into something else—a slower piece—still no good. Lyric's face turned red, Luna kicked her tiny legs like a furious elf.

I shot Ivy a panicked look. "Ivy, fix it."

She muttered under her breath, thinking fast. "Alright, let's try something weird."

She launched into the piece she'd been practicing earlier that night—something obscure, twisty, not even remotely baby-calming by normal standards. The notes wove together in a hypnotic, offbeat rhythm. And just like that—the twins went still.

Lyric blinked slowly, her tiny mouth forming a perfect little "o" of wonder. Luna let out a tiny, content sigh. Both babies stared like they were watching music physically float through the air. Mom pressed a hand to her heart, exhaling deeply. "Ivy, you are never leaving."

Ivy laughed but kept playing, letting the music work its strange, inexplicable magic. I sank down beside her, rubbing my hands over my face, more relieved than I could say.

"Remind me to always have you on call," I muttered.

Ivy smirked. "I'll send you my rates."

From that day forward, the twins needed Ivy's cello music every afternoon like clockwork. Both Mom and Dad had been recording Ivy. I had too and we'd compiled a good selection of playlists. There was *Twin Tranquilizer, Opus 1; Lullabies Only Work if They're Weird; Cello Sorcery for the Sleep Deprived; Twins Loony Tunes; and Girls Just Wanna Have Fun (but They've Got to Sleep).*

We kept adding to the collection. Every strange, soothing, inexplicably perfect track. Ivy's cello became the soundtrack of chaos being calmed.

61

No Repeat Performances

Ivy

Every few days, I had to switch up what I played for the babies. If I repeated something too much, the twins lost interest. Classical lullabies never worked for long. It always had to be something strange. Something unexpected.

One day I played something that sounded like eerie movie music, and the twins stared at me like I was casting a spell. It was bizarre. But it worked.

Week one: Shostakovich and gentle chaos.

Week two: Modern minimalist etudes that made the house feel like a dramatic documentary.

Week three: Gregorian chant meets kazoo covers (an experiment I refuse to talk about).

And, of course, the cats. Not real cats. YouTube cats. Cats playing piano. Cats meowing in harmony. A cat-synth remix I found late one night during a very intense emotional crisis.

"They like the ambiguity," I said once, seriously, as Luna contemplated the sounds of a tuxedo cat awkwardly pawing out *Chopsticks* on a keyboard.

Aiden's mom didn't even blink. She might've been afraid she'd fall asleep if she did. "If it works, it works."

I nodded solemnly. "They're evolving. I have to keep up."

One afternoon, I came over triumphantly with a CD Aiden and I had created when we were missing our front teeth. We had no business making a mix at that age, but it turned into a chaotic masterpiece: lullabies, pop songs, a dramatic reading of *Goodnight Moon*, and Aiden rapping the alphabet. I swore the twins would love it.

I popped it into the old CD player I found buried in the back of the closet. It whirred and clicked. A few hesitant skips. I leaned in, whispering to it like an old friend.

"Come on, girl. You've got this."

Aiden shot me a look, a smirk pulling at his lips. "You talk to that thing like it's alive?"

"I'm trying to revive it," I said seriously. "It's ancient but powerful."

After a few more clicks and groans, the CD finally started playing. Aiden's baby voice rapped the alphabet, followed by a slow lullaby—barely audible under the static. The twins went silent. Wide-eyed, they stared like they were deciphering the mysteries of the universe.

Aiden groaned. "Please tell me you're not going to play the whole thing."

"You mean the raw emotion of baby-Aiden's rap? It's a masterpiece."

"'Q-R-S-T-U-V,'" he muttered, covering his face. "I can't believe we used to sing that to ourselves."

"Well," I said, grinning, "the twins definitely respect the dramatic phrasing of 'X-Y-Z.'"

62

WEIRD TRICK SHOTS

Aiden

I adjusted my hold on Lyric, cradling her against my chest as she let out a tiny, frustrated squeak. Her little body felt impossibly small, her warmth sinking through my shirt. Luna was already settled in Mom's arms, looking more like a satisfied burrito than a human. Lyric, though—she had other ideas. Sleep wasn't on her agenda. I bounced her gently, shifting my weight from foot to foot.

"Okay, kiddo," I murmured, glancing toward Mom, who shot me a tired but grateful smile from the couch. "Let's see if we can work some magic, huh?"

I started with Basketball Dribbling Patterns, swaying side to side in time with an imaginary crossover.

"Right... left... right-right... slow it down... there we go."

I adjusted the rhythm as I felt her tiny fists relax against my chest. It worked about half the time, and tonight, I got lucky. Her little sigh of contentment felt like a victory.

When that only half-worked, I moved on to Ceiling Fan Commentary—a crowd favorite. I tipped my head back, eyeing the slow, hypnotic spin of the fan.

"And there's the Lakers in transition," I whispered dramatically. "Bryant swings it to Gasol—back to Bryant! Oh, the crowd is on their feet, folks!"

I softened my voice, adding just enough excitement to hold her attention.

"And there's the shot... it's good!"

Lyric let out a tiny noise, barely more than a breath, but I could swear it sounded approving.

When that wasn't enough, I pulled out the Finger Puppet Solution. I lifted my pointer finger and wiggled it like I was about to take the game-winning shot.

"Magic Johnson sets up at the top of the key," I whispered, curling my finger like it was spinning the ball. "He fakes the pass, drives the lane—no-look shot—bucket!"

Nothing. Lyric was still awake, though her eyelids drooped. Time for the nuclear option.

I lowered my voice, barely above a hum, and started the Basketball Lullaby Medley.

"Basketball, basketball, swish so far," I murmured, fitting the words into the rhythm of *Twinkle, Twinkle, Little Star*.

The weight of her small body settled deeper against me, her breathing evening out.

I kept going, switching seamlessly into *Row, Row, Row Your Boat*.

"Dribble, dribble, down the court, smoothly as can be..."

By the time I got to *Merrily We Roll Along*—or rather, "Takes the shot, takes the shot, nothing but net"—Lyric was officially out.

I let out a slow breath and glanced toward Mom, who had been watching from the couch with the softest look on her face.

"You've got a gift," she whispered, carefully adjusting Luna in her arms. "A weird one."

"Yeah," I exhaled. "Weird but works."

Mom smiled. "They love you, Aiden."

I looked down at Lyric, her little fist still gripping a piece of my shirt, her tiny breaths warm against my chest.

"Yeah," I admitted, "I love them too. Can't wait to work on their jump shots."

63

Short Listed

Ivy

Rory's house smelled like citrus tea, old books, and rosin dust—a scent that had settled into the walls after years of music lessons and late-night composition sessions. The air always felt electric here, like creativity lived full-time in the corners.

I adjusted my cello's endpin, letting it sink into the worn groove on the floor. A memory of all the students who'd come before me. Across the room, Rory lounged in her favorite oversized armchair, one leg slung over the armrest, a chipped mug in hand.

"That was solid, Ivy." She lifted her mug in a toast. "Your phrasing? Beautiful, beautiful."

I grinned, loosening my bow and stretching my fingers. "Still needs work."

"It always does," she said, sipping her tea. "That's the trick. Music never really feels finished. You just get better at making peace with the unfinished parts."

I let that sit for a second. "That's... kind of terrifying."

Rory smirked like she'd been waiting for me to say it. Then she pulled a flyer from the table beside her and handed it over.

"Good. You'll need that mindset," she said. "Because I have an invitation."

I blinked at the paper. "What's this?"

"Chamber concert. A visiting violinist from Dickinson State is doing a short residency, and she asked me to help put together a small ensemble of advanced students for a winter performance." Rory leaned forward, her eyes bright. "She wants you in the group."

I froze. "Me?"

"You," she confirmed. "She's planning a story-driven setlist. Strings only—mostly classical with a few contemporary pieces arranged for small ensemble. She's seen clips from last spring's recital. She asked for names. Yours was the first I gave."

I looked down at the flyer again, my throat suddenly tight. "You think I'm ready?"

"I know you are," Rory said, her voice firm. "You've put in the work. And more than that? You listen. You don't just play—you make people feel something."

My cheeks flushed. "Is it weird that I kind of want to cry a little?"

"Not at all," she said, smiling. "That means you're doing something that matters. You'll still have to audition, but you're on the shortlist. I'm pretty sure you'll be picked. There will probably be more opportunities with her coming up. She's a ND native and has been working on compositions inspired by indigenous and folk music. And, she's committed to working with youth orchestras."

I ran my fingers along the edge of the flyer again.

A real performance. A chamber concert. With professionals. Maybe a chance to work with her more.

"I'll do it," I said softly.

"I know," she replied, raising her mug again. "That's my girl."

Aiden

I was halfway through a set of free throws—driveway time approved by Dad—when I saw Ivy heading over from her house, curls bouncing, hoodie sleeves shoved halfway up her arms.

She was glowing. Not just smiling—glowing. Her whole face lit up.

Yeah. My heart definitely did the flip thing again.

I let the ball bounce off and wiped my hands on my shorts as she stepped onto the edge of the court.

"You've got a look," I said. "Should I be scared or impressed?"

She rocked back on her heels, barely containing her grin. "I have news."

I raised an eyebrow. "Good news?"

"Great news," she said. "Rory's helping coordinate a winter concert at Dickinson State. It's for a visiting violinist—she's putting together a chamber group."

"That's awesome," I said. "You're in?"

Ivy hesitated just a beat. "I'm on the short list. I still have to audition next week. But Rory thinks I'll be in."

My eyebrows shot up. "Wait—this visiting violinist saw your spring performance and asked for your name?"

She nodded.

"That's like Steph Curry watching your game film and going, 'Yeah, I want that kid on my team for pickup.'"

Ivy laughed, eyes bright. "I mean...slightly less three-point range, slightly more Bach."

I stepped closer and hooked my finger through her belt loop. "So...does this mean I have to wear a tie and sit still for, like, an hour?"

"You're so dramatic," she said, laughing. "You'd be happy to do it...for me."

"I would," I said, softer now. "For you."

She was close—just a few inches away—and for a second, neither of us said anything. The wind tugged at her curls, and I had this sudden urge to reach out and catch one. Tuck it behind her ear. Let my hand stay there. But I didn't move.

She looked up at me then, eyes soft and searching, like she was trying to decide something. Then she stepped back, just a little, but enough. Her smile stayed, but her guard was back in place. "You've got free throws to finish."

I nodded, swallowing whatever that moment almost became. "Right. Go be fancy."

She laughed again as she turned. "Wish me luck."

"Always."

I watched her jog back to her house, curls bouncing. And it hit—she'd come over to share good news with me. She'd included me.

64

Not a No Show

Ivy

The community center felt enormous. The space amplified footsteps and insecurities shouted a little louder. My cello felt heavier than usual. Nerves attacked me as usual. I glanced around at the scattered chairs and simple wooden stage.

"Next up, Ivy Preston," the coordinator called, her voice kind but brisk. The walk to the stage felt longer than it should have. I adjusted my stool and glanced at the two people seated at the front row table.

One of them, a man with glasses perched low on his nose, scribbled notes on a clipboard without looking up. The other, a woman with a warm smile, nodded encouragingly. I latched onto that smile like a lifeline. I steadied the cello between my knees, placing the bow on the strings.

My audition piece was a variation of - Bach's Cello Suite No. 1 in G Major, Prélude —a deceptively simple piece that allows individual playing to shine. The first note was always the hardest.

Once the sound filled the room, something shifted. The notes crowded out my nerves and I could focus.

The melody flowed. Each note resonated humming in the room. Halfway through, I glanced at the judges. The man had stopped writing. His pen hovered mid-air. The woman's head was tilted, smile softer now, eyes following the rhythm of my bow. They were listening. Really listening. As the final note faded, the silence rang louder than the music.

I lowered my bow, heart pounding in the stillness. The man scribbled something. The woman clapped gently.

"Thank you, Ivy," she said, voice warm. "Beautiful work."

I nodded, managing a quiet "Thank you," and stepped off the stage. My hands were shaking, but whatever happened next, I'd played my heart out.

***

My phone buzzed.

> **Jordan:** How'd it go? I predict you crushed it.

> **Me:** It wasn't perfect, but it felt good. Thanks for believing in me.

I glanced out the windows of the center, trying not to feel disappointed. Aiden had been showing up more lately—but maybe not for this. I couldn't expect him to be everywhere and be everything.

Aiden

Dad dropped me off at the community center with a knowing smile. "You've got this," he said. "Just let her know you're there for her."

"Thanks, Dad," I muttered, grabbing the small gift box from my backpack before stepping out of the truck. I paced near the entrance for a few minutes, waiting for Ivy. When she finally came out, her face lit up with surprise when she saw me. For a split second, I wondered if I'd made a mistake showing up, but then her expression softened.

"You're here?" she said, her voice hesitant but warm.

"I'm here," I replied, holding her gaze. "I wanted to be."

She hesitated, then nodded. "Okay." We walked side by side for a few moments, the tension between us less heavy than it had been before. I gestured toward the restaurant down the street.

"Wanna grab some fries or a shake? My treat." Her lips twitched into the beginnings of a smile.

"Okay. But I want both. Auditioning is a workout and I'm starving."

I laughed, "Deal."

***

Ivy

The familiar smell of greasy food and coffee hit me as we stepped into the small restaurant. We'd both been here dozens of times. Aiden slid into the booth across from me, looking more relaxed than I'd seen him in weeks.

"So," he said, leaning forward as the waitress set down our food. "How'd the audition go?"

The question caught me off guard—not just that he asked, but honestly cared. I hesitated, then started talking. He heard about my nerves, the piece I played, the judges, the nice judge who smiled at me, the moment both judges seemed to be listening intently. Almost tripping over my cello case. When I finished, he smiled.

"I knew you'd crush it."

"You weren't even there," I teased.

"Doesn't matter," he said, shrugging. "I knew."

***

As we finished our fries, Aiden reached into his pocket and pulled out a small box. He slid it across the table toward me, his expression nervous.

"What's this?" I asked, my fingers brushing the soft velvet.

"Just... open it," he said, rubbing the back of his neck. Inside was a delicate necklace with a silhouette of a seeded dandelion. My breath caught. The tiny etched seeds looked like they were floating away, just like the wishes we used to make as kids.

"I thought it might remind you of those dandelion wishes we used to make," he said quietly. "Back when... you know, things were simpler."

I blinked, suddenly feeling the sting of tears. "Aiden, it's beautiful."

He smiled, a little sheepishly. "I just wanted to say I'm proud of you. For the audition. For everything." For a moment, I didn't know what to say. But as I looked at him, I saw something I hadn't seen in a while—genuine effort. He wasn't just showing up this time. He was trying.

"Thank you," I said, my voice soft but steady. "This means a lot."

***

"You've gotten quiet on me. What's up?" Aiden asked, his tone soft, curious. I hesitated, tracing a finger along the edge of my milkshake glass.

"It's nothing." He leaned forward, resting his elbows on the table.

"Ivy, come on. I know you. What's going on?"

The way he looked at me—earnest and concerned—made it impossible to keep dodging. I took a deep breath, letting the words tumble out before I could overthink them.

"When I got back from music camp, I saw you downtown. With Whitney." Aiden blinked, caught off guard.

"Whitney?" I nodded, my cheeks burning. "You two looked... close. I don't know, it just threw me off, I guess."

His expression shifted from confusion to realization, and then to something close to embarrassment. "Oh. That."

I braced myself for his answer. "Whitney just... kind of showed up," he said, scratching the back of his neck.

"I was going to grab some groceries for my mom and there she was acting like we're old friends." I can't help but smile at his obvious discomfort.

"She kept trying to, I don't know, hang all over me," he continued, his voice laced with exasperation. "I didn't know how to leave without being rude. Trust me, I was counting down the seconds until I could escape."

He paused, a wry grin tugging at his lips. "Honestly, I think she saw the summer as her big opportunity. You weren't around, and when you are around, I don't think she realizes I barely notice her."

The words hung in the air, casual but revealing. A flicker of something warm rippled through me. Aiden laughed, shaking his head. "She thought I'd changed my mind about ignoring her. But no. Whitney's just... Whitney."

"She's not exactly subtle, is she?"

"Subtle?" Aiden snorted. "She's about as subtle as Tyler's three-point celebrations."

I laughed, felt the tension ease. Part of me lingered on his words, that quiet admission about how he barely noticed Whitney—especially when I was around. As the conversation drifted back to jokes and fries, I glanced at Aiden across the table.

He was grinning at something he'd just said, but there was a softness to his expression that made my chest ache.

Maybe Whitney saw a door open this summer. But with Aiden sitting here, laughing and making me feel like the center of his world again, I realized it was never open at all.

65

TALKING TO THE GRASS

Aiden

When I found her in the music room, the soft sound of her cello wrapped around me like magic. I leaned in the doorway, watching her play. How had I never noticed how beautiful she looked while playing? I used to think Ivy was cute. But now? She was stunning. Like—actual string section angel levels of stunning.

In my head, I swear a few emojis floated by. One gave me a thumbs-up. Another nodded like, *finally.* The emojis were happy with me.

"Aiden."

I didn't move.

"Aiden," she said again, louder this time. She was already setting her cello down, her eyes full of quiet amusement.

I blinked. "Yeah. Yes. Totally fine. Just—music appreciation moment. Very advanced stuff."

"I finished playing a while ago," she said, smiling. "I've been trying to get your attention for at least a minute."

"You sounded amazing," I said quickly. "Just took me a second to rejoin reality."

She closed and fastened her cello case.

"So what's up?"

I shrugged, suddenly awkward. "I just—wanted to see how you're doing. I know you asked for time, and you've been at our house a lot helping with the girls, which is great, but burping babies and poopy diapers don't really count as quality time and..."

I stopped myself, exhaled. "I miss you. So much."

Her gaze dropped, but she smiled. "You managed a few weeks, Superstar," she teased. A blush crept up her neck. "I've missed you too."

I rushed in—too eager, I knew. "Are you walking home? Can I walk you?"

"Yes and yes," she said with a giggle.

It was a perfect fall day—crisp air, orange leaves underfoot. We strolled toward our neighborhood, but my heart was pounding like I'd just finished suicide sprints.

I could feel it pounding in my chest, in my ears. Was I having a heart attack? I was fifteen. That didn't happen, right? Of course it would happen now. Ivy and I had just started figuring things out, and I was going to keel over mid-sentence like some kind of walking cautionary tale.

Boy dies of heart failure on stroll home from school. Girlfriend-to-be horrified but not surprised.

Girlfriend to be? Yep, that's what I wanted and a felt a cold sweat break out. Not exactly how I pictured this going.

"Aiden, are you okay? You're breathing kind of funny."

"Yeah. No. I don't think so, Ives. I think I'm having a heart attack." I pressed a hand to my chest. "Feel my heart. It won't slow down. I'm serious. This is how it ends."

"You're not having a heart attack," she said, already rolling her eyes, even as she reached for my arm. "Sit down before you actually pass out."

She steered me over to the nearest patch of grass like I was a grandma at the state fair.

"Head between your knees," she added.

I obeyed, because that's what you do when a girl smarter than you is helping you to avoid a heart attack. Even if said girl is also the one causing the medical event. She knelt in front of me, hands on my shoulders, voice gentle.

"You're okay. It's gonna be okay. Just keep your head down. Breathe."

She sounded exactly like she did when Luna was overtired and needed to be rocked. Which was...not my proudest comparison. I took another breath. Then another. Eventually, my heartbeat stopped trying to break the land-speed record. I tried to lift my head to look at her, but every time I did, my heart started slamming around again like it was trying to escape. So I gave up and talked to the grass instead.

"Yeah. I'm just... really nervous."

"You? Nervous? I don't think I've ever seen you like this. You're always Mr. Calm and Collected."

"Maybe because this is the first time I've felt unsure about anything."

"Unsure? About basketball? Aiden, you know..."

"No, Ives," I interrupted, still not looking up. "Not basketball. Something bigger. You."

She almost tipped sideways. I couldn't lift my head, but I saw it happen in my side vision. Made me feel a bit better that I could knock her sideways with my words. I looked at her sideways. Her confused expression was adorable.

"Me? What do you mean?"

"I don't want to take you for granted again," I said. "Having you as my best friend—that means more than basketball. No...," I held up a hand blindly as she started to interrupt, pretty sure I was waving it somewhere near her knee. "It's not basketball *and* you. It's you, *then* basketball. Took me too long to realize it. But it's true. I'm not asking for anything more right now. I just want our friendship back. Okay, Princess? Just want to spend more time with you."

She froze, then let out a slow breath, her face softening. "Yeah, sounds good to me."

It was another ten minutes before I could stand up without feeling dizzy. And I couldn't look at her too closely all the way home.

66

The Universe Finally Takes a Time Out

Aiden

The days that followed felt like muscle memory.

Little things came rushing back: the way her curls framed her face, how her nose scrunched when she focused, how her laugh could light up a room. We'd always been best friends. But now? My heart pounded every time she looked at me. I tried to say something—tried to tell her what I was feeling—but the universe kept interfering.

The first time, we were under the oak tree by the soccer field. Sunlight filtered through the branches. It was perfect.

"Ivy," I began, leaning closer. "There's something I've been meaning to tell you, and—"

A lawnmower sputtered to life, roaring like a jet engine.

Ivy tilted her head, eyes dancing. "You were saying?"

I sighed. "We'll talk later."

The second time, we were watching Ty and Aria's pickup game at the park.

"Ivy," I started, gripping the bench. "I've been thinking about something, and I really need to—"

"HEADS UP!" Tyler yelled.

A basketball came flying at us. I barely ducked in time.

"Sorry, man!" Tyler called.

"No problem," I muttered, shoving the ball back.

By the third time, I was desperate. We were walking home again, and I was determined not to let anything stop me.

"Ivy," I said, voice steady. "I really need to tell you something, and I need you to just—"

"Don't move," she whispered.

"What?"

"There's a wasp on your shoulder."

Panic shot through me. "WHAT? A WASP? WHERE? GET IT OFF!"

"Don't freak out!" she said, already laughing. "Just stay calm."

"CALM? THERE'S A LITERAL TERRORIST WITH WINGS ON ME!"

"Okay, okay, hold still," she said, biting her lip, failing miserably to hide her laughter.

I swatted it anyway. The wasp buzzed off, and I stumbled back like I'd been tackled.

Ivy doubled over. "Oh my gosh, Aiden, I think you screamed louder than I've ever heard!"

"Nature hates me," I muttered, brushing imaginary bug guts off my shirt. "I was finally going to say something important and the universe sent a wasp."

"You want to try again?"

"At this point? The universe is clearly out to get me."

Today, I wasn't letting anything stop me.

As we neared her house, I grabbed her hand and pulled her to the side.

"Aiden, what—?"

"Ivy, I need to talk to you." I gently placed my hands on her shoulders, backed up, and threw my arms into a time-out sign. Then I looked up. "Time out, universe. Just one freaking time out."

She blinked, lips twitching. "You just called a time-out on the universe?"

"This!" I gestured between us. "This conversation. I keep blowing it. I've double-dribbled with my words, committed an illegal screen because I keep blocking my own points, and let's not forget traveling—because my brain is running all over the place."

Ivy burst out laughing. "You're not even on a court and you're fouling yourself. How does that even happen?"

"Hey, it's what I know!" I said, grinning. "But seriously, I think I'm about to foul out. You're the ref in this situation."

She softened. "I don't know, Superstar. I think I can let one more technical slide... if you just say it straight this time."

I laughed. "No more turnovers. No more fouls. I'm going for the game-winning shot."

She rolled her eyes, but smiled. "Good. I'm getting tired of watching you trip over yourself."

I took a breath. "Ivy, you're my best friend. But it's more than that. You mean everything to me. Not second to basketball—not second to anything. You come first. Always."

Her cheeks flushed, and she gave me the kind of smile that could knock the wind out of me.

"I feel the same way," she said.

I nearly collapsed against the house from the relief.

"But," she added gently, "let's not label anything yet. Okay?"

"Okay, but—"

"I feel more, too. I just...I need to go slow with you."

My forehead creased before I could stop it. She took a breath.

"The hurt of the past months—it's not just gone. I wish I could say I'm not afraid anymore, but I am. Less than I was. Fear isn't in control. But rebuilding? That'll take time."

I reached for her hand. "I hate that I made you feel like that. Made you doubt. Made you afraid to trust me. I'm sorry, Ivy. Truly. I'll go slow. I'll show you."

"Thank you for understanding."

"Can I hug you?"

"Yes. Of course."

I pulled her in, arms wrapped tightly around her. I hoped she could feel how much I meant it—how sorry I was. How much I never wanted to lose her again.

"I didn't realize hugging someone fun-sized would be this hard," I muttered. "Next time I'm bringing a box."

"Well, if you start to feel faint, go ahead and fall to the hard ground, because I'm too little to catch you," she said, before slamming her full weight into my gut.

"Oomph. Little but violent," I wheezed, pretending to be winded as I held her tighter, then finally let go. I didn't want to. But I knew I had to earn her trust back.

And when I did?

It would feel better than any three-pointer. It would feel like winning everything.

67

BOOPED

Aiden

I jogged down the driveway, spotting Ivy waiting at the corner. Her arms were tucked against the crisp morning air, curls glowing in the early sunlight like a halo she didn't know she wore. "You're late, Superstar," she teased as I caught up.

"Had to secure the breakfast of champions," I said, holding up a crinkled paper bag. I pulled out a powdered donut, wiggling my eyebrows. "Figured you'd need some sugar to keep up with me."

Ivy rolled her eyes but still plucked a donut from the bag, taking a slow, deliberate bite. Her lips pressed together as she chewed, her lashes flickering slightly—like this was some gourmet delicacy, not a gas station pastry.

"You know these are my favorite," she murmured, almost to herself.

My chest tightened, though I played it off with a shrug. "Yeah, I know."

She glanced at me then, her expression unreadable, but something about it made my stomach do this weird, twisting thing—like I'd just missed a step walking down the bleachers. I shoved another donut toward her, breaking whatever the moment had been. "Here, for endurance. Long walk ahead. Wouldn't want you lagging behind."

"Oh, *please*." Ivy scoffed, snatching the donut anyway. "I'd like to see *you* keep up with *me*."

I smirked but didn't argue. We fell into our usual rhythm—footsteps in sync, the familiar path to school stretching ahead like it always had. But something about today felt...different.

Or maybe it was me. Every time Ivy laughed at something I said, I caught myself watching her too long. Every time our arms brushed, I had to fight the impulse to shift closer instead of away.

She popped the last bite of donut into her mouth and dusted powdered sugar off her hands, smirking at me. I smiled back though my stomach felt kind of weird because the soft, unexpected way she'd giggled earlier.

We reached the school gates, and my brain was still trying to untangle that thought when Ivy turned to me, mischief flickering in her eyes.

"Race you to the entrance."

I barely had time to register the challenge before she took off, curls bouncing as she sprinted ahead.

"Oh, *hell no*." I grinned, launching after her.

She was fast—always had been. But my legs were longer, and even though she zig-zagged to throw me off, I caught up just before we reached the doors. We skidded to a stop, laughing breathlessly.

"So close," Ivy panted.

"You let me win," I accused, trying to ignore the fact that we were standing way too close.

She rolled her eyes. "Sure I did."

My gaze flicked to her lips before I could stop myself.

I took a half-step back, clearing my throat. "Well, *fun-size*, looks like I'm the true *champion* this morning."

I expected her to push back, but she just tilted her head, considering me. Then she reached up and *booped* my nose.

Booped.

"I let you have this one," she said lightly, "but next time? No mercy."

She turned and disappeared through the doors before I could react. I stood there for a second longer than I should have, something *new* twisting in my chest. It wasn't just the race. Or the donuts. Or the way she smiled when she thought I wasn't looking.

It was just everything.

68

What a Chair Angle Says

Ivy

Aiden caught my eye as I pulled books from my locker. He leaned against the lockers down from me. So good at it he was close to getting a varsity letter in locker leaning.

"Hey, Princess."

"Hey back, Hotshot."

The nickname escaped before I could lasso it. Too cute? Too much? Should I move to another hallway? Aiden's grin widened, hazel eyes sparking. That lean. *What was it about leaning against a locker that made a boy irresistible?*

"Hotshot, huh?" he mused. "Is that a promotion or a demotion from Superstar?"

"What?" I blurted, slamming my locker and confidently striding in the absolute wrong direction.

Aiden gently caught my arm. "Uh, Princess? History's the other way."

I froze mid-step. "Right. I was testing you."

"Sure you were," he said, grinning as we walked.

In history, I slid into my seat, determined to focus. Which was a silly goal at the moment. Every time I glanced his way, he caught me. And if he smiled? Yeah. Forget it. My brain packed its bags and left for summer break early.

After history Aiden walked me to next class like it was a totally normal thing.

"Well, this is me," I said, awkwardly adjusting my bag like I was about to board a flight instead of go to class.

He smiled, easy. "See you later." Then he winked.

My neural connections short-circuited. I think I whispered, "Okay, later," or "Later gator," or maybe I just stood there trying to get my feet to work. I watched him disappear down the hall, then let out a breath I didn't realize I had been holding. My lips curved into a helpless smile as I stepped into class.

***

Aiden

At lunch, Ivy slid into her usual seat. I was towed along in her gravity. Tyler glanced between us, then set down his drink like, straightened up, and looked around like he was about to launch into a TED Talk.

"Well, well, well," he said, loud enough for the whole table to hear. "If it isn't our two favorite childhood besties, finally staring their destiny in the eyes."

Ivy blinked. "I'm sorry, what now?"

He pointed at her with a carrot stick. "You've been orbiting each other like confused satellites for months. But recently? I've observed changes."

Jenna leaned in. "Please continue."

"Exhibit A: he now waits for her after class like a lost Labrador. Exhibit B: synchronized lunch tray placement. Exhibit C: the chair angle of intimacy."

I raised an eyebrow, mid-sip. "Chair angle of intimacy?"

"Aiden, you automatically angle your chair towards Ivy when you sit down," Emilia chimed in.

"See, even our viewers in farm country know what the chair angle is. Look it up."

Maddie nodded. "Showing some astute observational skills Ty."

"Thank you," he replied.

I smiled and shook my head. "Will we be getting a written report from you?"

Tyler shrugged. "Sure. Or an article submitted to the school newspaper. I'll keep you posted."

Ivy sighed. "It's not that big a deal."

Tyler pointed a carrot stick at her like a microphone. "Miss Preston are you fielding questions from the press this afternoon."

Ivy huffed, shrugged, but the smile gave her away. "Fine, we're just figuring things out."

Tyler leaned back, supremely satisfied. "Breaking news confirmed. Soft launch successful."

I caught Ivy's eye across the table. She nudged my foot under the table.

I nudged back.

***

Aiden

Later, by her locker, Ivy gave me a look.

"What's up with the weirder-than-usual faces from Tyler?"

I leaned against the locker next to hers. "I think he's just...happy we're getting along again."

She raised an eyebrow. "That's all?"

I hesitated. "He's also thrilled I'm not calling the Tyler Relationship Hotline every three days."

Her mouth twitched. "Wait—you actually did that?"

"It was less a hotline, more like a roast line. I'd ask what to do, and he'd just say, 'Wow. You're really this clueless?' Every time."

Ivy laughed. "So now he's giving you the official *perhaps you're not stupid* nod?"

"Hey—I said clueless, not stupid."

Right on cue, Tyler strolled past, walking backward like it was how he usually moved through the halls.

"She could've gone with 'idiot,' if we're splitting hairs," he called. "But don't worry, Pedersen—you've graduated. No more training wheels. Just don't crash."

He gave Ivy a mock salute. "Also—he's crazy about you. So there's that."

Ivy's cheeks flushed, but she was smiling now. Tyler turned the corner like he hadn't just emotionally sucker-punched me and moved on with his day.

"Tyler's been playing part-time life coach for a while," I said, rubbing the back of my neck. Then I looked at her—really looked at her.

"And…he's right. I am crazy about you."

Her breath caught. Then she smirked. "Okay, got it. You're cray-cray," she said, turning toward class. I followed, still grinning. I'd take it.

69

I GUESS TIME OUT'S OUR THING

Ivy

The late afternoon sun cast long shadows across the pavement as I waited outside the gym doors. Aiden's basketball practice had run long, and the stragglers were finally trickling out—some still in jerseys, others laughing about something that had happened on the court.

I shifted my weight, adjusting the strap of my bag, my thoughts tangled in a loop I couldn't undo. I knew Aiden and I had managed to find our way back to one another, knew we were more. Knowing it and believing it enough to silence my doubts were two different things. Movement from the doors pulled me out of my head—and then I saw her.

Whitney sauntered out, ponytail swinging. She barely looked at me. But the glance she *did* give—that faint smirk, that dismissive once-over—landed like a spark against dry tinder. I knew that look. It said, *You hesitated. I wouldn't have.* It said, *If you hadn't come back, I might've stayed.*

I stiffened, watching her flip her hair and link arms with a teammate, her laugh trailing like perfume. I exhaled slowly. I *shouldn't* care. But I did. A part of me might still be wondering whether Aiden—so easygoing, so generous with his attention—had ever *considered* it.

"Hey."

Aiden's voice cut through the noise in my head. Just like that, the tension in my shoulders eased. He stepped in front of me—basketball bag slung over one shoulder, hair damp from practice, jersey untucked. No distractions. Just that easy smile meant for *me*. Whitney's smirk vanished from my mind. This was what mattered.

He paused, studying me. "Timeout."

I blinked. "What?"

"Timeout," he said again, leaning closer, voice low and warm. "On whatever spiral is happening in that brilliant, overthinking brain of yours."

I frowned, not sure whether to laugh or scowl. "You don't even *know* what I'm thinking."

"Maybe not exactly," he said, grin tugging at his mouth. "But I *do* know you. And I know when you're stuck. So...clear the court. What's up?"

I hesitated, fingers tightening around my bag strap. "It's nothing."

He tilted his head.

"Okay, maybe not nothing," I muttered. "I just...I keep wondering if I really *understood* what we talked about. If I *understand* what's happening now."

His hazel eyes stayed steady on mine. "What's happening is still what we talked about," he said gently. "Us wanting more with each other."

"It's been good," I admitted, feeling my cheeks warm. "Really good. But..."

"But you're worried I'm just being my charming self?" he finished, amusement flickering in his eyes.

"Something like that," I said, dropping my gaze.

Aiden shook his head, like I'd just said something completely backwards.

"Ivy. Timeout again."

I let out a small laugh. "Is this a thing now?"

"Totally a thing," he said, grin softening into something quieter. "And for the record? You're *not* reading too much into anything."

His words settled around me like a warm scarf. But one fear still sat lodged in my chest, unspoken.

I took a breath. "What if...I'm too much work for you?"

His expression didn't shift, but a flicker of surprise passed through his eyes. He tilted his head, like he couldn't believe I'd even ask.

"What?"

I forced myself to keep going. "You make things easy, Aiden. You always have. You know how to just *be*. And I—I don't. I get stuck. I overthink. I make everything complicated. What if one day you just...get tired of it?"

He didn't answer right away. That was worse than anything he *could've* said.

Then he stepped closer. His voice was quieter now. "Timeout."

"Again?"

"Yeah," he said, eyes still on mine. "First, there was nothing easy about the past six months, and you hung in there for me. I made it difficult, Ivy. And, you know I overthink too, right? You don't think I've been going round and round in my brain wondering how I could have been dumb enough to let you start slipping away?"

I opened my mouth. Closed it again. He exhaled, running a hand through his hair.

"You wanna know what I think is *work*? Pretending I don't care about you as much as I do. That's work. *This*? This is just us."

Something in my chest twisted tight. I'd spent so long afraid I was the problem—afraid *I* was the one making it hard.

"I don't get tired of you, Ivy," he said. "Not when you're overthinking. Not when you're stressed. Not when you throw midnight classical music rants at me. That's part of the deal. And I want the *whole* deal."

My breath caught. "You swear?" I asked, voice barely above a whisper.

His grin tugged at the corner of his mouth. "Swear it's true… or a killer wasp will get me."

I laughed. It wasn't just a laugh—it was a release. And when I reached for his hand, I didn't hesitate. I felt sure.

70

DECIDING TO BE BRAVE

Ivy

Textbooks were scattered across the couch, highlighters uncapped, but let's be real—we weren't actually studying. We'd gotten sidetracked reminiscing about the treehouse disaster of 5th grade.

"We had structural vision," Aiden insisted.

"We had *delusion*," I corrected.

My mom never directly called us out, but she always seemed to know. Like the time she walked in, dropped a plate of snacks in front of us, and said, "Figured you two might need a study break."

Aiden, completely unbothered, grinned. "You're the best, Mrs. Preston."

She smirked at me before leaving the room—her message loud and clear. We still called it studying, but we knew better. When the sun dipped low, Aiden stretched.

"Should probably head home before my parents send a search party."

I walked him to the front door.

"Wanna walk me home?"

"You live next door."

"Yeah, but I like the company."

I rolled my eyes but grabbed my hoodie anyway. We wandered out into the crisp night air, quiet settling between us like a comfortable old song. At his front steps, he turned, still grinning.

"Thanks for the study session. We should definitely do that again."

"Oh yeah. We got *so* much done."

"Next time, I'll bring flashcards."

I laughed, shaking my head. "Go inside, Aiden."

He did—but not before walking *me* back home. We lingered on my front step longer than we needed to. Lingering in that space between now and what's next.

***

The gym echoed with the squeak of sneakers and the sharp bounce of basketballs—the soundtrack of a world Aiden fit into like it was made for him. I'd never been to one of his open gym practices before. Watching him now—fluid, confident, totally in his element—reminded how much this sport suited him.

Aiden spotted me immediately, flashing that easy, lopsided grin that always made my stomach flip.

"Didn't think you'd actually come."

One of his teammates clapped him on the back. "Aww, little Aiden's got himself a girlfriend now." Aiden didn't correct him.

I took a seat on the bleachers, watching him sink shot after shot. I'd always known basketball mattered to him. Knew he was good. Knew he loved it. But seeing him out there with his team—it hit differently. After practice I waited for him to finish up in the locker room. He caught my eye as he pushed through door.

"Hey, you waited."

"I did."

"You ready to walk home, girlfriend?"

I froze for a minute. I saw the feeling and sincerity on his face. I didn't correct him. Deciding to be brave I reached for his hand.

"Ready when you are. Boyfriend."

71

GERM FREE AND HYGIENIC

Ivy

The festival wrapped us up in the easy comfort of fall. Chill, but not cold, air touched our cheeks. Hay crunched under our shoes. Cinnamon-scented breezes floated past, and gooey caramel apples waited to be consumed.

We met our friends at the festival entrance. First, we wandered as a group, but soon broke off to explore booths and food stalls in pairs. Aiden pulled me toward the food stands first—pizza, obviously. He leaned back against a table, looking more relaxed than I'd seen him in weeks.

"You've been balancing everything so well—basketball, family, us."

I squeezed his hand. "I'm proud of you."

He laced his fingers through mine, smiling. "Trying my best."

He slid his arm around my shoulders, steering me toward a line. "Hayride?"

I pretended to think. "Only if you promise not to push me into the hay."

"No promises. But if you fall, I'll go with you."

And with the way his fingers curled effortlessly around mine, I knew he meant it.

***

The friend group reconvened later at my house. Dad had a fire going in the pit, and Mom had snacks waiting inside. We huddled around the flames, mugs of hot chocolate in hand, marshmallows on sticks.

Aiden made sure I had a blanket around me before sitting beside me, slipping our joined hands under the fabric like it was second nature. We laughed, trading stories from when we were kids, roasting marshmallows, and debating the correct chocolate-to-marshmallow s'mores ratio.

Tyler, with his usual dramatic flair, tried balancing four marshmallows on one stick. One caught fire, of course, and instead of handling it like a rational person, he waved it in a panic—nearly lighting his sleeve on fire.

Emilia groaned. "Why are you like this?"

Tyler just grinned, popping the charred marshmallow into his mouth. "Adds flavor."

Aiden laughed beside me, his grin easy and unguarded. And with every passing minute, I felt myself falling even harder. One by one, our friends called it a night, until it was just Aiden and me by the fire, huddled beneath the blanket, and the sky scattered with stars.

***

"Aiden," I said, breaking the comfortable silence.

He turned, firelight flickering in his hazel eyes. "Yeah?"

"Do you still have boy cooties?"

He blinked, then chuckled, amused. "No, I promise. I outgrew those."

"Hmm." I pursed my lips. "What about yucky boy germs?"

He raised an eyebrow. "Also germ-free."

"That's good." I nodded solemnly, fighting a giggle. "I don't want to catch cooties or get sick from gross boy germs."

Aiden gave me a mock-offended look. "Hey, I'm not gross or yucky. I happen to be extremely clean and hygienic, thank you."

"Hmmm." I tapped my chin. "You'll have to prove that."

Aiden smirked. "And how exactly should I do that?"

"Think for a minute. I bet something will come to you."

He leaned in, voice low. "How's this for a start?" He kissed my forehead gently.

I sighed. "That works. But I don't think forehead germs are the dangerous kind."

"Okay, fair." His smile widened. "Now what?"

I tilted my head. "Well... you could try that again. Just... somewhere more likely to make me sick."

His expression shifted, his gaze deepening. He brushed a hand through my hair, leaned in, and kissed me. It was soft. Unhurried. But there was more behind it—something real. Something that made my heart thud so loud I was sure he could hear it. When we finally pulled away, I tried to look unaffected. I failed completely.

"Sadly, one kiss won't prove you've shaken off the cooties," I said, voice a little breathless.

Aiden chuckled, brushing his thumb along my cheek. "Alright, scientist. What's your next step?"

I smiled, bold now. "We apply the scientific method. We could try a longer kiss—purely for research."

"For science, huh?"

"It's a solid hypothesis. My guess? The cootie levels won't change."

"Guess we'll have to test it."

He leaned in again. This time it wasn't just sweet. It was certain.

When we pulled back, our faces still close, Aiden smiled. "Now do you believe me?"

I pretended to consider. "Not quite. Might need a few more trials to be sure."

He grinned and kissed me again.

***

When we finally came up for air, Aiden shook his head, laughing. "I can't believe I ever thought kissing was gross. Though I stopped thinking *you* were gross in fifth grade."

I froze. "Wait. Fifth grade? You *liked* me in fifth grade?"

His ears turned pink. "Yeah. But I didn't know how to say it. And I still just needed my best friend."

I laughed, thinking of our awkward fifth-grade selves. "We were pretty clueless, huh?"

"Not anymore."

He pulled me closer. "And Ivy, you know I've only ever been interested in you, right?"

"Really? Never any other girl?" I let out a dramatic sigh. "Do you know what I've had to hear every day since sixth grade? Girls wanted all the Aiden, all the time. And yet somehow I survived. And—well, I guess we figured it out."

Aiden grinned, squeezing my hand. "Never any other girl, cause I only ever had eyes for one girl."

I swallowed, his words hitting deeper than I expected. We had figured it out. And it was worth every second of waiting.

NOVEMBER

72

1980's Basketball Vibes

Ivy

The buzzer blared. Game over. North Riverbend had held on. The gym erupted—cheers, stomping feet, students rushing the court. I stayed where I was, watching Aiden slap palms with his teammates, his grin big but tired. Then, in the middle of it all, he looked up. His eyes found mine. A quick glance, a smile tugging at one corner of his mouth. He jogged over, cutting through the chaos like it didn't exist.

"You were loud," he said, stopping just below the bleachers.

"You were good," I shot back.

He reached up just far enough to grab my hand for a second. His palm was warm and a little sweaty.

"You here—that helped."

I rolled my eyes. "I yelled the same way last game. You nearly fouled out."

"Timing," he said with a shrug and another crooked smile. "Tonight it worked."

Someone behind him called his name. He gave my hand a quick squeeze before letting go. "Don't disappear, okay?"

"I'm not going anywhere."

He nodded and turned back toward his team. As he disappeared into the crowd, I sat down, sign still in my lap, a fluttery ache blooming in my chest that I wasn't even pretending to ignore.

Maddie nudged me. "That was weirdly romantic."

"Shut up," I said, but I couldn't stop smiling.

***

Later, at The Round Up—the team's favorite postgame hangout—I was tucked beside Aiden in a booth overflowing with teammates. The place buzzed with post-win energy: fries passed hand to hand, milkshakes slurped, jokes flying nonstop.

One of the seniors clapped Aiden on the back. "Nice game, McHale."

Aiden groaned. "No. Don't start."

"Oh, it's started," another teammate said, grinning. "Old-school footwork, weirdly calm under pressure, zero flash. You're officially the team grandpa, Oldtimer."

Tyler leaned over with a smirk. "Don't pretend you weren't dying to yell *'Clear out the paint!'*"

Aiden dragged a hand down his face. "The man had moves. Just because he didn't do windmill dunks—"

Nick cut in. "Hey, no one's denying his talent. Just a little...eighties." Then he turned to me like I'd have an explanation.

I grabbed a fry, popped it into my mouth, and said, "Three rings, seven All-Star nods, and part of the most dominant frontcourt in league history." I elbowed Aiden lightly. "But if they're going to give you a nickname, don't let them go with *Oldtimer*. That's weak."

Aiden looked at me warily. "Got a better idea?"

I smirked. "Torture Chamber."

The entire table paused.

Tyler frowned. "Wait, what?"

"Something to aspire to. Make guarding you actual suffering. Like McHale and Barkley."

That earned a couple mock-oohs, a few knowing chuckles, and one milkshake salute. Aiden stared at me.

"You've been waiting to say that, haven't you?"

I grinned. "Timing is everything."

Across the table, one of the seniors clapped Tyler on the back. "Nice block tonight, *Little Tyler*."

Tyler groaned. "Seriously? I'm not the little anything."

Nick pointed toward the older Tyler, who raised his milkshake in solemn acknowledgment. "Seniority, man."

Aiden leaned in close, voice low. "You actually called me *Torture Chamber* in front of people."

I bumped his knee under the table. "You're welcome."

73

PICKING THE BETTER BRICKS

Ivy

The waiting of the past turned into minutes of being together. Hours of being Aiden and Ivy. School. Basketball for him, cello for me. Studying—actually studying, because our grades depended on it. Spending time with Lyric and Luna. Cheering Aiden on at his games. We carved out moments, stitched them into days.

But real life didn't slow down just because we thought we'd finally figured things out. Rehearsals stacked up. So did exams. Practice. He missed my calls. I missed his texts. We both missed each other more than we said out loud. And neither one of us had yet learned the communication skills we needed when things stopped fitting together so easily.

It wasn't dramatic. There was no big fight, no slammed doors, no sudden silence. Just a slow shift. The space between us started growing—quiet and unnamed.

Aiden

It wasn't like she vanished. We still walked to school hand in hand. Still sent late-night texts. Stole kisses between classes. Sat near each other at lunch—when we were both actually there. But a distance was growing, unchecked by either of us.

Ivy was busy. Seriously busy. Between rehearsals and everything she was juggling for the ensemble performance, I barely saw her. She missed two of my games. Both times, she sent a "Good luck!" with a smiley face. I told myself not to take it personally. So I didn't. At least, not out loud.

***

Aiden

But we'd started building a wall brick by brick of *Can't talk, rehearsal's running late* texts, the rushed goodbyes, the way she sat at the far end of the lunch table, scribbling through her music notes. It all started to feel like a wall between us—one we both pretended not to see. And I didn't say anything.

I didn't want to be that guy. The clingy one. The insecure one. The one who couldn't handle her having her own thing. So I bottled it. On afternoon, I was walking to math and a couple of cheerleaders passed by and called out, "Great game last night, Aiden!"

I smiled, nodded, kept walking. Across the hall, Ivy was at her locker. She didn't look up. I didn't stop. I didn't say anything.

***

Ivy

I saw him. Of course I saw him. He'd played last night. I'd meant to go, but rehearsal ran long, and by the time I looked up, it was already the fourth quarter. I'd sent him a "Good luck!" earlier—with a smiley. That counted for something, didn't it? I figured I'd catch him at lunch. When I got there, he was already deep in conversation with Nate and Drew. I sat at the other end of the table with Aria and Jenna, opened my music notes, and tried not to look up too much.

I didn't want to be the girl constantly chasing attention. Not when he was surrounded by teammates and people who always showed up for his games. Later, walking between classes, I passed him near the math wing. Two cheerleaders behind me called out, "Great game last night, Aiden!"

He nodded. Smiled. Kept walking. I paused at my locker, pretending to dig for something I didn't need. He didn't stop. Didn't say anything. Not even a hey. I didn't say anything either.

74

SEEING BUT NOT SAYING

Aiden

The girls had been coughing for a couple of days. At first it was just congestion—nothing dramatic. But by midweek, they were both fussy and warm, and Mom was checking their temperatures like it was her part-time job. By Friday, she had the RSV info page from the clinic open on her phone like it was a weather alert.

Ivy's concert was Saturday night. I kept telling myself they'd be okay by then. Or okay enough. I'd show up, sit near the back, find her afterward, and tell her how incredible she was. I wanted to be there.

But Saturday came, and it was bad. Lyric's breathing had gone shallow and fast. Luna wouldn't stop crying—red-faced, tight-fisted, full-body wailing that didn't ease, even in Mom's arms. Dad was pacing the living room with the nurse line on speaker while I rocked Lyric against my shoulder.

I didn't think about the concert. Not once during that hour. By the time things calmed—both girls finally asleep, Mom sitting down with her eyes closed—I looked at the clock. Past ten. Ivy's performance was over.

I sat on the couch with my phone in my lap, staring at the lock screen like it might tell me what to say. Then I opened our messages and typed:

> I'm so sorry I missed it. The girls were really bad tonight—breathing stuff. We thought it might be RSV. I wanted to be there. I hope it went amazing. I'm proud of you.

I didn't know if it was too much or not enough. I hit send anyway.

Ivy

I stepped off the stage, heart still racing, hands tingling from the adrenaline and bow pressure. The applause had faded, but the aftershock still buzzed in my chest. It hadn't been perfect. But it had been good. Better than good. Rory gave me a quiet nod as we exited the wings—a small half-smile that felt like something real. I'd worked hard for this. Rehearsals, late nights, sore fingers, skipped hangouts—I'd earned this moment.

I scanned the crowd instinctively. The lights were still up. Families were hugging near the back. But Aiden wasn't there. I blinked. Looked again. No tall figure near the door. No Mustang jacket. No hands-in-pockets half-smile. Nothing. I tried not to let the feeling settle in too deep. Maybe something came up. He said he'd be there. He wouldn't just... not show up. Right?

I stepped into the hallway to breathe. My fingers still tingled. Jordan found me before I'd even taken two steps, a bouquet of white tulips in his hand and a grin on his face.

"For the girl who didn't just play," he said, "but performed."

I smiled, a little stunned. "These are beautiful."

"Sarah's idea," he admitted. "But I picked the color."

We stood for a photo. Sarah snapped it. Jordan made a goofy face in one. I smiled politely in another. I kept looking toward the door. Still waiting.

Aiden

I stared at my phone way too long after I sent the message. No read receipt. No typing bubbles. Nothing. It was late. I told myself she'd probably gone to bed. Big night. Exhausted. Surrounded by people. She'd reply in the morning. I believed that for about four hours.

Around midnight, I gave up on sleep. The girls were finally out—soft, congested breathing through the monitor—but my brain wouldn't shut off. So I scrolled. Jordan's post hit like a sucker punch.

@basslineandbaseball: *Proud of this one for absolutely crushing her performance tonight.*

I froze mid-scroll. The photo: Ivy with her cello case slung over her shoulder, hair frizzy like it always got after she played. A bouquet of white tulips in her arms. She looked radiant. Tired, but glowing. And Jordan was standing next to her. Close. No one else in the frame.

The next three photos didn't help—her laughing at something off camera, the two of them holding drinks, one where she looked away like she was mid-movie moment. No sign of Sarah. No caption explaining anything. No mention of me.

I checked Ivy's stories. Just concert clips. Music stands. A blurry ensemble bow. Still nothing back from my text. I locked my phone. Unlocked it again. Checked the message. Still unread. My chest felt too tight for how quiet the room was. Maybe she hadn't noticed I wasn't there. Maybe she had—and didn't care. Or maybe she was exactly where she wanted to be, tulips in hand. With someone else.

Ivy

I saw his text the next morning. It was buried under group chat pings and a test study group reminder.

> I'm so sorry I missed it. The girls were really bad tonight—breathing stuff. We thought it might be RSV. I wanted to be there. I hope it went amazing. I'm proud of you.

I stared at it for a long time. Of course I felt awful. He wasn't ignoring me. He wasn't ditching me. He'd been holding babies, probably scared out of his mind, trying to stay calm while listening to his little sister struggle to breathe.

But still—

He hadn't told me beforehand. I would've understood. I think. But I didn't even know he wasn't coming until I realized he wasn't there. Until after. When the lights came up and I was standing alone.

I typed out a reply.

I'm glad the girls are okay. It went well.

Too flat.

I missed you.

Too much.

I settled on:

> I get it. Hope they're doing better today.

I hit send and shoved my phone in my bag. At school, I told myself to act normal. Smile. Head down. Don't overthink.

***

I was walking toward first period when I saw them—Aiden and Whitney—talking near the lockers by the main stairwell. She was smiling. He said something. She laughed, brushing her hair behind her ear. He didn't touch her. Didn't lean in. But they were standing close. I stopped.

I don't even know what I'd been expecting—an apology? An explanation? Some kind of quiet, steady look that said *I still care*? Whatever it was, this wasn't it. He didn't see me. I turned down the side hall and didn't look back.

75

TEXT INTERVENTION

Aiden

The ball left my fingertips. Clean release. Clank. Tyler caught the rebound. "That's six."

I shook out my arms. "Just tired."

He tilted his head. "Tired or emotionally blocked?"

I ignored him. I wasn't thinking about Ivy. Not about how she'd missed the last game. Not about how her *"Good luck tonight"* text came with a cheerful little smiley face—like something you'd send a coworker, not someone you'd kissed under a blanket with firelight shining through.

I took another shot. Clank. Tyler didn't bother chasing it. "Let's call it."

I nodded, grabbed my water bottle, and followed him off the court. We pushed through the gym doors into the cold night air. I rolled my shoulders, trying to shake off the tension. Not that it helped.

Tyler shoved his hands into his hoodie pocket. "So. You gonna halt the spiral and figure out what's going on with Ivy?"

I exhaled. "I don't know what to say."

"That's... kind of the problem, dude."

My phone buzzed.

> **Josh:** smiley face, thinking face, phone, violin, camera

Tyler peeked over my shoulder. "You just got cursed-phone'd."

I frowned. "Translation?"

He nodded solemnly. "That's: 'Hey bro, I bet you're spiraling about that Jordan post with Ivy.'"

Yes, Josh. I'd seen it. And yeah—I'd been spiraling.

***

> **Me:** You do this on purpose.

> **Josh:** smiley face

> **Me:** WHAT DOES THAT EVEN MEAN.

> **Josh:** smiley face

Tyler tilted his head like he was analyzing game film. "Hmm. That's the 'hey buddy, maybe use your words' smile."

I scowled. "It's just Josh messing with me."

> **Josh:** smirking face

Tyler whistled. "That one's saying, 'I know things you don't.'"

Josh: raised eyebrow face

Tyler nodded. "Now *that's* concern. As in, 'Are you really gonna keep pretending you don't know what's wrong?'"

Me: STOP TEXTING ME RANDOM EMOJIS.

***

Josh: broken heart, wise wizard, sparkles, flashlight, cloak

Tyler nodded like it was obvious. "Yep. That's definitely: 'You're breaking my heart. You know I'm just trying to teach you, young padawan.'"

My phone buzzed again. Josh had added me to a group chat. Then added Molly. Renamed it: Aiden's Feelings Matter (with a heart). I stared. "What?"

Tyler glanced at my screen. "Oh, man. You just got group chat trapped."

Molly: Sigh. Guess I'm the translator now. Hi Aiden. Josh wants you to know his phone now can't text any actual words to you, so please don't block him.

Josh: big puppy eyes

Josh: frowning face

Molly: He also wants to know how things are going with Ivy.

Molly: He says thank you for understanding.

Josh: smirking face

Molly: That means: 'Be honest with yourself.'

Tyler covered his mouth, trying not to laugh. "Josh got his girl running PR for him. That's commitment."

Tyler: Just answer the question, Aiden. Everything good with Ivy?

I glanced at Tyler literally standing beside me.

"You're in the chat?"

Tyler grinned. "Obviously."

Tyler: Guys, Aiden's spiraling after spending the night staring at and misinterpreting a post with Ivy in it. He's not using his words again.

Josh: smug face, clapping hands, sparkles

Molly: Don't rub it in, Josh. Focus.

Josh: heart eyes, blowing kiss, sparkles, engagement ring

Molly: Josh, it's completely inappropriate to text about proposing to me in the middle of Aiden's emotional crisis.

Tyler: Isn't that just your way of saying she's the one?

Molly: Maybe. But this is Aiden's heartbreak moment, Josh.

Josh: heart eyes, flexed bicep, shooting star

Tyler: Translation: If Josh can win someone as amazing as Molly, there's hope for you too, bro.

Josh: raised hands, confetti

Molly: melting face, sparkles, soft smile. Okay, that was kind of sweet.

Josh: trophy, clapping hands, crying face, film camera, Oscar statue, thumbs-up

Tyler: And Josh is ready to direct your comeback story.

I locked my screen before I could actually hurl it into the parking lot. Close call. Tyler laughed. He'd caught me pulling my arm back before I shoved my phone in my pocket.

"Yeah. That would fix everything."

***

Ivy

I sighed, thumbing over to my messages. No new texts from Aiden. Then again, I hadn't sent much to him. I almost typed something. Good luck at practice? Too basic. Hey, I miss you? Too much. Do you ever feel like you're drifting from someone even when you don't want to? Way too much.

I deleted the draft and set my phone on the nightstand, groaning. I sat up and stretched, trying to shake off the tiredness when a blaring guitar riff ripped through the silence, followed by an overdramatic wail—something about never giving up, even if you're stuck on a metaphorical train ride to personal growth, all delivered in a power-ballad explosion of 80s optimism and mullet-fueled enthusiasm.

At full volume.

Reaching for my phone, I knocked it off the nightstand to the floor. It kept blasting the most aggressively motivational rock anthem in existence. I slid to the floor and swiped it silent. Still on the floor, I unlocked my phone.

Jordan: Tyler says you're definitely a small-town girl.

Jordan: Headed somewhere real.

Jordan: Then your train derailed in Spiral-town.

Jordan: Now you're acting like you were born to sing the blues.

Jordan: Which we both know is a lie.

Jordan: That is not your genre. So Tyler called in the Big Strings.

Jordan: Just a little gift to match your energy lately.

Me: BLOCKED. And you're responsible if bad things happen because I. Just. Stop. Believing.

Jordan: WAIT—before you do, serious question: were you about to stare dramatically at the ceiling and overthink your entire life?

Jordan: Like, literally as we speak?

I froze. Because I wasn't at the moment, but I would have gotten there. Give me five minutes, and I'd have been lying on my bed, internally composing a full symphony of hypothetical worst-case scenarios. I sat up, grabbed links, and created a group chat.

Me: Enjoy your consequences. [Link to *Train*] [Link to *Blondie*]

Jordan: NOOOO NOT *50 Ways to Say Goodbye*

Tyler: I never found Blondie threatening before.

Me: Getcha. Getcha. Getcha.

Jordan: Tyler, stay strong. Don't stop believing in our cause.

Tyler: Too late. She's terrifying.

Me: One way or another, you pushed a girl to the edge with a rock ballad about eternal hope.

Me: And I chose violence.

Tyler: Ivy. Please.

Me: One way or another, I will remember this.

Jordan: She's quoting lyrics. We're doomed.

Tyler: This is psychological warfare.

Me: Poetic justice. Believe it.

Me: And if you push me again, Jordan's going down singing *help me, help me* in my emotional hurricane.

Tyler: We are NEVER doing this again.

Jordan: Never is a strong word.

Me: *One. Way. Or. Another.*

Tyler: I AM LEAVING THIS CHAT.

Jordan: Don't stop believin', Tyler.

Tyler: STOPPPP.

Me: Yeah, Tyler. Don't. Stop.

Tyler: I HATE BOTH OF YOU.

Me: Congratulations. You've unleashed an unholy mashup of feelings and 80s revenge.

76

MIGGY SAYS, "LAME."

Ivy

Emilia didn't even let me finish putting my books in my locker before she grabbed my wrist and pulled me into an empty classroom.

"Okay," I protested. "This is dramatic, even for you."

She shut the door behind us, crossed her arms, and pinned me with a look so sharp it made my stomach twist.

"Tonta," she muttered, shaking her head. "Estás tanpreocupada por que pase lo mismo que lo estás haciendo pasar."

I blinked. "English?"

"No." She leaned against a desk, eyes still narrowed. "Porquesi te lo digo en inglés, lo vas a ignorar."

I sighed, rubbing my temple. "Em, I don't even know what you're talking about."

"Oh, sí lo sabes." She lifted an eyebrow. "You and Aiden are doing the thing again."

"The thing."

She threw her hands up. "¡El ciclo! The cycle, Ivy! The one where you assume, he assumes, and instead of talking, you both just drown in your own insecurities until someone else has to come in and fix it."

I flinched. "That's not—"

"It is that," she interrupted. "You saw him talking to Whitney and what? Decided to go home and suffer in silence instead of asking him about it?"

I hesitated.

She groaned. "Dios mío, esta chica…"

"That's not fair," I argued. "You didn't see them. She looked right at me and—"

"And you let her get in your head." Emilia's voice softened, but the disappointment in it still stung. "Ivy. You're acting like she controls the narrative here. Like you and Aiden don't have a say in your own story."

I swallowed hard, arms tightening around myself.

She sighed. "And if you'd talked to him, you'd know he finally told Whitney to leave him alone."

I stiffened. "What?"

Emilia nodded. "He did it nicely, of course. But he was firm. So firm that maybe it even scared her." She crossed her arms, tilting her head. "But you wouldn't know that, because instead of talking to him, you went home and let your anxiety write the worst possible version of events."

My stomach clenched.

He told Whitney off.

And I'd been lying awake, spiraling, for nothing.

"Mira, I know you're scared," Emilia continued. "But you're so afraid of losing him that you're pushing him away. And if you don't stop, you're going to end up making your worst fear come true."

My throat felt tight. "I don't know how to fix it."

She let out a breath, then placed both hands on my shoulders. "You talk to him, Ivy."

I nodded, even though the knot in my stomach refused to loosen.

Emilia squeezed my shoulders once before stepping back. "Good. Because Tyler and I actually like each other, and if you and Aiden's weird inability to use words messes that up, I will make your life very inconvenient."

I let out a watery laugh. "Noted."

She studied me for another moment, then sighed. "Do you need me to call you *mi niña* and give you a comforting forehead kiss or are you good?"

I rolled my eyes. "I'm good."

She huffed. "Fine. But fix it, Ivy."

Then she left, the door swinging shut behind her, leaving me alone with my thoughts. And I hated how much I knew she was right. I hated that I was stuck in place, trapped between what I wanted and what scared me most. I hated the way my pulse stuttered at the thought of losing all the reconnection we'd fought to rebuild.

But worse? Worse was the fear that if I tried to fix this—if I made the wrong move—I'd lose it all anyway.

***

Aiden

"Okay, no offense, but you're an idiot."

Two fries came at me before I could reply.

"You're not giving me time to take offense. Stop throwing fries at me!"

Tyler leaned back in the booth, crossing his arms. "Are you ready to listen? Hearing aid on, Oldtimer?"

I sighed, dragging a hand down my face. "What is it, Ty?"

He popped a fry in his mouth, chewing pointedly before continuing. "You're being dumb about Ivy. Again."

I stiffened. "I'm not—"

"You are." He pointed at me with another fry. "You saw a post after her concert and didn't ask about it. She saw you with Whitney and didn't ask about it. And now you're both miserable because instead of using your words, you're making up your own sad little stories in your heads."

I clenched my jaw, staring at the table.

Tyler sighed dramatically. "Dude. You are literally causing the thing you're afraid of. Self-fulfilling prophecy, man. Look it up."

I exhaled sharply. "It's not that simple."

"Actually, it is." He leaned forward, propping his elbows on the table. "You love Ivy, Ivy loves you, and instead of remembering that, you're sitting here stress-eating fries like a tragic protagonist in an angsty romance novel."

I scowled. "That's not—"

He threw another fry at me. "Fix it."

I caught it, sighing. "How?"

"Talk. Ask. Stop assuming. Act like big kids and use your words." He gestured between us. "Emilia literally just gave Ivy this exact same speech, and I'm not gonna let you mess it up for me when that girl has finally stopped running away from me."

I snorted despite myself. "So this is about you and Emilia?"

"Absolutely," he said without hesitation. "But also, I care about you, man. And I care about Ivy. And you two deserve to be happy."

I swallowed hard, staring at the fry in my hand.

Tyler took a sip of his drink, then added, "Oh, and by the way? If Ivy had actually talked to you, she'd know you finally shut Whitney down."

"Finally."

Tyler smirked. "Yeah, I think she's off your back. I guess you were scary in your Mr. Nice Guy firmness. Terrifying firmness even."

I rubbed the back of my neck, not meeting his eyes. "She was really pushing it."

Tyler laughed. "Yeah, no kidding. But Ivy doesn't know that, because you haven't told her."

I sighed, dragging both hands down my face. "I hate when you're right."

"I love when I'm right." Tyler grinned, then suddenly perked up. "Oh, speaking of people who are talking about their feelings, I have something to show you."

He pulled out his phone, thumb flying over the screen before turning it toward me.

Miggy's name was at the top of the messages.

***

> **Miggy:** What's wrong with basketball dude?

Tyler: Aiden?

> **Miggy:** Yes. He looks sad.

Tyler: He's just being dumb. We're working on it, buddy.

> **Miggy:** Ivy looks sad too. Is she being dumb too?

Tyler: You gonna be mad at me if I call your cousin dumb?

> **Miggy:** Not if she is.

Tyler: They won't use their big kid words and talk to each other. They're pouting.

> **Miggy:** Lame.

Tyler: You got that right.

Miggy: Sofía's sad because Ivy's sad. I don't like it when someone makes my little sister sad.

Tyler: We're working on it, buddy.

Miggy: Good.

Tyler grinned. "See? Even Miggy thinks you're being an idiot. And apparently, you're breaking Sofía's heart in the process. Nice job, man."

I blinked at the screen, then looked at Tyler. "That kid is scary."

"True that. I picture him taking over the world someday."

I shook my head, but a laugh slipped out. "I kinda want to cry because he said I'm lame."

"He's not wrong. And you're about to get lamer." He scrolled through his social media feed before turning his phone back to me.

"You saw the post with Jordan, spiraled, didn't ask a single question, and completely missed the part where it's very clear those pics were posted by Sarah —his girlfriend, who went to Ivy's recital with him and gave her the flowers." Tyler wiggled the phone in front of my face.

"You know, Sarah—the girlfriend of Ivy's friend, who is also good friend to Ivy."

I kept staring. I knew Ivy and Jordan were just friends. I knew that. But I'd still let that post mess with my head, twist into something it wasn't.

Tyler sighed. "You two are exhausting."

I rubbed a hand over my face. "Yeah. I'm exhausting myself."

"So, what are you gonna do?"

I let out a breath, then nodded. "I'm gonna talk to her."

"Good." He grabbed a fry off my plate. "Now stop looking so moody. You're ruining the fries."

77

Barn Trap Plan for Dizzy Chickens

Tyler

I barely had time to sit down the next day at lunch before. Emila dropped her tray onto the table like the school food was highly offensive.

"They are so dumb," she said, sharp and exasperated.

I took a sip of soda. "I assume we're talking about Aiden and Ivy?"

"Who else?" She dropped onto the bench across from me. "Ivy *knows* she needs to talk to Aiden. But is she going to do it? No. Wanna bet she's hiding in the library inventing sad little scenarios to torture herself with?"

I snorted. "That's funny. Aiden's doing the exact same thing. Guy has proof Ivy wasn't doing anything sketchy, and he's still brooding like he's the lead in a bad indie film."

Emilia groaned. "It's like they *want* to suffer."

I leaned in. "So, do we let them work it out on their own, or do we speed this along before I lose my mind?"

She narrowed her eyes. "What do you have in mind?"

I grinned, pulling out my phone. "Funny you should ask. Because a certain little someone named Miggy already thinks we should intervene."

She started laughing as she scrolled. "First of all, my little brother is legendary. And a little scary. Second—what exactly are we thinking here?"

I drummed my fingers on the table. "We need to get them alone. No distractions. No easy escape. No background characters to stall or deflect."

Emilia raised a brow. "So what? Lock them in a supply closet?"

"I was thinking a little bigger." I smirked. "How do you feel about using a barn?"

She tilted her head, already smiling. "Kittens."

***

Ivy

There were no kittens. Emilia had lured me out by mentioning a litter of barn kittens. I folded my arms and stared her down. "What are you doing, Emilia? There aren't any kittens."

She smiled sweetly, looking far too pleased with herself. "Oh, they're around."

Before I could demand kitten appearances, the barn door slammed behind me. A lock clicked into place.

"Emilia!" I spun around, rattling the door. "Emilia, you let me out right now!"

From the other side, she sighed loudly like I was the unreasonable one. "Ivy, you and Aiden are a disaster."

"Excuse me?"

"A forty-car pileup on I-94," she added helpfully. "We're done watching it happen."

I gave the door a frustrated kick. "Ow!"

"Stop kicking the door, Ivy. I'm not letting you out until you and Aiden figure it out."

"Since I'm the only one locked in here, how is that supposed to happen?"

Her voice turned smug. "Oh, you should be getting company any minute now."

I heard a thud and a voice from the far side of the barn.

"What the—Ty! I bet Barn Ball isn't even a thing!"

Aiden

I should've known Tyler was scheming when he suggested hanging out at the Preston farm.

"Dude, you've just got to come out and play Barn Ball. Robbie and my dad used to play it. It's a blast."

Like an idiot, I went along—Golden Retriever brain. Say the word "ball," and I'm in. Barn Ball? Sure. Result? Me—locked in a barn. With Ivy, who very pointedly was not talking to me.

I sat on one side of the barn, staring at a loose knot in the wood. Ivy sat across from me, her finger drawing idle shapes in the dirt floor. She wasn't looking at me. I wasn't looking at her. Total silence. Except for the judgmental rooster crowing somewhere in the distance. Probably bragging about how he had better communication skills.

"This is dumb."

"You're dumb." She muttered it—pretty sure that's what I heard.

Before either of us could say another word, the barn door opened. Dramatically. With a long, drawn-out, ominous squeak. Miguel stomped in, and Sofía toddled behind him, hugging her stuffed bunny tight.

Miguel squinted. "Okay. Farm Security is here."

I groaned under my breath.

Miggy pointed accusingly. "Use your words yet?"

Ivy cleared her throat. "We were going to."

Miguel sighed like this was the most exhausting shift of his career. "Emilia says you're bad at it. So we gotta check."

Sofía bounced on her toes, enthusiastic. "Yeah! Check!"

Miggy paced like a tiny interrogator, then jabbed a finger at Ivy. "Okay. Ivy, you still wanna like Aiden even if he stays a clueless basketball dude?"

Ivy's cheeks flushed. "I—uh—"

"Sí or no, Sondita," Miggy said, cutting her off.

She mumbled, "Yes."

Miggy turned to me. "Aiden, you still wanna like Ivy even if she didn't rescue you from Whitneyland?"

I felt my ears heat. "Wait—Whit—what?"

Miggy narrowed his eyes.

I answered, quick. "Yes."

Miguel gave a slow, theatrical sigh. "You guys are a mess. This is real bad."

Sofía scowled at us and chimed in, "Bad!"

Miguel shook his head like we were hopeless. "Did you say nice stuff yet? Like 'I don't hate your face' or 'there's no boogers in your nose'?"

Ivy crossed her arms. "That's not exactly—"

Miggy held up a hand. "Shh. My turn to talk."

He turned to Sofía. "Officer Fia, what's next?"

Sofía clutched her bunny. "Mah-weed?"

Miguel shook his head gravely. "No, gross. That means kisses. They gotta stop being dizzy chickens and use their words."

Sofía wrinkled her nose. "No diz-chickys."

Miguel pointed between us. "You two are in time-out. Eleventyhundred minutes."

He fixed us with a firm stare. "Use the minutes to think hard 'bout your choices. And use your words like big kids."

I raised a brow. "Or?"

Miguel's finger hovered in the air. "I call... Mi abuela. Both of 'em."

Ivy gasped. Now she looked nervous. Miggy crossed his arms.

"Talk. Don't talk. Make a good choice."

Then he and Sofía marched out, their little boots thudding across the barn floor.

"No tak! Bad!" Sofía called over her shoulder as they left. The barn door clicked shut.

Ivy

I waited a beat longer just to make sure Miguel and Sofía were really gone. I turned around slowly. Aiden was already looking at me. Somehow, even after everything, we both laughed. Of course this would happen to us.

"Did you call me dumb, Ives?"

I kicked at the floor. "Maybe. You started it."

I stopped kicking, realizing I sounded like a four-year-old. He gave me a look that was more fond than annoyed, and for a second I thought maybe this wouldn't be so hard. But then the quiet came back, and all the words I hadn't said piled up next to me.

"I don't understand myself sometimes," I said. "For years we've talked about everything. I've never worried about telling you something. Except maybe when I say anything about—" I lowered my voice, "—cramps. And you look like you're going to pass out."

"Yeah. You've always been the one I could talk to about...pretty much anything. Except us. I can't talk to you about us. Not even can't—afraid to. Afraid my words would push you away. Worried I'd say the wrong thing and you'd think you'd had enough."

I folded my arms—not because I was mad, just because I needed to hold something in place. "You seriously thought that? That I'd just...walk away?"

452

He didn't answer right away. Just looked down at his shoes like they had something wise to say. Then his eyes met mine. "I convinced myself you wouldn't want to hear me out."

I took a deep breath and let it out slow. "I haven't been making it easy for you to get your words out, I know. But here's the thing, Aiden—it will never be your choice of words, or how many or how few you use. It's the effort you put into making space for me in your life."

"Ives, look at me."

I met his gaze.

"You don't just have a space in my life. You're woven into it all. You're in every play in my playbook. If you pulled back—if you took yourself out of my life—everything would be off. Whether I saw it immediately or not, it'd be one technical after another until I couldn't keep going."

I blinked, trying not to cry like some overly dramatic movie character—but the tears were there anyway. Stupid, stinging ones.

"I don't need to be your sole focus; I don't need to be what everything is about. I just need to know there's room for me, even when our lives fill up. And I know I haven't made it easy for you to tell me. But I've always supported you. I've always pulled for you. I've known you'd succeed. I'm not giving up now."

He took my face in his hands. "I'm sorry I doubted that. You've been there. And I trust you'll still be there."

I put my hands over his. "I've seen you eat mud and put peanut butter in your ears. I'm not going anywhere now."

Aiden laughed softly, his forehead resting against mine for a second. "That was one time. And technically, the peanut butter was a dare."

"From you to yourself," I reminded him.

He smiled, and I could feel it in his hands—how steady they were now. Like we'd both finally stopped bracing for impact. Then he reached into the pocket of his hoodie and pulled something out. Small. Worn.

"Thought maybe he should come home," he said.

I gasped. "Mr. Basketball!"

I didn't even try to play it cool. I cradled him like a newborn. "Ohhh, Mr. Basketball," I whispered. "I've missed you so much."

Aiden tilted his head. "You know I was the one carrying him around, right?"

"Doesn't count," I said, stroking the faded seams. "He was emotionally hollow without me."

That's when I noticed the tiny piece of paper pinned to his side. I unpinned it and unfolded it.

I LOVE YOU.

Everything stilled.

"Aiden?" My voice barely made it past my throat.

He swallowed. "Yeah..."

My heart bounced in spiccato rhythm—fast and bright and a little wild. "I love you too," I said, breathless but sure.

I'd thought it in some form on every walk to school, in every puff of breath that sent dandelion seeds sailing, in the quiet and the ache of missing him. But saying it now—here—it felt like the dandelion notes finally dancing free, sparkling in the sun.

A laugh bubbled up—half joy, half disbelief. "Were you seriously waiting for the perfect moment, Pedersen?"

He groaned. "Maybe, yeah...gesture timing's not my strength."

I stepped closer. "So...Miggy told us we have to talk. He also told us to stop being dizzy chickens."

Aiden grinned. "Just let me emphasize that I may have been dizzy poultry for a short time, but if so—I was a rooster. A buff rooster. And you, you're beautiful even in dizzy chicken form."

"Hmmm, okay. I think I don't hate your face, Mr. Rooster." I looped my arms around his neck. "And because you do such a good job keeping your nose booger-free, I want to do this."

I rose up on tiptoe and pressed a soft kiss to his lips. He followed me as I pulled back.

"Miguel said we needed to use our words."

"He didn't say we had to use English or Spanish. Or even speak out loud."

He leaned in for another soft kiss. "I like your face."

Another. "You don't smell bad today."

Another. "That was, good job—you don't have bad breath."

I looped my arms tighter. "Got it. I think we should be done with the small talk and get down to the serious stuff."

We did get serious. We talked until our eleventy-hundred minute time-out was officially over—barely stopping until we heard Sofía outside.

"Dey's kissin'!"

And then Miggy, "GROSS! Cover the cows' eyes!"

We broke apart, laughing. Time-out over. And if we forgot to use our words for a few more minutes...well, that was between us and the barn kittens who finally showed up.

78

THE REALITY OF BARN BALL

Aiden

The second the barn door opened, I stepped into the sunlight like I'd just been released from cow scented prison. Ivy followed close behind, cheeks pink, eyes suspiciously bright.

Tyler stood in the yard. Waiting. Hands on hips. Smirk fully deployed.

"So, Pedersen," he called, "You think Barn Ball isn't a thing?"

I squared up, arms crossed. "I take it back."

"You doubted the legacy," he said, voice mock-serious. "You mocked the hay-bale bucket."

"You've never talked about it before," I muttered. "It sounded made-up."

He stepped closer, narrowed his eyes. "You know what this means."

It meant *Aiden vs. Tyler -The Fake Stare-Down of the Century.*

Ivy sat down on a hay bale and stage-whispered to Emilia, "This is where David Attenborough would have a voice-over, 'The bro-bonding friendship ritual of rural North Dakotan boys. A scene as old as time.'"

Tyler jerked his chin toward the barn. "You and me. One-on-one. No time-outs. First to five. But no points if the chickens panic."

Miguel popped up out of nowhere. "I ref!"

Sofía followed, arms wide. "Me, me, me," while blowing air kisses.

I looked over at Ivy and saw that she and Emilia were walking away arm in arm. Ivy waved a hand in the air, totally unbothered.

"Good luck, Aiden. Watch out for manure. And may the hay be ever in your favor."

79

EPILOGUE

Ivy

The list of things Miggy told us after he found out Aiden was my (gag) boyfriend:

- "No kissing at the farm. Ever." Unless we want the cows to faint. Apparently, cows are very delicate.

- "If basketball dude wears stinky gym shoes, he stays in the barn." Fair.

- "We have to play trucks with Sofía once a week to stay good people." Aiden takes this very seriously. He made a pit stop on the way to our second date to buy her a new dump truck. I'm pretty sure it's Miggy's way of making sure he gets time with Aiden, without saying it out loud.

- "Basketball dude needs to eat all the veggies on his plate." Miggy says it's because basketball guys have a basketball brain, and the veggies get them closer to a baseball brain.

- "Aiden has to hold a baseball for at least an hour a week to get baseball in his brain. That stops from getting big and orange." The baseball must be extra special. Conveniently, Miggy has one. And conveniently, it always comes with Miggy attached.

- "Only I can call him basketball dude." Exclusive nickname rights.

- "I'd like this better if he played a real sport. Like baseball." Miggy is still holding a grudge against basketball, and honestly, he might never let it go.

- "If you marry him, invite the llamas." (There are no llamas at the farm. Yet. Miggy has a dream.)

- "No kissing during family dinner." He says this twice a week. Loudly.

- "If he makes you sad, call me right away. I punch good." He demonstrated his punching skills on a hay bale.

- "He's okay, I guess. For a dizzy chicken." High praise.

***

Honestly? I can't argue with most of these. Miggy's got the science covered, the clones on standby, farm security fully briefed, and, apparently, a lifetime rescue plan in case I ever let Aiden get trapped in Whitneyland again.

Turns out, the best lists are made together. Hard moment by hard moment, happy feeling by happy feeling, memory by memory. And if you're lucky, there's a four-year-old who's going to rule the world, helping you write your list.

Molly: Hi Aiden, Ivy, Emilia, Tyler, Jordan, Sarah. Josh asked me to text you.

Josh:
(heart eyes, cello, sparkles, crown, explosion, rainbow, fire, unicorn, dancer, princess, music notes, 100 percent, speaker blasting sound.)

Molly: Yes, Josh. Love you too. Knock it off now please.

Josh: (Screenshot of conversation with Miggy)

Josh:(heart eyes, double hearts, face melting, sparkling stars, fireworks, hands raised in celebration, shooting star, lucky clover, gold medal, ring, infinity symbol, face screaming in joy, exploding heart, confetti.)

Sarah: Aw, he's telling Molly "You are so amazing, my actual heart might detonate from love. I'm basically the luckiest potato in the basket and I don't deserve your sparkle."

463

Ivy: Molly, he's so sweet with you. But why does Josh have Jordan's, Sarah's, Emilia's, and my numbers?

Molly: Sigh. Yes, he's sweet. But Josh. I need you to Focus. F.O.C.U.S. Sorry, Ivy – I have no idea about your phone numbers. I'm just the translator.

Molly: Josh says *"Thought everyone should see this."*

Aiden: Emilia, how did your little brother get Josh's number?

Tyler: I told you. Josh's phone knows things.

Josh: (pointing finger, screenshot, bugged-out eyes, brain explosion.)

Molly: Josh says, *"Just read the convo."*

Screenshot Text Log

Miggy: Hey. This is Miguel Cabrera.

Miggy: Are you the guy teaching basketball dude to not be so dumb?

Josh: (Thinking. Basketball. Idea. Into brain. Improvement.)

Miggy: Okay. Good. Basketball dude and Ivy need to use their words. You gotta tell him that.

Josh: (Thumbs up.)

Miggy: They're being dizzy chickens now. Dizzy chickens aren't no good. They lay scrambled eggs.

Josh: (Goats watching. Under control.)

Josh: (Dizzy chickens. Reset. Brains. Confirmed?)

Molly: Josh is checking that the dizzy chickens have their heads on straight.

Aiden: I'm assuming I'm one of the dizzy chickens even though I'm a studly rooster?

Josh: (Chickens. Young apprentice. Spiral. Lightsaber wisdom. Face the truth.)

Molly: He says, *"Face the truth, young padawan. I said chickens. I meant chickens."* But he acknowledges your confidence.

Jordan: Rumor here in Dickinson is that the chickens are walking in straight lines.

Aiden: Again, rooster.

Ivy: Hush, Aiden. It's chickens for the sake of Miggy's farm-grown idiom.

Tyler: Dude, we all know you're a bold mustang, but that kills the folkish feeling.

Emilia: Let the metaphor live, cowboy.

Sarah: Honestly, I think Miggy's the only one qualified to assign animals.

Josh: (Goats. Chickens. Roosters. Mustangs. All bow to Miggy.)

Molly: He says animal classifications fall under Miggy's jurisdiction. As does your redemption arc.

Aiden: Again, Miggy *and* Josh? How?

Ivy: Jordan and Sarah?

Josh: (Mind link. Signal. Juice box hotline. Wizardry. Don't ask.)

Molly: He says: *it's complicated. And classified. But juice boxes may be involved.*

Josh: (Juice box. Calendar. Travel. Goats. Meet. Epic.)

Molly: And he wants to meet Miggy when we're home over our next break. Also, he says: *it will be legendary. Possibly world-altering. Proceed accordingly.*

Ivy Recommends

DISCLAIMER: All media listed here was considered family-friendly and age-appropriate at the time of viewing. Some content may now be ad-supported, subject to regional availability, or hosted on platforms with mixed content policies. Viewer discretion is advised when accessing third-party sites. This is a real disclaimer about real videos on real websites. Ivy's commentary is fictional. The documentaries and platforms, however, are not. Links worked at time of publication.

Classic Chronicle: How the Smiley Face Was Created

Ivy's Take: Short but impactful history of the most over used and misunderstood emoji in history.

https://www.youtube.com/watch?v=PHkUqIh2Oyw

Dakota Mysteries and Oddities

Ivy's Take: Delves into the strange and mysterious tales from North Dakota.

https://www.youtube.com/watch?v=rh_pyJG99W

Generations of Victory

Ivy's Take: Even if you're not into football, the passion is contagious. A touchdown of storytelling.

https://www.youtube.com/watch?v=

The Green Planet BBC, 2022 – narrated by David Attenborough)

Ivy's Take: High-definition drama. Attenborough whispering encouragement to a cactus. "10 out of 10, cried for a tree. Don't @ me."

https://www.bbc.co.uk/programmes/m0013cl7

Jacqueline du Pré: Genius and Tragedy

Ivy's Take: A poignant look at the life and career of the renowned cellist. "Her music speaks volumes; her story, even more." Heartbreaking and beautiful.

https://www.pbs.org/video/jacqueline-du-pre-genius-and-tragedy-6bgci0/

Ken Burns' The National Parks: America's Best Idea

Ivy's Take: Explores the history and significance of America's national parks. "Makes you want to hug a tree and thank a ranger." Status: Inspirational and enlightening.

https://www.pbs.org/kenburns/the-national-parks/#watch

Ken Burns' The Roosevelts: An Intimate History

Ivy's Take: A comprehensive look at the Roosevelt family's impact on America. "History told with heart and depth." Must-watch for history buffs.

https://www.pbs.org/show/roosevelts/?source=googlehome&action=play

Kingdom of Plants 3D

Ivy's Take: It's Attenborough, but inside a giant greenhouse. Plants plotting in 3D.

https://www.youtube.com/watch?v=9tgpy9yQF8s

Plants Behaving Badly

Ivy's Take: True Crime, but plants. Carnivorous and deceptive species doing the most. "This is the kind of energy I brought to the dandelion massacre."

https://www.amazon.com/Plants-Behaving-Badly-Season-1/dp/B0CVWBMNXN

North Dakota State Bison Draft History

Ivy's Take: North Dakota doubters. Read this. Then I'll talk to you.

https://247sports.com/team/north-dakota-state-bison-football-314/draftpicks/?year=alltime

North Dakota: Discover the Spirit

Ivy's Take: A promotional video showcasing North Dakota's attractions. "Makes you appreciate the hidden gems of the state." Nostalgic and informative.

https://www.youtube.com/watch?v=IUvnmcr_KGY

The Private Life of Plants Ivy's Take: Time-lapse footage of plants behaving like passive-aggressive roommates. "More drama than a lunch table breakup. Highly recommend." Legendary. May have cried over a climbing vine.

https://archive.org/details/the-private-life-of-plants

Refuge of the American Spirit

Ivy's Take: A 17-minute film offering insights into Roosevelt's time in the Badlands and the park's history. Ivy's Take: "Short, sweet, and surprisingly moving." Perfect pre-visit primer.

https://www.nps.gov/thingstodo/watch-the-theodore-roosevelt-national-park-film-refuge-of-the-american-spirit.htm

Rostropovich: The Genius of the Cello (2011)

Ivy's Take: Explores the life of one of the greatest cellists, Mstislav Rostropovich. A masterclass in passion and perseverance. Inspiring.

https://www.youtube.com/watch?v=tKQpR7aO1SM

Smiley Program – The History of Harvey Ball's Smiley

Ivy's Take: The surprisingly earnest backstory of a yellow circle that changed the world. "Should not have made me emotional. But it did." Archival gold.

https://www.youtube.com/watch?v=i2OSsN--itk

Talent Has Hunger (2016)

Ivy's Take: Follows cello instructor Paul Katz and his students over seven years. "A testament to the transformative power of music education." Uplifting.

https://www.imdb.com/title/tt5176762/

Theodore Roosevelt National Park (1994) – PBS Nature Scene

Ivy's Take: A serene exploration of the landscapes that inspired Roosevelt's conservation efforts. "Ideal for calming the mind while contemplating life's complexities." Classic nature walk with a historical twist.

https://www.pbs.org/video/theodore-roosevelt-national-park-1994-chnvxd/

A Brief Look at the Rules and History of Barn Ball

Play this fictional and, probably, dangerous in real life, game entirely at your own risk.

Invented by Robby Preston and Adam Alred, perfected by Tyler.

A not-quite-sanctioned sport involving a basketball, two hay bales, a feed bucket, and an unreasonable number of barn-specific rules.

Objective: Get the ball in the bucket or bounce it through the upper hay-bale gap without breaking a window or starting a chicken riot.

Known Rules (as enforced by Tyler):

- Buckets are goals. So are gaps in the hay bale stack—those are worth two.

- If a goat knocks the ball in, it still counts.

- You can rebound off barn walls, but do not let your ball get anywhere near The Beast.

- "Pitchfork!" is a freeze command. If someone moves, they're on fence post duty.

- If the ball lands in a feed trough, everyone resets and yells "Cow out!"

- Arguing with the ref (Tyler) results in a penalty: playing air kisses with Sofía for three minutes.

- Bonus point if a rooster crows when you score.

- Loser is on manure duty. No exceptions.

From the Book:

Copacabana – Barry Manilow

I'm Gonna Wash that Man Right Out of My Hair – from *South Pacific*

Carnvial of the Animals – Camille Saint-Saëns

Serenade for Strings in C major - Piotr Ilyich Tchaikovsky

William Tell Overture Finale- Gioachino Rossini

Danse Macabre – Camille Saint-Saëns

Flight of the Bumblebee - Rimsky-Korsakov

1812 Overture Finale - Piotr Ilyich Tchaikovsky

Queen of the Night Aria – Wolfgang Amadeus Mozart

Leaving on a Jet Plane - Peter, Paul, and Mary

Footloose- Blake Shelton

Yakety-Sax - Boots Randolph

Also Sprach Zarathustra – Richard Strauss

Prehistoric Park Original Soundtrack – Daniel Pemberton

Bach: Cello Suite No. 1 in G Major, Prélude - Yo-Yo Ma

One Way or Another – Blondie

50 Ways to Say Goodbye – Train

Don't Stop Believin'- Journey

***

Cats Sing Classical Music - Mozart - Eine Kleine - Cats Version
https://youtu.be/kpTiwUTCyvA?feature=shared

Kazoo Orchestra does Tchaikovsky! The Nutcracker Overture
https://youtu.be/c6ayAkdjOv0?feature=shared

From the Author:

Almost Missed Our Shot – Writing Playlist

1, 2, 3, 4 – Plain White T's

100 Years – Five for Fighting

a Thousand Years

Always and Forever – Canaan Smith

An Old-Fashioned Love Song – Three Dog Night

arms – Christina Perris

At Last – Etta James

Can't Help Falling in Love – Haley Reinhart

Crazy Little Thing Called Love – Juice Newton

Dandelions – Ruth B.

Do You Believe in Magic – The Lovin' Spoonful

Favorite Girl – The Icarus Account

Footloose – Kenny Loggins/Blake Shelton

How Sweet It Is – James Taylor

I Won't Give Up – Jason Mraz

I'm a Believer – The Monkees

Love Grows (Where My Rosemary Goes) – Edison Light House

Love's Been a Little Bit Hard on Me – Juice Newton

Need the Sun to Break – James Bay

One Call Away – Charlie Puth

Rhythm of Love – Plain White T's

Still Right Here In My Heart – Pure Prairie League

Sunlight – Plain White T's

The Power of Love – Huey Lewis and the News

The Way I Am – Ingrid Michealsen

Unchained Melody – The Righteous Brothers

Whatever It Takes – Lifehouse

ACKNOWLEDGEMENTS

My mom always hoped her kids would collaborate on a project such as writing a book. I wish I could share this with her now. My imperfectly perfect parents gave me what I needed for life, some of which I only see now. Miss you all the time. There are so many people sharing their knowledge about independent writing and publishing. They've made this possible. A note to M. Rowley who's more family that medical provider to our whole family. Thank you for hearing us. LaRayne, the first person I trusted to read a rough draft. And you liked it! I don't think you know how much that mattered. Julian of Norwich left us these words, "All shall be well, and all shall be well, and all manner of thing shall be well." I love this as a way to remind myself that the love of God is all-encompassing, there will be a day when everything will be alright – no matter how it all feels now. And everyone who makes the world better for children in the here and now, thank you. We're in this together.

About the Author

M.C. Danielsen writes heartfelt YA rom-coms with equal parts humor, emotional depth, and small-town charm. A lifelong North Dakotan at heart, she pays close attention to the smaller places that often get overlooked. Her current series delivers authentic rural vibes, slow-burn romance, and fiercely loyal friendships.

Her stories follow girls finding their voice, boys growing into heart, and the emotional chaos that comes with figuring out who you are—especially when feelings, playlists, and group chats get in the way.

When she's not writing, you can find M.C. playing merge-three games, rabidly cheering for the Minnesota Twins, the Minnesota Vikings, and the Buffalo Bills by marriage (she admits they're worth following).

By training, she's an expert in child development, trauma, and resilience. She believes every teen deserves a safe place to land and to have people who light up when they walk into the room. She's certain that today's young people are capable of more than any generation before them.

Also By

Releasing September 24, 2025

Finally Found the Words

Riverbend High Happy Endings Book 2

***

Releasing October 29, 2025

Saw You From the Start

Riverbend High Happy Endings Book 3

***

Releasing December 3, 2025

Help Me Change My Mind

Riverbend High Happy Endings Book 4

***

Releasing January 14, 2026

Not the Ending I Saw

Riverbend High Happy Endings Book 5

www.ingramcontent.com/pod-product-compliance
Lightning Source LLC
Chambersburg PA
CBHW020007120726
47903CB00004B/1180